DIEGO'S SECRET

When one does not take a stand
against injustice, they tacitly
support it

[signature]

2/20/19

Bryan T. Clark

Cornbread Publishing Inc.

Diego's Secret

Copyright© 2018 by Bryan T. Clark

Published by: Cornbread Publishing Inc.
Fiction / Contemporary / Gay & Lesbian / M-M Romance

Cover art by: **Kristallynn Designs**
Cover content is for illustrative purposes only, and any person depicted on the cover is a model.

First Edition: May 1, 2018
ISBN: 0997056266
ISBN-13: 9780997056266

DIEGO'S SECRET

By Bryan T. Clark

When two men from different cultures meet, there may be sparks, but what about their values, principles, and social circles? Can love win over attitudes, judgments, and pre-conceived perceptions?

Eight years ago, at the age of seventeen, Diego Castillo came to the United States illegally from Mexico. Working long hours in the family landscaping business, he now shares a tiny apartment with his two machismo brothers in Southern California. Diego has worked hard to keep his desires for other men a secret from his brothers. He's worked just as hard to keep his undocumented status a secret from the world he now lives in.

Thirty-two-year-old Winston Makena is beautiful, intelligent, and intimidating. He was born with a silver spoon in his mouth, but no amount of money can relieve the enormous grief he is suffering from his husband's sudden death. He is one of Diego's best accounts and lives a life in stark contrast to his gardener's. Winston's wealthy upbringing has influenced his ideas, leading him to certain biases.

Winston believes he could never love again. Diego believes that his family's lives depend on him keeping his secrets. What neither of them know is that the heart knows no such boundaries. Will social divisions, ideology, and secrets destroy both their chances for happiness? Can love really conquer all?

The heart has its own language.
—Rumi

ACKNOWLEDGMENT

In writing fiction, I believe I, as an author, have a profound responsibility to my readers to deliver a fictional story in which the truth still lies somewhere in the pages. Although **Diego's Secret** has a backdrop of Hispanic culture, immigration status issues, and a bit of Spanish language, it is not meant to be a representation of the Hispanic culture in general. Nevertheless, it was important to me, as a writer, to ensure that the book accurately portrayed the people and their beautiful culture, as well as some of the issues that one in the Hispanic culture might face. I would like to thank *Irene* and *Izzy* for being invaluable advisors to me on Hispanic cultural issues and for ensuring I was educated and got it right on the many important issues.

1

From the expansive entryway of the house, the sound of glass shattering echoed through the long halls. The heavy draperies in the office were still drawn from the night before. The house was cold—lifeless, as if the once-vibrant estate had been stripped of its soul and abandoned.

Winston's heart faltered in his chest as he attempted to draw a full breath. He would have screamed, like a lion in the jungle who has made his kill, if only he could breathe.

"Winston?"

He heard his name, followed by the sound of heels striking the Italian marble flooring. The steps quickened towards him, confirming that he was no longer alone.

"Winston . . . Are you okay?"

There was enough light in the study that Winston could see Ann the moment she appeared in the doorway. She stood still, her eyes scanning the room in search of him. She was his business partner, his closest friend, and the last person he wanted to see.

Obstructed by the giant mahogany desk, Winston's six-foot-two frame kneeled to pick up the remnants of what had been a Monique Lhuillier Waterford vase, a gift from Parker for their ten-year anniversary. A million crystal shards covered the Persian carpet that lay over the hardwood floor.

Ann stepped into the room. Her brow wrinkled in concern. "What happened?"

She must have let herself in the front door, which hadn't been locked in months. In the condition he had been in lately, someone could have held a party in the nearly six-thousand-square-foot house and he might not have known it. With every breath, he fought to hold back the nausea that swelled in his throat. If allowed, his grief would take over his entire being with more ferocity then he could control. He couldn't let that happen. Breaking the four-thousand-dollar vase had been his only means to release the building pressure.

Avoiding eye contact with Ann, Winston carefully put the largest pieces of crystal into his palm. He used his elbow to keep his dog, Lucy, from stepping in it. "I dropped a vase." Under his breath, he added, "I pretended it was Parker and smashed it against the wall."

He had forgotten that Ann was coming over this afternoon to drop off some contracts that needed his signature.

"You dropped it?" She shifted her weight and leaned over the top of his desk.

Her Chanel perfume dominated Winston's space. It was her trademark; it was too much, overpowering. Picking up on her tone, Winston knew she wasn't buying his story. As his best friend since college, she would often say that she knew him better than he knew himself. Maybe she did, but she wouldn't get much from him today. "Yeah, I dropped it!"

"Do you want to talk about it?"

Ann's eyes bored into him, sending him scrambling for a better excuse. If he looked at her, she would press on. "No . . . I don't want to talk about it!" What could they possibly talk about that hadn't already been said? He should have told her to send the contracts by messenger. Putting a handful of broken glass onto a coffee table, he kept his eyes on the floor.

"Honey, I know you're hurting. I'm sorry I can't make it go away. I wish there was something I could say or do . . ." Ann's voice trailed off into silence.

The silence didn't work for Winston either. "I can't believe he left me. Gone, just like that!" The anger swelled in his chest. He was unsure of what had brought on the onslaught of emotions he'd felt this last week. Until a week ago, he had thought he was doing well. Throwing himself into his work had mostly succeeded in distracting him from grieving the love of his life.

"He didn't leave you. Parker died!" The sorrow in Ann's voice came across loud and clear.

"What's the difference? He's not here now, is he?" She wasn't going to win. Not today. It was his right to be angry. These days, it was the only emotion that eased the pain deep within him. He wanted to lash out at someone or something, and today he had chosen the vase.

Picking up the last of the glass that he could see, he decided to save the vacuuming for his housekeeper. He was not a hundred percent sure that Monday was even her day, but he figured that he had cleaned up enough that Lucy wouldn't get cut.

Ann laid a folder on top of the cluttered mahogany desk and made her way around towards the window. With both hands, she peeled the heavy drapes open, sending a flood of light into the impressive wood paneled study.

"Jesus, what are you doing?" Winston shielded his eyes from the burst of light as if it was a gigantic fireball about to roll over him.

Stepping into his personal space, Ann stared at him for a second. Her lips pressed together as she fanned her face with her hand. "Are you drunk? It's one o'clock. Have you had breakfast?"

Winston took a seat behind his desk, attempting to put some space between them. The light buzz pulsating in his forehead said that she was right. As he thumbed through the stack of papers in the folder, she took her usual seat on the couch across the room. Without looking, he knew that she was staring, undoubtedly waiting for elaboration and penitence.

"Yes . . . No . . . No, I'm not drunk, and yes, I ate. I had a mimosa with my eggs, if that's okay with you." He closed the folder. He couldn't remember a thing that he had just read. He would examine it again when Ann left. Right now, he couldn't even focus on the clock in front of him. He was lost in a sea of hopelessness.

"Did it have any orange juice in it?"

"Ann . . . Please, I'm just not feeling it today." He finally made eye contact with her. She was wearing the beautiful white and blue kimono that he had convinced her to buy last year when they were in Japan. She was easily the most beautiful woman he knew. Her brown skin was flawless; her need for makeup was minimal. The day they met, she had reminded him of a young Diana Ross, her hair thick and as black as coal. With her long lashes that framed her smoky brown eyes, she could have graced any magazine cover. At thirty-seven, she was that girl that women loved to hate and men couldn't get enough of.

Winston sat behind his desk, staring out the window across the lawn and pool. There was movement. Either the gardener or the pool person was doing something in the yard. Sighing under his breath, he realized that he was a stranger in his own house. He remembered how, on the day after Parker's accident, it had taken him hours to find Lucy's dogfood. When he had finally located the fifty-pound bag in the garage, he had decided that keeping it there made no sense. Why wouldn't you store it in the kitchen, where she actually ate? For the past ten years, Parker had taken care of everything: the bills, running the house, and Winston.

Devastated by Parker's death, Winston was now lost in his own world, which Parker had created and managed. All Winston had been required to do was live in it. This had worked for them both.

"Are you listening to me?" Ann's voice came out of nowhere. She was staring at him, her eyebrows arched. Her crossed legs revealed the red soles of her beautiful Christian Louboutin pumps.

Winston snapped back into the present, the last place he wanted to be. "What? I'm sorry." Eyeing his empty champagne glass, he thought about offering her a mimosa. He was certainly ready for another. Adjusting himself in his chair, he forced a smile. "So, how's William doing?"

Ann rolled her eyes. "Ugh, he's driving me crazy with this new juice diet. He has juiced everything in the house. Last night, for dinner, we had what he called his 'super meal.' Apples, carrots, kale, and beets. Thank God he didn't insist on sitting at the table and drinking it together." She laid her arm across the back of the sofa as she turned to the window. The lines in her neck were beautiful as she stretched it for a better view of the gardener. "Hmm, he's kind of cute. What's his name?"

"Who?" Winston had no idea whom Ann meant. Was she planning to stay the entire day? Surely not. There had to be plenty of work at the office that required her attention.

Turning back to Winston, she smacked her lips exaggeratedly. "Is he looking for new clients? My lawn could use a good mowing."

"Really? I don't want to hear about what *your* lawn needs." Although his thoughts were fuzzy, he would rather talk about work than his best friend getting her *lawn* mowed. "What's going on with the Harper Gala? I was supposed to call Christian last week and finalize the count. Last I heard, there will be four hundred guests. Have you talked to the caterer about the veal?" The Harper Gala was one of the biggest who's-who events they had landed since starting the business almost seven years ago. At the moment, it was just a blur to him.

Standing, Ann glanced at the young man outside before walking over to Winston's desk. "I talked to Christian last night. We're at six-fifty." She traced her fingers through Winston's tousled mass of black hair. "You need a haircut."

Winston's ink black hair against his steel-grey eyes often left people unaware that they were staring at him. Since his early childhood, people had incessantly reminded him of how beautiful he was.

"Six-fifty? The Corinthian Ballroom will only hold four-eighty-five!" Winston wiggled out from under her assault and sat up in his chair. Tapping on his laptop keyboard, in seconds he brought up the configuration of the Royal Peaks' six ballrooms. His eyes darted between the various pictures on the screen. "Can you call and book the Tuscan room instead? It holds eight hundred. We're going to need it after all. Damn it. I knew I should've booked that room in the first place! Why didn't you call me?" Winston was eager to focus on something other than his sorrow.

"Done!" Ann held out her hand to stop his rant. "I already talked to Karen at the Royal Peaks, and after a couple of calls, she was able to get us into that room. The caterer is on board with all of Christian's requests. The veal is a non-issue. They got it."

Winston leaned back into his chair. "What about the wait staff? We'll need more. The guests will be waiting for their dinners for hours."

"Winston, I've got it under control. I'm not your secretary; I'm your partner. This is not my first party, you remember." Her voice was cold as she took a seat on the edge of his desk. "Look, I've not said anything to you before, but it's almost been a year since Parker died. I've been working my ass off—"

"Well, I'm sorry his death has inconvenienced you!"

"Don't come at me with that bullshit. I loved him too. But I didn't just lose him; I lost you. You haven't been in the game since he died. The last couple of months, I thought you were doing better, as if your old self was coming back. Now, I'm not so sure."

"But—"

Ann threw her hands up. "Let me talk! I get it, baby, I do. He was everything. Hell, I would have married him if my Wildebeest William hadn't come along! But here's the reality: he died, and he's not coming back. It's the shittiest thing I could say, but I love you, and I can't continue to sit back and watch you disintegrate into a bottle of vodka. You're not even a drinker."

Fighting tears, Winston held his tongue. He knew that, when she was fired up, there was no stopping her. Only once before had he been on the receiving end of her wrath, and he had vowed never to let it happen again.

Ann continued, "I need you to take some time off, some real time. Let me handle the business. I'll keep you up to date on anything important, but I need you to focus on you. See a doctor. Go on vacation.

Go visit your mother in Montana and get to know your newest stepfather, what's his name . . . *Cowboy Dick?*"

"Cal . . . His name is Cal Richardson."

"Whatever. What I'm trying to say is you need to take care of yourself. The world has not ended, although you may feel like it did. The sun is shining, and the rest of us are alive, waiting on you to come back. You're a beautiful man. You might want to start thinking about dating again."

Dating was the last thing on his mind. At thirty-two years old, he didn't care if he ever dated again. His heart couldn't take it. Thinking about the past few months, Winston knew he hadn't carried any of the workload. He had called Ann a week ago and said he was sick and was taking the rest of the week off.

"Yeah. I can't." The words came out of Winston's mouth before she was finished. "The Harper Gala needs us both. Perhaps after that."

"Bullshit! Who's the primary beneficiary for the Harper Gala?" Ann asked.

"Um . . . it's . . ." He was sure he knew this. If she would back off and give him a minute to think, it would come to him.

"You can't tell me one thing about one of the biggest events we've ever landed." Ann clasped her hands together. "Please, baby, let me handle this. Take some time and get yourself together. Come back after. Do it for me. Please."

Maybe she was right. Maybe he did need to take some time off. But he wasn't going to Montana. That was for sure. Winston tried to erase the thought of sitting in Montana with his mother and Cal.

That night, after a long, hot shower, Winston ran a towel through his hair as he stood in front of his bathroom's floor-to-ceiling mirror. Ignoring the trace scents of balsam and fir that permeated the room, he stared at the pale body in front of him. He turned to one side and then to the other. He was getting too thin. For being white, he once prided himself on his inherited round bubbly ass that now seemed to be disappearing. It didn't help that it was June and there wasn't a hint of a tan line anywhere on his pasty frame, not even a farmer's tan. Over the years, his youthful, athletic body and natural six-pack were getting harder and harder to maintain, but this last year, these last couple of months, everything about him was becoming harder to recognize. He ran his hand across his flat stomach and forced a smile at the mirror, almost as if he was smiling at a stranger. He couldn't re- member the last time he had smiled. *It may be time to join a gym.* Words forgotten as soon as he thought them.

Winston wrapped his robe around his body. Drawing the tie tightly across his abdomen, he glanced at the mirror one last time. Releasing an exasperating sigh, he tossed the wet towel on top of the hamper. It was only eight o'clock. There were four more hours before this day would end. A year ago, he and Parker would've been on one of their date nights, in the middle of a fabulous dinner some- where down in Beverly Hills or West Hollywood. A chuckle escaped him. Parker would have been going on about the wine or the cuisine. Parker had been a true foodie, talking about food as if he were dat- ing it.

Walking back into his office, Winston looked for the folder Ann had brought over. He would resort to his go-to means of making time pass: work.

After ruffling through the pile of papers on his desk several times, he realized that the folder she had dropped off wasn't there. His desk wasn't that messy at the moment. Actually, it was clean by his stan- dards. He remembered laying the folder next to his laptop. He rum- maged through the papers again, thinking he must have overlooked it. He wanted to review the numbers and check the caterer's order.

Nights were his worst times since Parker's accident. Darkness brought a hellish isolation in which their once-beautiful home be- came a tomb, an empty place that left him hollow. *Did Ann take the folder with her?* Sitting down in his chair, he logged into his computer and waited for the data to load. He hated this antiquated program.

He reminded himself that he had to hire someone to create new software for them. Words flashed in red across his screen: *Failed. Try Again?*

"Goddamn it!" Winston cursed aloud. Lucy raised her head at the pitch of his voice. "Sorry, girl." He watched her for a second or two before returning his attention to his laptop. Ann was right. He did need a break. Grabbing his phone, he leaned back into his chair. No messages, no texts, no updates on anything. A deep sigh escaped him. *Where could I go?* He vetoed each idea as quickly as he thought of it. No place sounded very interesting when he would be there alone. He could visit his mother. He hadn't seen her since the funeral. She and Cal had flown out as soon as they heard the news of the accident. His mother had stayed at the hospital with him, day in and day out, until the physician called a family conference.

"We've done everything possible," he told them. "As a family, you need to start thinking about what Parker would want." Words never to be forgotten.

Winston knew what Parker would want. They had talked about it a million times. The conversation was usually sparked by a television show or a news story.

Parker had been lying in his hospital bed for two weeks. He hadn't moved. The doctors and nurses had been hinting for several days that this decision was coming, but Winston had ignored them. Now, his mother, his stepfather, and Parker's parents, sister, and grandmother all sat staring at him as the doctor waited for an answer.

Was he to make this decision? To take Mrs. Leblanc's son from her, to cause a grandmother to outlive her grandchild? He had no proof that Parker would have wanted this; they had only laughed about not leaving one another on life support. *Goddamn, Parker, why didn't you write this down? You took care of everything but this. Goddamn you.*

Returning to the present, Winston walked into the living room and over to the bar. He had waited long enough for a drink.

Glass, ice, vodka, and a splash of cranberry juice for color. With his glass in hand, he followed Lucy down the hall to the back door.

She needed to pee. Normally, he would just open the door and let her go out, sniff flowers, and patrol the yard—whatever French Bulldogs did.

As he trailed her outside, a delicate balance of cut grass and jasmine filtered through his lungs, sending a sudden lightness into his head. Blindsided by the sweet perfume, he wandered farther into the yard. He was sure it was star jasmine. Looking around, he spotted the aromatic culprit bordering the back of the pool.

He had forgotten how beautiful Thousand Oaks was. The town's mountain terrain was peaceful and isolated from LA's traffic, which was just what he and Parker had wanted when they bought the house two years ago. The place was surrounded by foothills. Parker had said that deer and mountain lions lived in the area, but Winston had never seen either.

Taking a seat in a double lounge chair, he laid back and peered up at the sky. It was too early for stars; the sun had barely set. He could visit his mother. How bad could a few days in Montana be? Who names a town Marysville? Could the name be any gayer? *Yeah, I'm not going to Marysville.* Nevertheless, Ann was right. *I need to take some time off, figure things out, shake this depression thing that's got me.*

Across the pool, up in the hills, glimmered the lights of houses. Looking at the closest house, he saw movement through the large windows, but he was too far away to make out anything else. He didn't know any of his neighbors, if you could call them that. Every house sat on at least an acre or two of property, ensuring privacy.

Taking another sip of his drink, he relished the warmth and calmness that the cocktail provided. It was nice, sitting here. He should have brought his phone with him if he was going to hang out . . . just in case.

Maybe I'll come out here tomorrow and lie out. Tomorrow . . . A lifetime away.

2

Diego lay in bed, waiting for his older brother Rafael to come out of the only bathroom in their tiny, two-bedroom apartment in the predominately-Hispanic neighborhood in Maywood, California. Curled in the fetal position, his five-foot eight-inch body was nestled down in his twin bed. It was just past five-thirty a.m., and like clockwork, his eldest brother, Francisco, was yelling, his commentary likely heard by the other renters in the four-unit, two-story building in the heart of East Los Angeles County.

"Are you up?" Francisco yelled through the bedroom door. He spoke in Spanish as they usually did at home. "I'm running late. You need to take Rafael to school before you start this morning."

Diego drew a long breath. He was exhausted. He hadn't had a day off in three weeks. His gardening service, which the three of them had started after they arrived in LA eight years ago, was keeping him busy twelve to thirteen hours a day.

Francisco had left the business first, to open a garage where he did oil changes, minor repair work, and window tinting. About a year later, Rafael decided he wanted to go to the local college, so he too left the business and took a job working evenings at the Grind Coffee Shed.

Throwing off his blanket, Diego prepared himself to jump and go the moment Rafael came out of the bathroom. Wait too long and Francisco would be back in there.

While he waited, he examined one of his many landscape sketches pinned to the wall. The piece needed several changes before he would be satisfied, but that would have to wait until later.

When he heard the bathroom door's handle turn, Diego jumped out of bed. Meeting Rafael in the hall just as he was exiting the bathroom, Diego waited for his brother to get out of the way. Rafael stood a couple inches taller and was about ten pounds heavier than Diego, who, at one hundred and forty-five pounds, was the smallest of the three brothers. Rafael would seize any opportunity to demonstrate his machismo to Diego. It was too early for that bullshit.

"Sorry, *flaco*, for the smell. My stomach is jacked up." Rafael passed Diego without looking at him, heading back into their bedroom. "You got me this morning?"

"Yeah, I have to leave in ten minutes!" Diego shut himself in the cramped bathroom, pushing through the nasty stench his brother had left. He freed himself from his underwear as he stood over the toilet. *Ah, the feeling of relieving yourself after holding it for hours in bed.* This wasn't the first time; why he didn't get up and walk the five feet to the bathroom when he had to go was beyond him. As he thought about the day ahead, the door suddenly clipped him in his back. Francisco stuck his tatted arm in. "Need my belt." Grabbing the belt from the countertop, Francisco looked at him. "Hey, don't forget to go by and pay the rent. Rafael is short a hundred. Can you cover it?"

"No," Diego grumbled. That was a lie, but it was his knee-jerk response. He could easily cover it, but his older brother was short fifty to a hundred bucks every other month. Because Francisco had started the lawn company, he acted as if the income it drew was still his. Diego hated that, and it further pissed him off that Rafael went out on dates two or three nights a week. How much was that costing?

"Don't be a dick." Francisco's stout body jarred the door open a little more, hitting him again.

"Stop it!" Diego leaned back into the door, slamming it shut before tucking himself into his underwear. He splashed cold water on his face and hair and made quick work of brushing his teeth.

Tuesday . . . This would be his second day in Thousand Oaks. At least he wouldn't be pulling equipment in and out of the trailer all day. Mondays and Tuesdays were devoted to the two properties that he loved to work on.

It wasn't the usual cutting, edging, raking, and blowing eight houses per day, like he did the rest of the week. Instead, he got to maintain and work his magic on huge lawns with formal gardens. Creating a utopia for the rich. The fact that he was paid well to do it didn't hurt either. To tell the truth, Diego was enjoying the business more without his brothers. He spent his days alone, without having to listen to their idiotic caveman banter all day.

Diego knew that when Rafael was done with school, it would be his turn. He would love to return to school, maybe study landscape design. He had attended a workshop a year ago at the local community center where he first heard about the course of study. Several Latinos there had started out as gardeners and were now successful landscape designers.

"Come on, we got to bounce, *flaco!*"

"Alright, I'm coming!" Diego didn't know the exact time, but he knew they were running late. *How hard would it be to buy a clock for the bathroom? I'll stop at Dollar World and pick one up today, if I get a chance.*

Rushing out the door, he checked the trailer behind his truck, ensuring all the locks were intact and that his livelihood hadn't been stolen during the night. After a quick glance at the hitch and rear tires, he joined his brother in the crew cab of their 2001 Ford F150. Francisco had obtained the truck in a trade for their services several years ago, after threatening one of their clients who couldn't pay his bill. Thanks to Francisco's mechanical skills, the vehicle ran as if she was brand new. Diego dreamed of the day when he could purchase the new truck he had been eyeing on the Chevrolet lot. It was his dream truck, all black with black rims and silver pin striping.

"Are you in Thousand Oaks today?" Rafael asked, as he lowered his window and extended his arm to get some air.

"Yes." Diego fired up the truck and watched the gauges, hoping that everything was okay. As the cabin filled with Katy Perry's latest single, he saw that everything wasn't. "I need gas—and coffee."

"Do it after you drop me off. I don't want to be late." Rafael changed the radio station. "Why do you listen to that white music?" he asked in English. Of the three brothers, Rafael spoke English most confidently.

Diego ignored the comment. Anything was better than that ranchera music he and Francisco listened to day in and day out. He said, "You won't be late. It's barely seven. What time is class?"

In Spanish, Rafael answered, "Eight . . . I can't believe you drink that crap at the station. It's not real coffee."

Diego swallowed as if the bitterness of stale gas station coffee was scratching the inside of his throat. "Well, I don't have eight bucks to spend on a coffee at the Grind, and I don't get it for free." He would never admit that the coffee at the Grind was actually good. His usual gas station coffee was much less tasty, but it worked. "Francisco said you're short this month. You know that I have to pay the rent tonight."

"Yeah, my check was short. I only worked four days last week." Rafael settled on a station, and music filled the cabin. Threading his narrow fingers through his long, thick hair, he positioned Diego's rearview mirror so that he could see himself. He raked his fingers through his brownish-red locks a couple of times and leaned back, apparently satisfied.

You're full of shit, Diego thought. *What about the last check, or the one before that? What did you do with your money? You spend it on food, girls, and beer, and then I have to make up the difference.* Diego pulled away from the curb and merged the truck and trailer with the morning rush-hour traffic. Though he was a year older then Diego, Rafael was the least responsible of all of them.

"Did you save anything for Mom and Dad? Mom said Dad needed cash to fix their roof." Diego already knew the answer, but he wanted

Rafael to say it. Since arriving in the States, if the three brothers had done anything consistently, it was sending money back to Mexico to take care of their parents.

"I sent them something already." Rafael's voice told Diego he was lying.

Diego's attention was drawn to someone jogging on the sidewalk. He tried to leave at the same time every morning in the hope of seeing this jogger, whom he had nicknamed Mr. Legs. He had first spotted Mr. Legs about two months ago, jogging along Pomona Blvd. The man was tall and looked to be in his thirties or forties. The muscles in his thighs and chest danced every time he took a stride.

Diego would never forget the moment when he had first spotted Mr. Legs. Stopped at a traffic light, he had glanced over to the corner just as the man lifted his shirt to wipe the sweat from his face. Mr. Legs' deep and strained breathing had contracted and expanded his cut abs. He was beautiful. It was an image Diego had retained.

He had created an imaginary life for his mystery jogger. He was a banker with a wife and two kids. He jogged every morning. When he got home, his wife had breakfast on the table. They ate together, before he kissed his family goodbye for the day and left for work in his Mercedes.

Passing Mr. Legs, Diego took one last glance at him in his side mirror. The sight of Mr. Legs stretched the crotch in his pants every morning. He didn't know anything about the stranger other than the story he had made up for himself.

Right on time, at one o'clock, Diego pulled up to the gates of the Leblanc estate, put the truck in park, and got out to punch in the gate code.

He spent Monday and Tuesday mornings at another property, the Bernstein estate. The Bernsteins were congenial, but since Mrs. Bernstein had a standing two o'clock poolside bridge game every

Monday, she insisted that he split the work into two days, returning on Tuesday mornings.

After spending the morning at the Bernstein estate, he always made a quick stop at a taco truck. There, he got four tacos to go and ate them on the drive over to the Leblanc estate, a one-acre, meticulously landscaped piece of property. Thankfully, Mr. Leblanc was adaptable and allowed him to split a full day's work on his estate into two afternoons to accommodate the Bernsteins.

Two years ago, Diego and Mr. Leblanc had walked the grounds for several days, planning the landscape remodel. Mr. Leblanc had just purchased the property. He wanted to give the entire landscape a makeover, so the two of them discussed what would stay and what would go. They debated and finally agreed that the pool shouldn't be the centerpiece of the yard. "I want a yard full of color, flowers, things that draw your attention no matter where you are in it. I want a place where my husband can relax, where humming birds and butterflies come to hang out."

Husband? It was the first time Diego had ever heard a man refer to another man as his husband. At first, he thought he had heard wrong or had mistranslated the word in his head, but Mr. Leblanc said it again and again. He was referring to his partner as his husband, his *amor.* Diego had tried to stay focused on what Mr. Leblanc was saying. Never in his wildest dreams had he thought Mr. Leblanc was gay.

Diego parked the truck in the circular driveway and checked his face, mouth, and teeth in his rearview mirror for leftover tacos. Yesterday, he had taken care of the lawn and planter beds. Today, he needed to trim and shape the bonsai trees and hedges and tend to the assortments of annuals and rose bushes carefully positioned around the grounds. He loved spring. The weather was warming, and everything was blooming.

There was not a soul around as Diego unloaded his equipment. Even before Mr. Leblanc had died last year, the place had been quiet, but now it was a different, eerie kind of quiet. Before Mr. Leblanc had died, Diego had had several conversations with him about the yard, discussing plants, trees and landscaping ideas and future projects. He had appreciated the kindness of Mr. Leblanc, one of the few clients who acknowledged his existence.

He had met Mr. Leblanc's husband twice—or maybe three times. Once as they were loading luggage into the trunk of their car—they said they were flying somewhere. London? Another time, the husband had asked Diego to move his truck so he could get his car out. Oh, and then the third time, Diego had seen the husband and a beautiful African American woman sitting by the pool, working on their laptops.

Since Mr. Leblanc's death, the property had been like an abandoned zoo: some of the animals were still present, just enough to show that there was life here. Direct deposits of three hundred and fifty dollars kept coming every month, so Diego kept working.

His phone vibrated in his jeans. It was a text from Francisco. *Don't forget to pay the rent.*

Surveying the yard, Diego stuffed his phone back into his pocket. The lawn needed fertilizer, the boxwoods that bordered the driveway needed trimming, and the willow trees in the middle of the driveway circle needed a good spring whack job. The willows in the back yard needed the same.

He worked for a few hours before pausing for a quick break. He headed around to the front of the house to retrieve the one-gallon plastic milk jug that he filled with tap water every morning. Pulling the plastic cap from the opaque container, he held it up and allowed the tepid water to ease his thirst. Afterwards, he checked the time on his phone: *4:18 pm.*

Shit. He had forgotten that he had to leave early to get to the property manager's office before six. He hurried toward the back yard to grab his tools.

As he rounded the side of the house, Mr. Leblanc's husband appeared at the back door. A little dog charged past him and ran at Diego. The man spotted him and waved dismissively. "Sorry about that. I thought you were gone. Letting her out to pee. Lucy, come back!"

Diego kneeled as Lucy reached him. Petting the dog, he snickered at the stupid pink ribbon on its collar as it rolled over, wiggling in the grass. *I guess it's a girl.*

He stroked the little dog several times before looking back up at the man, whose loose-fitting black gym pants and wrinkled white tee shirt hung on him like he was a ragdoll. His face lacked any emotion; his eyes stared right through Diego. Perhaps the blower had woken him. *Surely not. It's four o'clock.*

"Do you speak English?" The man remained in the doorway. "*Habla usted Inglés ?*" he repeated.

Diego's ears perked. The man's Spanish was good. "*Si, hablo Inglés.*" Standing up, Diego watched the little dog run off to do her business. He waited nervously for the man to say something. Anything would have been better than the silence that descended as the man's sunken eyes burned into him.

"Oh, I'm sorry. I wasn't sure," the man finally replied in English.

Had you ever bothered to have a conversation with me, you would have known I speak English. Diego tried not to roll his eyes. He'd been rolling his eyes all of his life. It was his reaction to stupidity, but it tended to get him into trouble. In fact, when he was a child, his mother had often pulled his ear for the disrespect. Diego noticed that the man had a towel and a book in his hand.

Lifting his baseball cap, Diego ran his fingers through his long black hair, brushing the curls out of his face. The man made him nervous, just standing there.

Within seconds, Lucy reappeared, trotting up the walkway towards the house. She squeezed past her owner and through the door. "Have a nice day." The man waved and shut the door without waiting for a response.

Diego shook his head. He didn't have time for weird; he had to get going. Quickly gathering his things and packing the trailer, he sped off in the hope of making it to the property manager's office before it closed.

3

"I can't believe I just stood there staring at him. Ann, he was beautiful." Winston switched the phone to his other ear so he could hold it with his left hand. Popping his Lean Cuisine into the microwave, he set it to heat for three minutes. "I was heading out to lie by the pool. When I opened the door, *bam*, he was right there."

"Was it that same gardener? The guy from yesterday?"

"I don't know, maybe. He's very attractive—and I love his broken English. His voice is deep, with a thick accent. Sexy!" A sudden heaviness in Winston's chest caused him to lean against the counter. It was guilt. He shouldn't be talking about this guy as if Parker . . . And there was another kick to his gut. "Hey Ann, can I call you back? My dinner's ready." It was as if a cut had been reopened, but instead of blood, it was pain rushing to the surface. He was learning to apply the compress quickly, to stop it before he bled out.

"No worries. I'm glad you agreed to take some time off. I wish you were going somewhere, but we can do baby steps. I'll call you later this week."

"Okay. Love you. Goodnight." Winston quickly hung up before Ann could deliver her famous line: *Before I let you go . . .*

His stomach was in a knot, and the smell from his Chicken Alfredo was nauseating. One minute he was fine, and the next, the simple thought of Parker cast him into a sea of guilt. His mind jumped from Parker to the gardener, then back to Parker, and then again to the gardener.

In his denim jeans and a loose-fitting forest green long sleeve shirt, the gardener couldn't have been more than five-seven or five-eight. Winston had found his deep voice and accent a sexy surprise. His hair was a midnight black and hung over his collar. Yet it was those dark brown, almost black, eyes framed by thick black brows that made him most interesting. But, no doubt, he was young, a baby.

A ding from the microwave signaled that Winston's food was ready. He carefully removed the cardboard container that held his dinner. Tearing the plastic film from the top, he let steam billow out. As it cooled, he fed Lucy and went to make himself a drink. Standing in front of the liquor cabinet, he decided to give his liver a break tonight. A glass of iced tea actually sounded better.

With his dinner in front of him, he grabbed his phone from the counter. The thought came to him to check the gardener's website. There might be a picture of him there. *What was the guy's name? Gonzalez, Hernandez, Mendoza?* With his right thumb, he typed:

Gonzalez lawn care . . .one hundred and two hits. Too many to search.

Hernandez lawn care . . . Twice the number of hits.

Lawn service thousand oaks . . . one hundred and sixty-four thousand hits. *Jesus.*

Hot gardener los angeles . . . Naked girls in bikinis popped up. *Okay, he was definitely not a female.*

Hot male gardener los angeles . . . His screen quickly filled with pictures of guys holding clippers and pushing lawn mowers. *Hmm, this may be something.* He scrolled through the pictures. The guys were unquestionably hot, but none of them looked like his gardener.

After a half hour of searching through pictures of sexy male gardeners, he grabbed his room-temperature dinner and took it to the living room for an hour of CNN.

After the top of the news, his mind drifted. *Parker would be okay with me dating again, right?* It would be weird dating someone, being out with someone other than Parker. They were supposed to be together forever. In one of their private jokes, Winston had always said he wanted to die first so that he could haunt the house and scare off any young men creeping around for a sugar daddy. *It's been almost a year. When is it okay to date again?* Was it wrong to think about dating? Was it cheating? He laughed under his breath. He couldn't believe his gardener was invoking such thoughts. He had thought about no one like this—not before Parker had died and certainly not after.

Winston took to his yard for the rest of the week. He made extensive use of the pool and the warm sun, working on his tan. The only time he had ever spent in his own yard was during BBQs, pool parties, or while having cocktails with Parker in the evenings. He had never lain out for hours by himself. Now, he was even napping out there.

He stayed outside until about five o'clock each day. The sun was doing his mind some good. With renewed clarity, he began mapping out his future and what it might look like with the love of his life gone.

By the time Monday rolled around, Winston had a routine figured out: breakfast first, then emails, morning talk shows, and then out to the pool. His phone, iPod, and book in one hand, and a bottled water in the other hand, he set up his lounge chair at the far end of the pool with the house to his back. With a view of the mountain in front of him, he rolled up his board shorts until they almost reached his pelvic area, exposing as much of his pale legs as possible. He nestled deeper into his lounger before picking up his book to read. Within a couple of chapters, his eyelids grew heavy, causing him to lay the bulky hardcover across his chest.

Winston realized he must have dozed off when the sound of a mower being fired up out front jarred him from his nap. His cute gardener was back. With this realization, he felt a light fluttery in his stomach, followed with a concern as to how he looked.

Running his hand across his flat, sweaty stomach, he hated that he was so skinny. *At least I have somewhat of a tan going. It doesn't look that bad.* He repositioned his frame in the lounger for an even tan. He couldn't believe he was nervous and jittery over some guy—his gardener, no less.

It was about thirty minutes before Diego made his way around to the back. Behind the mower, he was wearing light-colored jeans and a V-neck black tee shirt. His baseball cap indicated he was a Dodgers fan.

Seeing Diego, Winston tried to breathe. The gardener was as cute as he remembered.

His eyes shielded by a pair of large sunglasses, Diego's head thumped to the buds in his ear. Wheeling the mower from the walkway to the far corner of the grass, he walked the length of the lawn before making a U-turn and heading back down. On his third pass, he finally glanced up. Seeing Winston, he came to an abrupt stop and turned off the blades of the mower. "I'm sorry. I didn't know anyone was back here."

Winston tried to play it cool. "How are you?" With a flurry of adrenaline rushing through his body, he released a concentrated breath. Winston couldn't avoid staring at the boot-cut jeans that molded themselves to the gardener's thighs. The man's small frame appeared solid, undoubtedly in shape due to the physically demanding labor of gardening. He was young, maybe in his early twenties. Winston's desire to know, touch, and understand more caused his eyes to linger, and an unintentional smile stuck on his face.

"Um, okay . . . I come back tomorrow. I cut it then, no problem." Looking down, Diego turned the mower completely off. Several short, jerky movements followed before his feet stilled behind his mower.

"No, that's alright. You're already here. I was about to go in anyways." Winston slid his feet down onto the patio and slipped into his flip-flops. As he stood up, he inspected his surrounding area before remembering he hadn't been wearing a shirt when he came out. He stepped onto the grass, closer to Diego. "I'm Winston, Winston Makena. I don't think we've ever officially met." Clumsily, he extended his hand to Diego.

Diego removed his work gloves before shaking Winston's hand. "Hello. Diego. Nice to meet you." Both held eye contact a little longer than normal as they shook hands.

Diego's grip was strong, his hands slightly rough from working. Noticing the thick, long curls sticking out from under the gardener's hat, Winston scrambled for his next words. His eyes darted down Diego's jawline, which was strong, defined, and filled with tiny, dark whiskers that cascaded down his neck.

As he released Diego's hand, the silence deepened between them. Winston swallowed, trying to moisten his throat. "Nice to meet—you." Lost for words, he stood there for a second or two. "Okay, I'll let you get back to work."

"Okay," Diego murmured.

With several long strides, Winston headed towards the house, where he was safe. He wanted to turn around and take one last look, but he didn't dare.

Diego called out to him. "Sir, how is everything? The yard, is it okay with you? You like?"

Winston turned as Diego removed his sunglasses, revealing his eyes. They were piercing. The sunlight rendered them a warm cinnamon that made Winston speechless for a split second. "Um, yes . . . The yard looks great. Thank you."

"I come back tomorrow to mow." Diego's forehead furrowed as he used a yellow handkerchief to wipe the sweat from his brow.

The tenor in his voice fell onto Winston's ears like a song. The deep thick accent, the slow drawl, brought his eyes to Diego's full lips; lips any woman would kill for; lips Winston suddenly wanted to kiss. The thought of actually kissing those lips caused the corner of Winston's mouth to twitch. "It's fine. I'm going inside." With the back door in sight, Winston retreated. Trying to control his breath, he exhaled slowly. His fantasy remained with him as he hurried to safety.

In the house, Winston fought the urge to go to the window and look. He couldn't believe how he was acting—as if he was twelve. He took a deep breath as he moved to the window and closed the blinds enough to shield him from sight. Scanning the yard, he found Diego raking a small flowerbed, clueless that he was being watched.

As he observed the young man, a contraction in Winston's stomach told him, *You're doing something wrong. He has to be straight. He looks straight. Damn, he's cute. Okay, that's enough. You're being creepy.* Winston forced himself to move away from the window.

4

Sitting at the table, Diego listened as Rafael and a shirtless Francisco argued over whose responsibility it was to put gas in the car. As always, when Rafael had returned the car that he and Francisco shared, the tank was empty. The three of them fought all the time about money.

Mayra, Francisco's girlfriend of three years, finally called a truce. "Okay, enough!" At just over five feet, she was a pistol and could handle all three of them. She had cooked dinner for the boys this evening, though she didn't officially live there. "You two fight like dogs and cats. Always . . . every night, you fight."

Francisco rubbed his bald, shiny head as he shot her a *mind-your-own-business* expression, a look she never heeded. Diego sat quietly, rushing to finish his dinner so he could retreat to his room. He used the last of a flour tortilla to mop up the remainder of his beans. He had about five minutes before Francisco and Mayra would start fighting.

Diego knew that neither of his brothers had room to talk about how the other spent his money. Rafael pissed it away like it grew on trees; Francisco had thousands of dollars in tattoos that covered his back and arms, and now he was having a piece done on his ribcage. Suddenly, Diego could not stop himself from jumping into their argument. He lashed out at Rafael. "Why don't you put gas in the car? You're being stupid!"

"Go to hell!" Rafael shot back, his face turning instantly red.

Diego had known that calling Rafael stupid would send him over the edge. Since the day their parents had put them on the bus for the three-day trip to the border, where the *coyotes* waited for them, the three brothers had fought like gladiators and yet had been each other's best friends.

When they had left Mexico, Francisco had been twenty; Rafael, eighteen; and Diego had just celebrated his seventeenth birthday. Old enough to take care of each other, they were in the hands of complete strangers and heading to the United States to live with their father's brother and his wife.

When they had arrived, Diego's uncle hadn't thought it was safe to register him or Rafael in public school. Instead, Francisco and Rafael worked with their uncle doing construction, and Diego went to work in the fields. Eight months after arriving, their uncle dropped dead of a heart attack. His wife had returned to Mexico, leaving the boys on their own. Shortly after this, Francisco had started Castillo Lawn Care with the help of his brothers.

Grabbing a tortilla from the middle of the table, Diego excused himself and fled to his bedroom to work on his drawings. Since Rafael worked in the evenings, he would leave soon, giving Diego the bedroom all to himself. For hours, Diego would sit and create lavish landscape designs on his sketchpad. With a stroke of a pencil, he had all the materials he wanted, whether they were rocks, ponds, or fountains. Self-taught, he dreamed of the day that his sketches would become real.

He hadn't been in the room but a couple of minutes when Rafael walked in to grab his shoes for work. "Can you give me a ride? Francisco says I can't take the car tonight." He plopped his long, skinny body down on his bed as he fished for his shoes underneath.

"Why?" Diego eyed his sketch as he put down his pencil.

"I have a date after work. He's worried I won't bring the car back before morning." Rafael's voice was agitated.

Diego didn't say anything. It was Rafael's own fault. How many times had they been forced to hunt him down in the morning so Francisco could drive the car to the shop? How many times had the entire house been in turmoil because of Rafael's selfishness?

"I'll be ready in five minutes." Rafael grabbed his toothbrush from his nightstand and headed to the bathroom.

Diego blew out a large breath. Exhausted, all he wanted to do was relax and draw. Picking the pencil up, he continued sketching out a large gazebo surrounded by water. He could at least finish the gazebo before his brother was ready to leave.

When Rafael reentered, his wet hair was pulled back into a tiny ponytail. Diego immediately caught a strong whiff of the knockoff Polo Red that Rafael bought at the flea market and that he chose to bathe in instead of taking a shower.

"Ready?" Rafael asked as he stood at the door, staring at Diego.

"Yeah." Diego pulled his tired body off his bed.

When they passed the front room, Francisco was on the couch watching the basketball game as Mayra cleaned the kitchen. Diego grabbed the keys to the car and, without saying a word, followed Rafael out the door.

"Who are you going out with tonight?" Diego's eyes dropped to the gas gage. The car was empty again. *Are you shitting me?* "Do you have any money for gas? We need gas." Diego tried to control his anger.

"No. That's what I was trying to tell Francisco. Put ten dollars in it, and I'll pay you back in the morning from my tips tonight."

If Diego wasn't putting gas in the truck, he was putting it in the car. He had forty dollars in his wallet and that was supposed to last him all week. If Rafael didn't pay him back in the morning, the rest of the week would be tight. Dipping into his hidden savings was not an option; he needed that money for his new truck. "So, who are you going out with tonight?" Diego pried. Was it the white girl Rafael worked with? He knew they were sleeping together. At least, they had been a month ago.

"You don't know her. She comes in the shop almost every night for a sugar-free vanilla latte. Her name is Kimmy. Hot little redhead." Rafael gave him a dirty grin. "You want me to ask if she has a sister?"

Rafael was messing with him again. Diego rolled his eyes. "No. I'm good. I'd rather not hang out with you any more than I have to." Rafael's question hadn't required an answer. This was what he did: pushed Diego's buttons for no particular reason.

"That's right. You like to do your shit in private—not let anyone know what you're up to. Where do you go? A hotel, rent a room by the hour?" Rafael poked at his side, causing him to slide closer to the door. "Maybe a prostitute? Is that what you like, fucking a prostitute?" Laughing, Rafael let out a moan, mimicking the sounds of someone making love.

Diego's grip tightened on the steering wheel. The jokes, the prying for information on who he was sleeping with. The truth was, Diego was a virgin. He had never had the same interest in girls as his brothers.

He used to think that he just wasn't ready yet. Then, at the funeral of one of his uncles, an older guy who had been staring at him motioned Diego to follow him into the church's bathroom.

Nervously, Diego had followed the stranger into the stall, where the man had sucked him off. That fifteen-minute encounter was better than any hand job he had ever given himself, and it opened a new world of possibilities. Fascinated by the idea that it could happen again, Diego had given little concern to the consequences of being caught.

After that day, he had paid careful attention to who was watching him, and lo and behold, they were all around him. At eighteen years old, he could walk into any crowded place and find someone who gave him that same *do-you-see-me* look. The stare that was too long to mean anything else. That someone was always a man. Women never ventured into his playing field; it was a man's game.

Now, eight years later, his sexual excursions occurred about once every two months or so.

After a fifteen-minute drive, Diego and Rafael arrived at the Grind. "I'll call you if I need a ride."

"Bullshit. I'm going to bed. Catch the bus." Diego's tone was clear. "Are you coming home before class in the morning?"

Shutting the door, Rafael leaned the top half of his slender body into the open window. "Can you give me a ride to class?"

"Yeah, no problem." Tomorrow's schedule flashed through Diego's head. The Leblanc estate, Mr. Makena. He had seen the name Makena on his checks a thousand times. Mr. Winston Willow Makena. He loved the name "Willow." *Winston Willow Makena*, he said again in his head.

Earlier that day, for a split second, he had thought that Mr. Makena was giving him *the stare* when they had met in the back yard. With his steel-grey eyes and that hair, he was even more attractive than Mr. Legs.

Mr. Leblanc and Mr. Makena lived in a different world than Diego. Rich people dated rich people. Mr. Makena, it turned out, didn't even remember that he and Diego had met before. It was foolish to keep thinking about it. He had heard Francisco tell Rafael a thousand times, *A dog never shits where it eats.*

Diego lingered until Rafael disappeared into the crowded shop. Checking his side mirror, he waited for an opening to merge back in with traffic. Mr. Makena was now stuck in his head, arrogant and unattainable.

The next day, as Diego pulled into the circular driveway, he eyed the silver Maserati parked there. As a car buff, he knew it had cost at least one hundred and sixty thousand dollars brand new. Moving the truck and trailer well past it, he checked his rearview mirror to ensure that his mouth and nose were clean. *Good to go!*

Before getting started, he figured he would take a quick look in the back yard to ensure nothing was happening that would be disturbed by the mower or blower. Circling the house, he heard music playing.

Sure enough, there was Mr. Makena on his stomach, his face buried in his folded arms. Diego studied the man, his eyes moving from his glistening back, waist, and ass down his long legs to his . . . big feet.

Swallowing hard, Diego rolled his tongue along his bottom lip. The moisture as he rubbed his lips together caused dirty thoughts. Mr. Makena was alone; there was no sign that anyone, perhaps another man, was sunbathing with him.

Diego hesitated. If Mr. Makena was indeed sleeping, he would let him nap. There was plenty to do in the front yard that didn't involve making a lot of noise or getting into another strange conversation.

With a sudden movement, Mr. Makena turned over onto his other side, his head now facing Diego. Within seconds, his eyes opened. It took a moment, but their eyes met. There was no avoiding him now.

Diego smiled and waved before making the decision to pull his earbuds from his ear. "Good afternoon, Mr. Makena."

The man raised his head. "*Hola. Como vas?*" A warm smile flashed across his face as he sat up.

"I'm—I'm doing good." Diego forced a smile as he lowered his chin and shrank back.

"Is my car in the way? I'm waiting on the detailer. He was supposed to be here before noon." Mr. Makena picked up his phone and looked at the screen. "Damn, it's after one. Where is he?"

Diego glanced at the man's chest. The small puff of dark hair between his nipples held Diego's attention longer than it should have. *So the Maserati is his. But a detailer? What kind of a person can't wash his own car?* "No, your car's fine . . . I mean okay." *Fine was the wrong word.*

A fine is something you pay. Embarrassed, he bowed his head, breaking eye contact. He hated English; it made no sense to him.

Rising to his feet, Mr. Makena stood next to his chair. His board shorts low around his waist, he slid his feet into his flip-flops. "Do you have a minute?"

"Sure." Avoiding eye contact, Diego looked instead at the large pink and yellow noodles floating in the pool.

Mr. Makena turned to take a sip of his drink. Diego's eyes probed his back. It was broad, tapering down to his waist. His suit hung on his hips, exposing a tiny strip of untanned skin. He was noticeably darker than he had been last week. "Um, is everything not okay?" Diego asked. That tiny sliver of untanned skin was distracting.

The man turned back toward him. "Oh yeah, everything's great. You're an amazing gardener. But I wanted to ask about flowers."

"Oh?" *Flowers?* Diego scanned the surrounding flowerbeds.

"Yeah, flowers. Can I buy some flowers and have you plant them? The yard needs more color. It's missing color this year." Mr. Makena's steel-grey eyes commanded Diego's attention.

"Well, um, sir, Mr. Leblanc he have me purchase what I need for the yard. You have an account at Joaquin's Nursery in town." Diego saw Mr. Makena's eyebrows and forehead taper. Was it because of his English, maybe he didn't understand.

"I didn't know that." Mr. Makena's face loosened. "That's perfect. Do I need to call and okay the charges?"

"No, sir." Diego removed his gloves and scratched the bottom of his nose. The heavy coconut oil coating Mr. Makena's chest tickled his senses. "Do you have an idea of what you want?"

Winston smiled. "I was thinking about something that complemented the purple lavender and yellow lilies." He diverted his eyes to the yard. "Maybe something red? Massive amounts of red everywhere. What do you think?"

Diego thought of the types of flowers blooming right now that came in red. "You want big, tall, or short?" Using his hands to demonstrate the various heights, Diego kept his eyes on the man.

"I don't know. You decide."

Pansies came to mind. Yeah, red pansies would look nice in the yard. He would have to put in a special order due to the volume he needed. "What about pansies? Mr. Leblanc loved the pansies we planted a few years ago. You not want them in the front too?"

"Yes, that would be nice, don't you think? Maybe lining the driveway." Mr. Makena walked toward the planter bed, pointing to where he thought the plants should go.

Diego didn't follow him. Instead, he used that thirty seconds to watch Mr. Makena's ass as it moved under his shorts.

The man jerked his head in Diego's direction. "What do you think of planting them all along here?" He pointed to another flowerbed.

Diego was sure Mr. Makena had caught him staring. Mortified, he avoided his gaze.

Mr. Makena folded his arms across his chest as he walked back towards Diego. "I'm stepping on your toes here. Of course you know where to plant them." He chuckled and smiled again, this time holding Diego's gaze.

Oh my God! Diego caught the *do-you-see-me* stare. He held his breath, not believing this was happening. There was no way. His skin tingled, and a lightness ran through his head as his pulse quickened. Was Mr. Makena coming on to him? He knew that smile.

Struck with an overwhelming desire to flee, he wondered what, exactly, Mr. Makena wanted. He couldn't imagine that Mr. Makena was actually coming on to a man covered in dirt and lawn clippings.

"Can I offer you some iced tea?" The pitch of the man's voice lowered. His eyes, again, held Diego's gaze a little too long.

A lump formed in Diego's throat. Mr. Makena was definitely hitting on him. Trying to breathe normally, he felt his heart pounding. "Um . . . No thank you, sir." Mr. Makena was his client. His mind raced with *what-ifs*.

The man smirked. "Sir? You make me think I'm as old as my dad. Please, call me Winston. I'm sure you won't get into trouble for taking a break. Have some tea. The yard looks incredible. There's nothing else that has to be done today."

Get into trouble? Was he talking about Francisco? No, Diego was sure they had never met. He had landed this and the Bernstein account on his own.

This guy is a dick. Was he insinuating that he worked for someone and couldn't possibly own his own company? Staring at Winston, he was going to pass on the tea. "Well, sir, I go to work. You have several broken sprinkler heads that need replacing in the front, and I need to trim the queen palms." Diego turned his attention to the four palm trees next to the house. "They have little seed pods that bloom and drop to the ground. I'm sure you not like the mess."

Diego stroked the back of his neck. His discomfort level was through the roof. The last thing he should do was follow Winston into that house.

"Okay, I understand." Winston lifted his shoulders in a half-shrug. "Well, I can't wait to see the flowers in the yard."

"Yeah, I call Joaquin's this afternoon and place the order. They have them in a couple of days, and I come back." Diego fiddled with his ear buds. He was ready to retreat back into his world.

"Great . . . Well, I have some stuff I need to do inside. It was nice seeing you again." Winston flashed a subdued smile as he extended his hand. "See you next week?"

Diego had enjoyed the absence of people at the Bernstein and Leblanc estates, the tranquil, uninterrupted time alone. But now, a part of him liked the thought of seeing Winston next week.

Just past midnight, Diego was still awake. He lay across his bed staring at his phone, scrolling through pictures of his cousins in Mexico sent by his aunt. Though he had left Mexico at age seventeen, there wasn't a day that Diego didn't think of his small village of Mezcala in the state of Guerrero. Sure, life was better here, but that place held his family, his friends, and childhood memories of playing in the Atoyac River.

He smiled as he remembered fishing from the bridge of that river with his *abuelo*, just the two of them. It killed him that he hadn't been able to see him one more time before he died. Knowing that the entire family had attended the funeral except for him and his brothers, he felt that he had never gotten closure. Maybe that was why he often thought of his *abuelo* as still alive. Diego would sometimes wonder what he was up to until the realization returned that he was gone.

The memory of his mother's *menudo*, cooking on the stove all day, suddenly penetrated his nose, sending a calmness down his spine.

Shifting his weight on the bed, he heard the metal-spring frame clang. The same sound came from Francisco's room when he and Mayra were having sex. The walls were thin in the two-bedroom apartment. He was thankful for the quiet old woman who lived in the unit under them. She and her two cats never made a noise. Diego shifted again on the bed. The clang triggered the urge to jerk off before Rafael came home.

He looked at the time in the lower corner of his screen. If Rafael was coming home, he would probably have been home by now. Usually, Diego didn't mind that his brother was a *perro*; it meant he didn't have to share the room or the bathroom with him on most nights. But tonight was different. Diego was missing having someone to chat with until one of them dozed off. The whir and rattle of the ceiling fan drew his attention. He watched the silver chain in the mostly dark room as it whacked against the light fixture. It was funny—he rarely paid any attention to that sound anymore. It had become white noise.

Diego listened for sounds from the front room. The muffled noise of guns firing on television told him that Francisco was still up, watching one of his favorite cop shows. Mayra was most likely draped across his lap in a light sleep.

Trying to shrug off his loneliness, Diego rolled over. Both Mr. Legs and Winston came to mind. *Who was cuter?* Hands down, it was

Winston. Those long legs, his glossy black hair, that oily chest. *Okay, then, between Winston and Mr. LeBlanc . . .* Winston won again.

Winston and Mr. Leblanc were the only gay couple Diego knew. In fact, they were the only gay *people* he knew. Francisco would freak if he knew about Winston. From the comments Rafael and Francisco made every time a gay person was on TV, Diego knew that they thought being gay was the same thing as being a pedophile.

Does Winston's family know he's gay? Diego didn't understand how it was that white families didn't appear to care about homosexuality. Every TV show had a gay person on it these days, surrounded by people who loved them. Maybe it was the fact that white people had money. People overlooked a lot if you had money.

His thoughts drifted to his dream truck. Oh, the things he could do if he had money. Would he bring his parents to the US, or would he return home? He bounced back and forth before realizing it was a win-win either way. Still, if he returned home, what about sex? He couldn't think of one gay person that he knew of in Mexico. No, he would definitely stay here.

He heard the front door open. It had to be Rafael coming home. Then he heard Francisco and Rafael talking. Minutes later, the bedroom doorknob turned, and Rafael entered. "What are you doing?"

Diego rolled over to face his brother. "Just lying here. How was work?"

"Okay." Rafael pulled his shirt off and stripped down to his boxers. Adjusting himself in his underwear first, he folded his jeans three times and tossed them at the foot of his bed. "Anything going on?"

Diego wished he were as cool and confident as his brother. Rafael had a better body than him, and he was taller, like Francisco and their father. His simple interaction with Winston earlier in the day had more than pushed him out of his comfort zone. "Just work. Mayra made *pozole* for dinner." Diego rubbed his stomach. "It was as good as Grandma's."

"Oh, she's rolling over in her grave, hearing you say that. Is there any left?"

"There was a whole pot on the stove. I had a couple of bowls, but there was a lot left, I think." Diego's eyes followed his big brother as he plopped onto his bed and adjusted his pillow.

"I'll check it out later," said Rafael.

Diego picked up his phone and looked at the time. "You're home late."

"Yeah, it was me and my boss closing tonight. The place was a wreck. We had one guy go home sick. The shop was so busy that we couldn't start on the prep work until after we closed." Rafael grabbed his phone from their shared nightstand. With a few clicks, he tapped out a text and then laid the phone at his side. "Then I fucked her." His phone buzzed, causing him to snatch it up and look at the screen. With a guffaw, he quickly pounded out a message.

"What? Where?" Diego sat up on his elbow. There was a flutter in his belly. Rafael's bravery continuously shocked him. The thought of having sex at work . . .

Rafael smiled. "Her office." He then launched into the graphic details of his evening. Diego listened, living through his brother's excitement. Somehow, what Diego did—going into public bathrooms with strangers—had always left him with a sense of emptiness. He felt a charge leading up to it, and then *bam*, it was over. It was meaningless, and each time, he told himself he would never do it again. Then, he would push it to the back of his mind, where no one would ever find it.

Threading a hand through his hair, he thought of Winston. Unlike strangers, Winston made him nervous for some reason. Diego would be lying if he said he had not had sexual thoughts about the man this past week.

There was no way it would ever happen. A good chunk of change was attached to that account—money he couldn't afford to lose.

Most of his clients made him nervous. The way they looked at him, spoke to him. Sure, they were pleasant, but it was hollow. What always came across was their posturing. They ensured that the roles were clear: they were rich, and he worked for them.

5

"Have you seen that cute gardener of yours lately?"

Ann's not-so-subtle change in the direction of their conversation was not lost on Winston. Pausing for a moment to shift his thoughts, he regretted calling her. He had made a total fool of himself when he attempted to talk to Diego last week. "I tried talking to him . . . I don't know, maybe it's too soon." Winston patted the end of the couch, signaling for Lucy to jump up next to him. Her little pink tongue dangling from her mouth, the tiny black and white French bulldog plopped her behind on the light-colored Monaco vintage rug instead.

Ann laughed. "Too soon for what?"

Hearing the sarcasm in her voice, he chose not to react. "I don't know." Drawing in a deep breath, he thought about how much he ought to share with her. What did he want, or better yet, what did he expect, from flirting with his gardener? It was crazy that Diego had even appealed to him; he was so young.

For ten years, Winston's heart had belonged to one person. They were going to be together forever. Guilt gurgled in his stomach like acid. *How could I be thinking about someone else so soon?* He tried to shield his mood from his friend. "I'm not interested in seeing anyone. I'm not ready."

"No one said you had to marry the guy. Be the little whore you were before you met Parker. Have some fun. You're not coming back to the office until you have some fun. You need to get laid for the hell of it. It would do wonders for your mood and outlook. How can you be creative at work with all that semen clogging your brain?"

"Ann!"

"Don't 'Ann' me. You know I'm right."

"He is cute." Winston unclenched his fingers, which had tightened into a fist at some point. He laughed at himself. "What am I supposed to say? 'Hey, you want to come in and have sex?'" He wasn't going to set himself up for rejection. *Why would he want to sleep with me anyways? He may not like older men, or white men for that matter.*

"Come on, I know you. You've got game. Don't pretend to be a shy little virgin."

Winston rolled his eyes. It was now his turn to change the subject. "Look, I've got to get going. It's almost noon, and I haven't even taken a shower yet." It was also Monday, and the very person they were talking about would be here soon. He wasn't sure what would happen, but week three had to go better. He would at least try to talk to Diego again.

Taking a long, hot shower, Winston did a little manscaping for the first time in months. Parker had preferred him clean shaven—really clean shaven, from his neck to his ankles. After Parker's death, Winston hadn't had the energy to do it as often as he should. Eventually, he had stopped all together. It evoked too many memories and feelings, and if he wasn't having sex, it seemed pointless.

He was out of practice, and the task took a lot longer than he planned. Once dry, he stood in front of the mirror above the sink. He turned his naked body sideways to examine it and poked at his boney hipbone. The tan helped to mask what he didn't like. Leaning toward the mirror, Winston ran his right hand through his hair, deciding how to fix it.

Ann was right; he did need a haircut. He had totally let himself go. He felt as if he was sixty years old instead of thirty-two. During his ten years of marriage, everything about his life had become a pattern. When had *they*, of all people, become so settled? That was one of the reasons they had moved out of LA: to escape the illusion that youth was forever.

He slowly ran his hands across his newly shaved arms. Their smoothness was surprising, but it also felt good and familiar.

A light-heartedness washed over him, and he exhaled. He changed his mind: he would lie out by the pool and surprise Diego again with his presence. He wanted to look nice—okay, cute. Quickly doing his hair, he then changed his clothes twice, first putting on shorts that weren't dressy enough before settling on a white polo shirt and a pair of Saint Laurent slim-fitting pants that complimented his thinness.

Shortly after one o'clock, he heard the clang of the front gate. Diego had arrived. It felt like show time. Winston smoothed out the front of his shirt, ensuring the tuck was even all the way around. Nervous, but ready, he took a deep breath and told himself that he had to try. *Just go outside and talk to the guy.*

With a stomach full of butterflies, Winston turned and left the safe haven of his bedroom.

By the time he got outside, Diego had already unloaded the mower and several other tools from the trailer. Removing a flat of red pansies from the bed of the truck, he had his back to Winston as he approached.

"Good afternoon." Winston fought to control his breathing and walk at the same time.

Diego spun. Both of his eyebrows shot up. "*Buenas tardes* . . . um, good afternoon."

"I see you found the pansies. They're beautiful." Winston found it easier to start with the flowers.

"You like?" Diego held the flowers out for Winston's inspection.

Winston felt a quiver in his throat. Flowers were the last thing on his mind. "Can I ask you something?"

Diego's nose wrinkled. Placing the flowers on the ground, he raised his chin before dropping his eyes towards Winston's powder-blue pants. "Uhh, yeah."

"Parker loved it when you planted those a couple of years ago. They're going to look nice in the yard." Winston rubbed his hands together as he admired all the flowers. Silence dropped between them as a noisy blue jay landed a few feet away. "You said the other day that Parker loved these flowers." Dropping his fingers towards the flat of bright red flowers, Winston choked on his words. "Um—what other flowers did Parker like?"

"Well, you have the jasmine blooming, the bougainvilleas are starting . . . and your crepe myrtles in front are going to be beautiful in a couple of weeks." Diego shrugged. "I think he . . . Mr. Leblanc very much liked the bougainvilleas in the yard."

Winston smiled. Diego was right. Parker had loved the dark raspberry flowers that filled the lattice against the back of the house. His eyes wandered over towards the bougainvillea vines. Sure enough, they were blooming beautifully. How had he missed that? A rush of adrenaline tingled through his body as he glanced around the yard, looking for whatever else he had missed. "He loved this yard. Thank you for always making it so nice."

"Um, thank you—for the work." Diego took a step back. His eyes looked away every time Winston's made contact. "Sir, *mi madre* once said that a flower will bloom at the right moment. When the time is right, it will reveal its beauty. It lives in the moment."

"Your mother was a wise woman, but please, stop calling me sir!" Winston certainly didn't need help feeling old. "I can't be that much older than you. How old are you, anyway?" He would have guessed twenty-two or twenty-three.

Diego's brows narrowed across his face. "Twenty-five."

"I'm thirty-two. Not old enough to be your father, so please stop calling me 'sir,' 'Mr. Makena,' or anything else you would call an old man." He smiled, and a tiny chuckle seeped out. "You're killing me with that stuff."

His joke didn't get a smile out of Diego, who said only, "I'm sorry." Diego's eyes dropped again to the flat of flowers, his face giving away nothing.

Winston hadn't meant to reprimand him. Trying to break the ice, he said, "Oh, I wanted to show you something."

Diego raised his head, allowing their eyes to meet for only a second. Then he broke eye contact and took a step back.

Detecting Diego's discomfort, Winston questioned his own words. "Um, there was something I wanted to show you . . . in the house." He pressed forward with his plan.

There was nervousness in Diego's eyes—in the way they fluttered, first looking at him and then anywhere but him. Winston thought that he should abort his mission before he made a fool of himself again. What had made him think, one, that Diego was gay, and two, that Diego would be interested in him? "I understand if you're busy," Winston said, stepping back and increasing the distance between them. There was that unnatural stillness again. "I'm sure your boss wouldn't appreciate me taking up your time. Sorry." He had to get out of there as quickly as possible.

"I have a few minutes." The expression on Diego's face softened as he tilted his head slightly to the left.

"Oh, good. We were talking about Parker. I wanted to show you something inside the house." Winston hesitated, second-guessing what he was doing. "I promise it will only take a minute."

Diego removed his heavy-duty work gloves and stuffed them into his back pocket. He followed Winston to the house, neither speaking until they reached the back door.

Before stepping inside, Diego kneeled down and began untying his bootlace.

Winston blurted, "Oh no! You don't have to do that. It's fine."

Diego looked up, revealing his narrowed brows. "No?"

Winston looked down at Diego's brown work boots. He couldn't help but see them as sexy. His eyes climbed up Diego's jeans, sending a rush of adrenaline through his body as their eyes finally met.

Diego held his stare. "My boots, leave them on?"

"Um, yeah . . . Don't worry about it." They were only going across the hall into his office. Who cared if Diego tracked dirt in? He was in the house and that was all that mattered.

Winston led the way into his office, stopping at a long, narrow glass table against the wall. There sat a porcelain vase, several framed pictures, and a tiny crystal clock. Hanging above the table were several certificates and awards.

Diego stopped directly behind Winston. Arms at his sides, he glanced around the room.

Pointing to a certificate on the wall, Winston glanced over his shoulder at Diego. "Parker got this a month before he died. It's his master gardening certification." Winston removed the certificate from the wall and handed it to Diego.

Diego eyed the certificate for a minute or two, his lips lightly moving. His expression softened as he continued reading the entire certificate.

"He loved gardening." Taking the frame, Winston returned it to its hook. Then his face stiffened. "The pansies made me think of this."

"I not know Mr. Leblanc loved gardening this much. He was a nice man." Diego's eyes took in the rest of the frames on the wall. "A couple of years ago, he . . ." Diego stopped. His brow wrinkled as if he was thinking.

"What? Go on." Winston's voice cracked as the words caught in his throat.

"I remember one day, maybe two years ago, when I pulled up, there were flowers planted everywhere. It would have taken me all week to plant that many flowers. He say he had done it himself. Say he was bored. He is the one who told me about the pansies, about them lasting all spring. Tell me they were your favorite flowers and how much you loved the color red." Diego took a step away from the wall and shoved his hands into his pockets.

With one hand, Winston straighten the frame back on the wall. He felt the enthusiasm draining from his body as his chest tightened. Parker's presence was in the room. Winston's eyes shifted to the doorway, fully expecting to see Parker standing there. "He would talk to anyone. I'm sure he talked your ear off." Winston again glanced back at the doorway.

"I not have a boss." Diego crossed his arms over his chest.

"Huh?" Winston was not sure what he had said. The only word he caught was boss. *"Jefe?"* he asked, translating the word into Spanish.

"I am my own boss. I own Castillo Lawn Care. That's me, Diego Jose Ramirez Castillo." Diego's chin thrust upward, his eyes locked on Winston.

"Oh!" Winston realized he had offended Diego. His eyes shifted to the man's clothes, taking a mental inventory of what he wore. "Is it a family business? Your *familia?*"

With an obviously fake smile, Diego shrugged. "At one time, it was my brothers and me. It's just me now." His voice trailed off as he brushed his palms together and nodded. "Mr. Leblanc made the sign on my truck door."

"The sign on *your* truck?" Winston turned towards the window, looking for the vehicle. His Parker never stopped surprising him.

"*Si.* Last Christmas, he say I should be advertising my business."

Looking back at Diego, Winston smiled. "I had no idea." That was just like Parker, to have something made for someone as if it was no big deal. They always gave the housekeeper a nice check for Christmas; he was sure they had taken care of the gardener as well.

"Did you and Parker talk often?" As soon as he said it, he wondered if Diego was going to take it the wrong way. Winston was interested in Parker: what he had said, what he had done, anything Diego could share.

Diego frowned. "Mr. Leblanc was a gentleman."

"No, I mean—" Winston tried to think of the right Spanish word. "*Hablo.* Did the two of you talk?" Pointing to his lips, he repeated,

"*Hablo?*" The commonality they shared in missing Parker caused a light flutter in Winston's chest, a pang in his heart.

"*Si, si.* He was friendly." Diego's smile intensified, revealing tiny dimples as his cheeks puffed.

Winston's eyes shifted from his dimples to his lips. The bottom one was slightly larger than the top. They were thick and kissable. He needed to look away but didn't. "Did you go to college for landscaping?"

"No, I learned everything I know by doing it. Of course, Mr. Leblanc teach me a lot. I would like to take some classes one day—at the college, maybe." He shrugged.

Winston noticed that he did that a lot, shrugged his shoulders. Then there was that thing he did with his hair—his fingers ran through his tousled locks every time he removed his baseball cap. It was sexy. The smile returned to Winston's face as he listened to Diego's adorable accent.

"I like my work. I like being outside all day. The weather doesn't bother me too much." Diego smiled slightly as he stepped closer to the wall, looking at the other frames. Spotting a diploma, Diego glanced over at Winston. "Did you go to USC?"

"Yeah, Parker and I met there. He ran track."

"Did you like it there, at the school?"

"It was alright. Why do you ask?" Winston had never given it much thought. "I went to Hawthorne Elementary, Beverly Hills High, and then on to USC."

Shoulders relaxing, Diego looked at another frame. "USC. It is a good school, no?"

"It is." Winston watched as Diego studied the diplomas and certificates. It was stupid to ask if he had gone to college. He barely spoke English. Winston wanted to ask where he was born, but he didn't want to make the guy uncomfortable with another stupid question. "And you? Where did you go to school?" That might tell him if Diego had been born here or in Mexico.

"In Mezcala, Guerrero."

"Is that in Mexico?" Studying Diego's face and his prominent jaw, which curved gracefully around his thin neck, Winston drank in the thick, midnight-black locks of hair that rested on the back collar of his shirt.

"Yes. In Guerrero."

"Do you mean Guerrero, the state?" Winston's attention was now drawn back to Diego's lips. His cheeks were a beautiful light caramel color and appeared soft. Winston wanted to touch them.

Winston forced himself to blink, but it didn't help. Diego's pretty eyelashes, draped over his brown eyes, mesmerized him, causing him to lose his concentration. Again, Winston felt the urge to kiss him and knew he had to look away.

"Yes, Mezcala is between Mexico City and Acapulco. You know?" Diego asked.

"Um, no. I've never been to Mexico." Winston's body temperature rose, his face warming due to Diego's proximity. Although he was paralyzed by the man's beauty, there was something else, deeper than beauty.

"Really? You should go. Do you like Mexican food?"

"You mean like tacos, burritos, and stuff?" Winston tried to focus on what Diego was saying.

Diego laughed as he shrugged yet again. "Seafood, frijoles, chilies?"

"Seafood? How is that Mexican?" Winston's ear smoothed out the thick accent, turning it into another thing that was attractive about Diego.

"Lobster, shrimp, fish . . . We make everything with it: empanadas, soups, ceviche, tacos, and tostadas." Diego's eyes sparkled as he gave a thumbs up. "The trucks, they deliver every day. Fresh from the sea, everything!"

Hearing the excitement in Diego's tone, Winston was drawn in. "Do you like to cook?"

"Me? No!" Diego laughed. "I make, how you say . . . P & J?"

It took Winston a second. "Oh, peanut butter and jelly!"

"Yes, yes, peanut butter and jel-ly." Diego's eyes lit up as he simulated spreading a knife across a piece of bread and then licked his lips. There was a softness to his smile, a boyish look that revealed more about him than he might have wanted to share.

"How old did you say you were?" Winston asked.

Diego stopped laughing and straightened his body. "Um, twenty-five. Why?" The corners of his mouth retained his grin.

The dark brown, almost black irises in his smoky eyes seized Winston. When he blinked, it gave Winston the millisecond he needed to break free of the trance. He retreated with a clumsy step backwards and a large breath to cleanse his lungs. "It's amazing that you have your own business and are so smart. You're mature for twenty-five."

"Um, yeah. I should . . . I have work to do." Looking at his watch, Diego glanced back at Winston before removing his ball cap from the small of his back. He hesitated for a moment before placing it on his head and adjusting the brow.

No, don't go! I want to kiss you. I want you to stay, but I don't know how to ask you. Winston's expression dulled. "Yeah, I have work I need to be doing as well."

Watching Diego's backside as he left the room, seeing how his ass molded the back of his jeans perfectly, Winston felt a pinch of guilt. He was a married man. The gold band on his finger said so. Unconsciously, his thumb flicked at the bottom of the band as he heard the back door shut.

6

Diego walked into the apartment a little after six o'clock. Francisco and Rafael were both sitting on the couch, watching yet another old re-run of their favorite show, *Alborada*, on MundoVision. The show reminded Diego of *The Three Musketeers*. The gorgeous Fernando Colunga, *Alborada*'s star, was the only reason Diego had ever watched. Mayra had her back to them as she stood in front of the stove cooking. Whatever she was fixing, the aroma made him instantly hungry. Though Diego was always thankful that she was in their lives, he often felt guilty that she cleaned hotel rooms all day and then came here to cook and clean up after them.

Stopping in front of the TV, Diego hoped the sexy Fernando would appear in one of his many shirtless scenes. As usual, he didn't have to wait but a second or two. Diego crossed his arms as he looked over at his brothers and then back at the screen. Fernando's sexy jet-black hair, brown eyes, and macho daddy swagger made Diego quiver. *Now that was a man!* Lost in a sexy daydream, Diego didn't hear Rafael address him.

"Cabron, stop dreaming of your boyfriend. Can you give me a ride to work?" Rafael asked. He grabbed Diego's ass. "Baby brother, you like that?"

Embarrassed, Diego jumped out of the reach of Rafael's long arms. Rafael didn't know he was actually checking out Fernando—he just wanted to get that rise out of Diego that both his brothers enjoyed so much. "Stop it!" Diego slammed his open palm against the back of Rafael's head, more in reaction to his comment then his assault.

"Francisco, Rafael . . . dinner's almost ready. Diego, go wash up, get ready to eat," Mayra instructed.

Diego knew she was intervening on his behalf. It wasn't necessary; he could take care of himself. With another quick smack to the back of Rafael's head, Diego shot past him and down the short hall to their room. With Fernando on the brain, he compared the TV star's looks with Winston's. Winston wasn't Mexican, for one thing. Maybe Italian or Greek, but definitely not Mexican.

Diego's interaction with Winston this afternoon replayed in his head. They had stood shoulder to shoulder, the woodsy, clean scent of Winston's cologne in the air.

There was something about the way Winston looked at him—something enamoring behind those stunning grey eyes. But as sexy as Winston was, Diego wanted to flee every time he was around the man. The dry mouth and inability to think made him nervous.

He remembered Winston's outfit. No doubt those blue slacks had been expensive. Even his plain white polo shirt looked different, crisp, like it had never been worn. Though Diego was poor, he could recognize quality—the way the fabric fitted to the contours of Winston's body, tailored without looking tight. Yes, it was quality.

Diego remembered visiting a shop on Rodeo Drive about a year ago. A girl who Rafael was seeing had worked there, and while Rafael was talking to her, Diego wandered the floor. He had stopped at an assembly of shirts folded neatly on a display stand. When he saw their prices, he couldn't get out of the store fast enough.

Waiting on the street for Rafael wasn't any better. Everybody that passed had stared as if Diego was wearing a clown outfit. It was clear the brothers didn't belong in that neighborhood.

Whatever Mayra was cooking caused his stomach to growl. With his work clothes off, he held his shirt to his nose, weighing whether he could get another day out of them. The shirt was definitely out, but the pants he could wear again.

Once inside the bathroom, Diego washed his face, arms, and hands in the rusty basin. Winston occupied his thoughts. They had encountered each other regularly for the last three weeks.

For years, it was Fernando that he had daydreamed about. More recently, it had been Mr. Legs. Two fantasies, both tall, dark, and handsome. Winston was a combination of them both. The fact that he was a client made him safe to fantasize about, untouchable.

After dinner, Diego retreated to his room, where he amused himself by playing on his phone. He had been in there about ten minutes when someone knocked lightly on the door. Not waiting for permission to enter, Mayra poked her head inside. "Hey, I'm taking off. I'll be happy to drop Rafael off tonight for you."

He smiled at her. "Thank you. That would be great." Why was she leaving? Were she and Francisco fighting? Diego studied her face.

"Goodnight," she said softly.

"Goodnight," he replied as she shut the door.

Diego settled back down in his bed, glad he didn't have to go out again that evening. Shirtless, he ran his hand across his stomach. There was no denying his attraction to Winston. Ordinary thoughts about the man quickly turned sexual. Diego wanted to touch himself. He listened for any noise from out front.

Then he lightly brushed his hand across his nipple. His breath caught. If Mayra and Rafael were gone, he was safe. Francisco wouldn't walk in on him; he was probably already asleep on the couch. Brushing his hand down his chest, he felt the coarse hair that led down below. Reaching for the drawstring on his sweatpants, he loosened the waistband. It had been a while. As he was about to slip out of his pants, Mayra's voice boomed, telling Rafael to hurry. Frozen, Diego knew it would have to wait.

Soon, he drifted off to sleep. The desire would have to be enough.

7

It had been four weeks since Winston first saw Diego in his yard, tending to his flowerbeds. Every Monday and Tuesday for the last month, he had been trying to figure out whether Diego was gay or not. There had been little, fleeting moments—a look or a smile—that said maybe.

The previous night on the phone, Ann had laughed at him when he explained his lack of progress with the Diego investigation. "I've never known you to be shy. I can't believe you haven't figured this guy out yet. You've turned into a groundhog, scared of your own shadow."

"What am I supposed to do? Reach out and grab the dude and plant one on him? See if he kisses me back?"

"No, but go talk to him. Find out what he likes."

Taking Ann's advice, that morning, Winston made several PB & Js: two with chunky peanut butter and strawberry jam, another two with smooth peanut butter and grape jam, and one with orange marmalade. Cutting them into halves, he arranged the sandwiches on a silver tray. Then he decided against the formal look and stacked them on a dinner plate instead.

From in the kitchen, he heard the metal clang of the front gate as it closed. It was after one o'clock. With an exhale, he wiped his sweaty palms down his thighs. Suddenly he thought, *What if he's already eaten lunch?*

This was stupid. What was he thinking? He was not going to carry a stack of PB & J sandwiches out to his gardener like Martha Stewart.

From the kitchen window, he saw Diego exit his truck and begin unloading his equipment from the box trailer. Winston glanced at the PB & Js. Was he really going to take them out? This was ridiculous, him standing next to a stack of sandwiches, peeping out the window. His heart was in his throat as he inhaled a forced breath, his insecurities bubbling to the surface.

Watching Diego's every move, Winston's heart continued to pound. *Take the sandwiches before he gets started*, he told himself. *It's a sandwich, not a marriage proposal.*

Before he could talk himself out of it, he had picked up the plate and walked out the front door. He was about fifteen feet away when Diego looked up and smiled at him. *Okay, this is good. Careful, watch your step, don't trip. God, wouldn't that be horrible?* "Hey there. I . . . I have something for you."

With the dinner plate just inches from Diego's chest, Winston watched as the man eyed the plate of sandwiches. Trying to be respectful, Winston reminded himself not to stare at the beauty before him. He glanced away, but it was only but a second before his eyes found their way back to Diego. This time, it was his flawless honey-brown cheeks. His skin shone perfection. There was no cream or amount of money that could give anybody skin that beautiful. You had to be born with it. Winston knew he was staring and felt thankful that Diego was avoiding his ill-mannered gaze.

"What is this?" Diego raised his head, his warm cognac eyes meeting Winston's.

"Um, last week, you said you liked peanut butter and jelly. I thought it would be a way to say thank you for planting all those flowers last week." Winston tried to control his breathing. "I wasn't sure what you liked, so I made a couple of different ones." He pointed to the top one. "This is strawberry with chunky peanut butter, and—"

Diego reached out and took the sandwich that Winston was about to describe. "Thank you."

"I wasn't sure if you had already eaten lunch. You don't have to eat all of—"

"Um . . . yeah, I had lunch before I come here." Again, a warm smiled curved the edges of Diego's lips.

"Oh."

"Mmm, this is good." Holding the sandwich up, Diego smiled. "You make a good sandwich. Thank you."

"You're welcome." A calming breath escaped Winston as he decided this had been a good call. "I made three versions, and I was curious what a real PB & J lover would prefer." Cracking a slight smile, he was stumped as to what to say next. What was he supposed to do with this mountain of sandwiches now? "Um, um, how was your weekend?" was the only thing he could think to say.

"Good. I work at my brother's shop on Saturdays."

"You have brothers?" His dry mouth was making it difficult to speak. Clearing his throat didn't help. He was going to die.

"Yes, two." Diego took another bite of his sandwich.

"Oh, are you the oldest?" Winston tried not to stare at the tiny bit of jelly at the corner of Diego's mouth. He wanted that jelly. No, he wanted to *be* that jelly.

"Francisco is twenty-eight, and Rafael is . . . twenty-six?"

"So you're the baby."

One of Diego's brows arched. "Baby?"

"I mean, the youngest," Winston clarified.

"*Si.*" Diego tapped himself on his chest with his index finger and nodded. "I am twenty-five."

There was a moment of silence apparently noticed only by Winston. Diego finished his sandwich and licked his lips clean. Winston held up the plate. "Would you like another?"

With one hand, Diego waved the plate off and shook his head. "No, no, thank you." He licked jelly from the tips of his fingers, and again, his mouth gave way to a nervous smile. "Thank you again for the sandwich. It was kind of you." His eyes darted towards his trailer.

Winston's eyes automatically followed and then returned to Diego as he released a silent, controlled breath. "I used to love these as a kid. I don't know why I don't eat them more often."

Diego again looked at the trailer. "Is there anything you would like me to do today? I cut the lawn. Make weed-eater today . . . No?"

"Whatever you have planned is fine. I . . . I . . . I have work to do inside." Winston fidgeted, shifting his weight from one leg to the other. His heart pounded. *Don't be a groundhog,* he told himself. "Okay . . . So . . ." His voice stammered, causing him to clear his throat yet again. "I'll let you get to work."

Diego nodded but didn't move.

"Okay," said Winston. *Okay, now that you have made a total fool of yourself, it's time to retreat.* Pivoting, he bolted towards the house. He wanted to look back, but he didn't dare. It had been forever since he tried to flirt with someone, and he was apparently terrible at it. Safe behind the front door, he leaned against it and closed his eyes. When, exactly, had he lost his mojo? He pictured himself as a groundhog.

With one eye shut, peeping through the blinds, Winston held his phone to his ear with his shoulder. He watched Diego strap a large blower to his back and begin blowing dust and dirt from the driveway. "Ann, if you could have seen it. I didn't know what to say. I'm a moron."

"I'm sure it wasn't that bad. But that's good."

"Um, why is that good?" Winston continued watching as Diego disappeared into the back of his trailer.

"Because it means you like him. If you didn't like him, you wouldn't care so much."

"I don't even know if he's gay."

"Well, there's something there, don't you think? Listen to your gut."

"Ann, I think I'm just horny. It's been a year." As Diego emerged from the trailer with a rake and a grey plastic trashcan, Winston adjusted himself in his underwear.

"Well, if that's it, I'm glad you're horny. It's progress. You need to go back out there and talk to him."

"I'm not going back out there." Winston thought of Diego's friendly smile. There was that spark in his eye, something that said Diego might not only be gay, but also interested.

Behind the blinds, Winston kept an eye on Diego while continuing his conversation with Ann. The whole thing was a little ridiculous. He was acting as if they were all twelve years old. Furthermore, Diego was the gardener and a baby. Was it the seven-year age difference? Surely not. Was it the fact that he was a gardener, or that he barely spoke English? *Love has no language, so they say.* Winston smiled at this absurd thought as he watched Diego rake out one flowerbed before moving onto the next.

"I have to go," Ann said. "I have a three o'clock with Christian about the Harper Gala."

"Oh, what's going on with that?"

"Not discussing that with you. You're on vacation—time off. I can handle it."

"I'm just asking."

"Okay, then I'm hanging up."

"Okay, okay. I'll talk to you later. Goodbye." Disconnecting the call, Winston realized that he needed some air. He had started taking Lucy to the dog park down the hill. It was about a twenty-minute walk. He had actually met some of his neighbors for the first time. Some knew Parker and had heard him talk about Winston. It was weird that, while they knew things about him, he didn't have a clue who they were. Had he been living in a glass bubble, a groundhog by nature?

Right now, he simply lacked the energy for a walk. He needed to start boxing up Parker's stuff on his side of the office. The Disabled

American Veterans were coming by at five to take the desk, the chair, and several other items to new homes.

Winston thought about fixing a drink. He hadn't had one in two weeks, and he didn't really want one, but that didn't stop the urge from hitting him several times a day. He pushed past the desire for a cocktail. For the first time in a while, a sense of normalcy wasn't followed by guilt.

When he could just shut off his brain, stop thinking for a moment, he found that he could actually breathe. This was impossible, though, come bedtime. The loneliness of crawling into an empty bed never got easier. Parker was supposed to be here, and no amount of alcohol could change that. It felt as if the bed was going to swallow him, drop him into some black, empty hole. Lying there, he simply waited for it to happen. Night after night, he waited.

Winston glanced at his watch, he knew that he had to start on the desk, or he would never have it ready for the Disabled American Veterans.

He worked at clearing out the desk before moving on to Parker's two filing cabinets. Soon, he was sitting in the middle of three piles of paper: to shred, to save, to further examine. Then he heard Diego closing his trailer.

Jumping to his feet, Winston wiggled his toes and steadied himself as he waited for his foot, which had fallen asleep, to wake up. The wall clock showed that it was ten to five. With no time to wait for his foot to wake up, he limped to the window and pulled back the sheers.

Yes, it looked as if Diego was leaving. Removing his gloves, he stuffed them into his rear pants pocket before reaching in and taking a water jug from the bed of the truck. Winston looked on as he took several large gulps of water before removing his sunglasses and hat. Splashing water onto the back of his neck and then across his mouth, Diego was oblivious that he was being watched. Winston couldn't let him leave without talking to him once more. So what if he was turning into a stalker? He had to go out there. He refused to be a groundhog!

Within seconds, he was out the door with the sandwiches, which he had bagged up. He hurried towards Diego, who was walking towards the front of his truck. Increasing his pace, Winston called to him. "Hey, Diego, I wanted to know . . . um, if you . . . wanted the rest of these sandwiches." He couldn't believe he had actually grabbed the sandwiches and was now offering them to the man.

Diego stopped and turned. Still reaching for the door handle of his truck, he looked at the bag of sandwiches.

Winston stopped less than a foot away from him. The flecks of gold in Diego's eyes dominated everything for a split second. "I'm never going to eat all of these," Winston said. "Thought you might want them. I thought, since you were such a fan of my cooking skills, you might like to take them."

A bright smile appeared on Diego's face—as if he was laughing inside. "I not say I was a fan, but they are my favorite."

Winston's heart jumped from his chest. *Yes, you did. You said you loved making peanut butter and jelly sandwiches . . . I think.* Forcing a smile, Winston lowered the sandwiches to his side. "Oh, I thought you said . . ."

"No, I say it was the only thing I make. You asked if I could cook." Diego's smile turned playful. "I say I not know how to cook, but I could make a P&J."

Winston stared into Diego's eyes. Had their color actually changed? He was sure their irises had been a dark, rich chocolate, but now they were a beautiful honey. They captured him, hypnotized him. Winston forced himself to blink, shaking the awestruck hold Diego had on him.

"Um, the other day . . . you said something about a flower blooming at the right time." Winston tried to recall their conversation. "You said something about living in the moment."

Diego's face relaxed as his smile reappeared. "Yes, *mi madre* use to say that a flower will bloom at the right moment. When the time is right, it will reveal its beauty. She say that flowers live in the moment."

Taking a large breath, Winston knew that he had to say this before he lost his nerve. "I was wondering if . . . you would like to have dinner with me sometime?" It was out there now. Good or bad, he was past the point of no return.

"Din-ner?" Diego tilted his head as his eyebrows arched.

Winston ran through his Spanish vocabulary, searching for the word for dinner. "*Cena?*"

"*Si, Cena.* Din-ner." Diego's face was stolid, his eyes fixed on Winston.

Oh, shit. I've made a fool of myself. He's straight. How can I clean this up? "Um . . ." Winston stuttered as a large truck pulled up to the front gate and blew its horn.

They both looked towards the gate and then back at each other. Diego's eyes were inquisitive. "Din-ner, yes. Okay."

Winston's heart raced as the truck's horn sounded two more times. "Yes," he said, "dinner, you and I." His eyes shifted to the truck, its engine rumbling as it waited. "I can text you later, arrange a place to go." He pulled out his phone and quickly scrolled through his contacts, looking for Diego's number. He didn't have it. "Here, give me your number." Winston handed Diego his phone. He forced himself to breathe as anxiety churned in his stomach.

Diego entered several digits into Winston's phone before handing it back to him. "This is my number. You call?"

"I'll text you."

"Okay." Diego smiled, his eyes lighting up, that tiny flicker of gold dancing. "I leave now. You have someone at your front gate. Tonight, you text?"

"Yes. They're here to pick up furniture. As soon as they leave, I'll text you. Is tonight a good night for you?"

"Tonight, yes, it's good for me. For you?"

"Yes. Okay. We can meet . . ." Winston looked at his watch. "What about eight o'clock? Do you live close?"

"I live in East LA."

"Okay, I'll text you with an address." Winston hesitated before extending his hand. Shaking hands seemed a bit formal. Was Diego a hugger or a shaker? Given the situation, a hug didn't feel appropriate either.

Within seconds, Diego answered the question for him by reaching for the handle on his truck. "I see you tonight. You text?"

Not a shaker or a hugger, Winston smiled at his adorable accent. "Yes, I will text you."

Diego stepped into his truck. When he fired it up, the rumble of its engine was nothing compared to the roar in Winston's chest.

Walking up the driveway to meet the Disabled American Veterans truck, Winston followed Diego's truck towards the front gate. He felt as if he was floating; his brain was on overload. Euphoria washed over him. He had actually asked Diego out. He was going on a date!

8

Arriving home, Diego went straight to his room. He immediately plugged his phone into his charger, wanting to ensure that he didn't miss Winston's text. Elated, he couldn't believe Mr. Makena had asked him out. He was sure it was a date. He had replayed the conversation repeatedly in his head, picking apart each word, ensuring he understood it correctly. Never having been on a date, he tried to picture the evening. Grabbing his wallet, he counted the cash inside. Twenty-seven dollars. He would need to stop at the ATM for more.

After exiting the shower, he returned to his room to finish getting dressed. He wanted to get out of the house before Rafael showed up. Neither Francisco nor Mayra were home yet either. It would be best if he dodged them all, so he wouldn't have to explain where he was going. They'd never stop hounding him if they suspected he was going on a date.

The plan was to leave the house and wait two blocks away, at the strip mall where he usually gassed up. There were many trees in the parking lot to hide his vehicle.

He heaved a sigh as he dropped the towel from his waist. Tossing it onto his bed, he began rummaging through his drawer, searching for the right underwear. He found his only pair of Andrew Christian briefs—his mother would die if she knew he'd spent thirty-four dollars on a single pair of underwear. Slipping on the tight red briefs, he carefully tucked himself in before raising them against his hipbones.

Two chimes from his phone caught his attention. Hoping it was Winston texting him, he grabbed the phone from his nightstand and tapped the screen to read it: *Is Molina's Cantina ok?*

Diego knew of only one Molina's Cantina, on Ninth Street in the Barnes and Noble shopping center. He hated that place. The food was Americanized and horrible.

He typed, *Ok with me. On ninth right?*

His phone chimed within seconds. *Yes. c u at 8 if that is still ok.*

Yes. c u then. Diego looked at the time in the upper corner of his screen before tossing the phone onto his bed next to his towel. He had to hurry if he was to get out of the apartment before anyone came home.

In less than five minutes, he had thrown on a pair of jeans and his nice blue button-down shirt. After brushing his teeth, he was safely out the door before anyone came home.

When he entered the restaurant, the host, a tall male Caucasian wearing black pants and a white dress shirt acknowledged him with a smile. "Ah . . . are you here with Mr. Makena? He is already here."

The host laid one hand at the small of Diego's back. "I'll show you to your table."

Looking around the dark and tacky dining room, Diego took a half step to his right, squirming free of the man's touch before falling in behind him. A thickness formed in Diego's throat as he realized the host was flirting with him.

As they neared the back of the restaurant, Diego and Winston spotted each other at the same time. Diego smiled as he watched Winston fight to catch the white cloth napkin that dropped from his lap when he stood.

"Hey, there!" Winston called as the host stepped in to assist him with his napkin. Gently shaking the square cloth, the man handed it back to him.

Diego noticed that Winston was wearing a tie and a dark navy-blue jacket. Although he was stunning, his appearance did little to relax Diego, who now second-guessed his own outfit. It had never occurred to him to wear a tie. He had only one, which he wore anytime a tie was required: church, funerals, weddings, *quinceaneras.*

"How are you?" Diego dragged the palm of his hand down the side of his pant legs to ensure that it was dry. They exchanged an odd handshake that began as a possible hug.

"You found the place okay?" Winston asked.

"I did." The employee pulled out Diego's chair for him. He had only seen this done for a woman. Was this man thinking of him as the woman in their couple? With a nod, Diego accepted the man's offering and sat down. When the host unfolded Diego's napkin and handed it to him, a second wave of embarrassment sent a flush of heat to his face.

Taking a step back, the host flashed a longer-than-normal smile at Diego before turning his attention to Winston. "Your waiter will be right with you." With a slight curtsy, the man walked away.

"I think he likes you." Winston guffawed.

Embarrassed by the guy's open display of affection, Diego couldn't think of anything to say. Obviously, the man didn't care that Winston was present. His boldness was disrespectful. A warm tingle swept across his face, knowing Winston had seen it too. Why would the staff disrespect Winston by hitting on him like that?

"Um." Diego's thoughts were scrambled; he wanted to punch the guy in the face. With Winston's intense gaze on him, he adjusted himself into the overly large chair. His knees were bouncing under the table. With his hands, he applied pressure to both his thighs to stop them. He noticed that Winston had already ordered a glass of red wine. "Have you been here long?"

"No. Maybe five minutes or so." Winston sipped the wine.

Diego was drawn into Winston's steel-grey eyes. They were striking against his black hair. The dry sensation in Diego's mouth became more pronounced. Several attempts to swallow did little to help. The last thing he wanted was red wine. He had tried it twice, and both times, it had landed on his tongue like dirt. He would take a soda; even a glass of water would be better.

"Have you been here before?" Winston asked.

The grey in Winston's eyes as he stared at him, seductively they once again disrupted his train of thought. "Um . . .once, a couple of years ago." Diego recalled the private party for which he and Rafael had been hired to help bus tables, keep up with the trash, and clean up afterwards. He had been excited when they were told that a free dinner and soda would be provided, but the excitement quickly ended when the poor, saltless attempt at Mexican food reached his taste buds. Diego took a deep breath as he recalled how hectic that night was. "A wedding reception," he said aloud.

"I wasn't sure what you liked. I figured this was a safe call." Winston handed him the wine list. "Here you go."

"Oh, I not want a drink." As soon as he spoke, Diego doubted his decision; a drink might calm his nerves a little. Reluctantly, he picked up the wine list and scanned the numerous wines; seeing chardonnays, cabernets, and two or three other categories he had never heard of. His eyes moved around the dining room, remembering that the restaurant had a full bar. He would order a shot of tequila.

"Good evening. My name is Josh, and I'll be your server this evening. Sir, can I get you something from the bar?"

Diego looked up at the voice to find a short round man smiling down at him. Hesitating, he waited for Winston to speak. With a nod, Winston signaled for him to go first. Diego grabbed the menu. "I'll have a cola . . . Do you have tequila?"

"Yes, we do. What would you like?"

Diego didn't understand the question. Thinking the man must not have heard him, he repeated himself. "I'll have a cola and a shot of tequila, but not inside the cola." His lack of confidence in his English sent his knees dancing under the table again.

"Tequila? You want a shot of tequila?" The man smiled, but it was clear by the look on his face that he was baffled.

"I think I'll have a shot too!" Winston chimed in. "Two Patrons."

"Yes, of course." The waiter straightened his back and nodded before stepping away.

"I'm not a big drinker either." Winston's eyes dropped to his glass. "Thought I would order a glass of wine before you got here to help calm my nerves, but I think I need a shot of tequila as well." He gave a tiny chuckle under his breath as he played with his wine glass.

"So you're nervous too?" Diego welcomed the possibility.

"Um, yeah. I haven't dated much. Parker and I got together in college. Before that . . . well . . . Maybe I'll hold off on that part of my life until our second date."

Second date? Would there be a second date? Diego tried to stop his legs from bouncing. His heart pounded. "So you and Mr. Leblanc were together a long time?"

"Yes, almost ten years." Winston broke eye contact to take a sip of his wine.

The waiter appeared with two shots of Patron, placing the first glass in front of Winston. "Gentlemen, are you ready to order?"

"Oh, no. We haven't looked at the menus. Can you give us a moment here? I think we're going to take our time tonight."

"Certainly." The waiter nodded before disappearing.

Winston reached for his shot of Patron. "Salud!"

"Salud!" Diego replied as he lifted his own shot to click glasses with Winston. Something about Winston taking charge and saying they would take their time set Diego at ease. The warm sensation of the Patron easing down his throat relaxed him even more.

"Well, I guess we should look at the menus," said Winston. "To be honest, it doesn't matter where I'm at—if it's Mexican food, I always order the same combination: a chicken taco, a shredded beef taco, and a cheese enchilada."

Diego looked down at the menus. "I guess I should look then." He took his menu and scanned the entrees and prices. "I guess I'll have the same thing. It sounds good." He didn't care. It didn't matter if the food was nasty; he was on a date with Mr. Makena.

"So, you said you have two older brothers. What about your parents? Are they living?"

What had made Winston think his parents might be dead? "I live with my brothers. My *padres* are in Mexico."

"Oh, so both your parents still live in Mexico?"

Diego held his breath. He knew what the next question would be: when and why had they come without their parents? He didn't share the fact that he was undocumented with anyone. Their lives and those of their parents depended on it. "Yes, they live in Mezcala. My mom's parents are old. They live with my parents too. My mom, she takes care of them. What about you? Do your parents live here?"

"No, my father died when I was a kid, and my mother has remarried twice since then. The second one died too, and now she's working on her third husband." Winston laughed. "She lives in Mon-tan-a."

"Mon-tan-a, why do you say it like that? Do you not like Montana?"

"There's nothing in Montana to like."

Diego didn't understand his answer. Had he asked the question wrong? He wondered if Winston meant that he didn't like his mother. Nervousness swept through him. "But your mom lives there. Don't you visit her?"

"Only if she was dying." Winston laughed. "I'm only kidding . . . That probably sounded bad."

Indeed, it did. That was his mother he was talking about. Maybe they didn't get along. Could it be because he was gay? Diego decided to keep the questions going. He found that conversations in English were simpler that way: asking a simple question was far easier than answering the many questions someone might ask. "Do you have brothers or sisters?"

Winston took a sip of his wine. "No. I'm an only child. But my best friend, Ann, she's like a sister to me. We've been friends forever." He stopped as the waiter suddenly appeared.

"Folks, are you ready to order, or did you need a little more time?"

Diego forced a nervous smile as his eyes moved from Winston to the waiter, and then back to Winston.

Winston sat up in his chair. "No, I think we're ready." With a hand gesture, he signaled for Diego to go first.

Diego straightened up as well and grabbed his menu. "Ah, um, I will have . . ." He couldn't find the combination plate they had talked about earlier. Nervously, he sputtered, "One taco de pollo, and one carne asada, and an enchilada . . . please."

"What kind of meat for your enchilada, sir?"

"Meat? Um, cheese, please." Diego repeated his order in his head, ensuring that he had said everything right.

"And for you, sir?" The waiter directed his attention to Winston.

Taking a breath, Diego listened as Winston gave his order.

"Okay," said the waiter when he finished. "I have two combination plates, both with one chicken taco, one beef taco, and a cheese enchilada? Can I get you anything else to drink, sir?"

Diego realized that the waiter was addressing him. "No . . . Um, water, please."

"Okay, I'll have your dinners right out." The waiter scribbled a second more on his pad before excusing himself.

Winston spoke. "Can I say, your eyes, they're beautiful. I can't stop staring into them."

Heat rushed to Diego's face. He was embarrassed by the compliment. He had never thought of his eyes as anything other than simply brown. Everybody in his family had brown eyes. "Thank you." He lowered his head, cutting off any further eye contact. "Your family—we were talking about your family."

"Oh, yeah. My best friend, Ann, ran track with my husband in college. I was at a meet to watch her when I met him. It was my twenty-first birthday. There was a bunch of us there. We thought she might break the USC record in the hundred-yard dash. I remember sitting in the bleachers and spotting Parker in the middle of the track. He was wearing a pair of tiny running shorts. I think I set a record for how fast someone could get from the bleachers to the middle of the track. I made a complete fool of myself meeting him."

"You called Mr. Leblanc your husband. Did you guys get married?"

"We did. We had a big wedding at Saint Leo's."

Diego didn't know the church. "Did you have a priest and everything?"

"Father O'Brian."

"So you're Catholic?"

"Yes, kind-of-sort-of. I'm Catholic, and Parker was agnostic. Saint Leo's is an Episcopal church."

Diego repeated *kind-of-sort-of* in his head, attempting to understand.

Winston continued, "I grew up in the Catholic Church, went to catechism, Mass every week, followed by Sunday school. My dad was in the choir. When I was younger, there was a time that I actually wanted to be a priest. That was before I found out they couldn't have sex. Little did I know that the church didn't enforce that rule."

Taken aback by how crassly Winston was speaking about the church, Diego hesitated before pressing on. It was a surprise to hear that Winston was a fellow Catholic. The fact that Winston had wanted to be a priest was even more surprising. "How long were you married?" This entire conversation was taboo. Openly talking about one's sexuality, the church, and sex in public created a nervous fluttering around Diego's heart. "You and Mr. Leblanc, did your families know about you guys?"

"Oh god, yes. His mother and sister took over and planned our entire wedding. My mother, I think, loved him more than she loved me. His grandmother flew in from London for the wedding." The pitch of Winston's voice had increased, and he was talking more quickly. His eyes lit up as he spoke of Parker.

Diego was silent as he listened to every word. The way Winston spoke of Parker was endearing. Parker was the one client that he enjoyed spending time with. Now, to hear Winston tell stories of who he was, he was not just the man who always took a few minutes to say hi, but a loving, caring husband; his death was far greater than Diego initially understood.

Winston talked about Parker and his family until the waiter appeared with their dinners. The two grew quiet as they dove into their meal.

The silence allowed Diego's mind to wander. He had never thought of himself as a jealous person; but listening to the way Winston talked about Parker, was he really jealous of someone who was dead? Taking a bite of his taco, he found that the meat and the manufactured crunchy shell were as bad as he remembered. Diego put the taco down and switched to the enchilada. It too was horrible. It had been drowned in tomato sauce. He couldn't believe people actually ate this stuff. The conversation, the food—at the moment, he would have rather been home alone, drawing in his room. He questioned his feelings. The night, the date—they didn't feel like he had thought they would.

"How's your dinner?" Winston asked, breaking the silence.

"Um . . . good. Yours?" Diego's eyes darted down to avoid Winston's gaze.

"Good." Winston took another bite, finishing one of his tacos.

With little appetite left, Diego opted to ask more questions. "Can I ask—what, exactly, do you do?" In all the conversations he'd had with Mr. Leblanc, neither he nor Winston's professions had ever come up. It was only clear that they were rich, the richest people he knew.

"I own an event planning business. We plan private parties and large events for companies. Ann and I started it about five years ago, and it took off."

"Do you work from home?" Not entirely sure what an event planner did, the fact that he owned his own business was another commonality between them. They weren't *that* different.

"No, we have an office in West Hollywood, on Sunset, down off of Doheny."

Diego tried to picture the area but came up with nothing. He wanted to know more about Winston. "So . . ." He paused to regroup. Unable to figure out his question in English, he decided to go a different route.

Winston waited, his fork close to his mouth.

"Um, why I not see you that much until a couple of weeks ago?" Diego knew he was saying it wrong, but it was the best he could come up with.

Winston laughed. "You want to know where the hell I've been until now, is that it?"

Though he was self-conscious of the question, Diego indeed wanted to know why, all of a sudden, he was seeing Winston every week. What had changed in his life? Was it Diego? Had Winston purposely made himself known because of him?

"I'm on vacation." Winston smirked.

This wasn't the answer Diego had been hoping for. "Did Mr. Leblanc work for the company too?"

"No, he was an attorney. An entertainment attorney. He was expecting to make partner with his firm right before the accident."

Accident? Diego hesitated before asking, "Is that how he died? An accident?" He recalled that he had been unaware of Parker's accident for several weeks. He had known only that there was more traffic than usual at the house. People came and went, and trucks delivered flowers and plants. He had only realized Parker was dead when, as he stood in the garden one Monday afternoon, the front gate opened and two limousines pulled in.

Seeing the car doors marked with Carlisle's Funeral, Diego stopped working and lowered his head as the automobiles passed him, parking in front of the house. Through his sunglasses, he cautiously watched Mr. Makena exit the first car with several other people. He noticed that Mr. Leblanc wasn't in either vehicle, and it hit him that Mr. Leblanc must have passed. Not long after, he went to pick up an order at Joaquin's Nursery, and the clerk expressed her condolences regarding the death of Mr. Leblanc.

Winston mumbled, "Yeah, it was a car accident. A drunk driver at two o'clock in the afternoon. The guy walked away with a cut above his right eye. He was an illegal. It was his fifth DUI." He sniffled and lowered his eyes.

Illegal. The word rang in Diego's ear. He knew without asking that the driver was Mexican. It was the way they always said it—as if the two words meant the same thing. Staring at Winston, he regretted that the conversation had reverted to Parker. The words *an illegal* continued to sound in his ear.

After this, Winston talked, and Diego partly listened, but the feeling telling him to run drowned out most of the words. When the check arrived, Diego waited for his portion of the bill. But Winston simply scanned the tab, shoved a credit card into the black folder, and placed it on the edge of the table.

Diego waited, unsure how to ask what he owed. Even if Winston planned to pay the whole bill, he should at least offer. It would be rude to assume he didn't have to pay for what he ate, even if the food wasn't worth a damn. Finally, he reached for his wallet and asked, "How much do I owe?"

"No, I got this. I was the one who asked you to dinner." Winston smiled as he placed his hand over the black folder.

"Oh, is that how it works?" Diego had to admit, it was better than being viewed as the female.

Within minutes, the check was paid, and the two walked out onto the street together.

"Where'd you park?" Winston asked as he fumbled in his pockets and pulled out his keys.

Diego looked both ways before pointing. "I think up that way. Around the corner." He was ready to end the night.

"This is me." Winston pointed to a black Rubicon Jeep parked in front of them.

"Cool. I not know you had a Jeep too. Do you like it?" Excited by the vehicle, Diego approached it, looking it over.

"Yeah, it's okay. I mostly use it for work." Winston stood next to Diego. "Tomorrow's Tuesday. Will I see you at the house?"

Diego remembered that he worked for the man. "Is there something you need done? I was planning to prune most of the bushes behind the pool since they not bloom anymore. Is that okay?"

"Of course. I wasn't asking about that." Winston stepped in a little closer, into Diego's personal space. "I wanted to see you again," he added in a softer tone.

"Oh?" Diego sensed danger. Was Winston going to try to kiss him right here on the street? Diego took two steps back, putting enough distance between them that it couldn't happen. There was no way he would let someone kiss him in public. He patted his jeans for his keys. "I'll see you tomorrow, no?"

"Goodnight." Winston smiled, looking as if he was going to say something else.

"Goodnight." Diego turned on his heels and walked as fast as he could to his truck.

Slipping into the safety of his truck, he watched as the Jeep crossed the intersection in front of him. His chest collapsed as he exhaled his breath and leaned back in his seat. The first part of the date had been great; he had loved sitting there talking, just the two of them. Then came that comment about illegals. He wasn't sure how to take that—it didn't sit right. He tried to dismiss it, giving Winston the benefit of the doubt and assuming that he had meant no harm.

It was their first date. Maybe it wasn't supposed to be perfect, and maybe there were things about him that Winston didn't like: his lack of a tie, his poor English. Maybe he had asked too many questions, stupid questions. Diego rolled his eyes, not sure he would get that second date after all.

9

Sitting in his office, Winston had struggled all morning to get a
handle on the household expenditures. He was shocked at the
amount of money they spent each month; he had no idea their
life had become so extravagant.

The thought of Diego crept in his mind, causing him to square
his shoulders and lean back in his chair. His mind drifted back to
their date last night. Since crawling into bed, he had been ripping
apart the evening, convincing himself that Diego was obviously not
into him. Too much of the conversation had been about Parker.
Truthfully, it was weird sitting in a restaurant with another guy. The
fact that he was strongly attracted to Diego didn't help.

He thought about texting Ann and telling her everything. The
fact that he had already had dinner with Diego after asking him out
yesterday would be mind-blowing to her. No, the last thing he wanted
to do was confess that he was an idiot groundhog.

Through the window, Winston stared at the dog groomer's van.
He hoped she would be finished before Diego arrived. He had about
an hour before Diego was due. The little old woman who ran the
business was sweet and all, but she talked more than she groomed.
There was always an hour-long conversation before she ever got started on Lucy.

When Parker was alive, they used to flip a coin to see who would greet her. Winston couldn't hate on her too much, though—when Parker died, she had stepped in, sending over a couple of pre-cooked meals each week, homemade breads, pies, and cookies.

He remembered how, during those long days and nights at the hospital, whenever he texted, she had dropped everything and gone to the house to let Lucy out or to feed her.

The stack of bills was never ending, he needed to make a chart of all of their bills and their due dates. Sitting up in his chair, he opened an Excel file on his laptop.

He now knew that the fresh veggies delivered once a week weren't free and that the total combined cost of employing a housekeeper, a gardener, and pool service was likely more than most people's monthly income. The one service that was definitely not needed was the man who showed up every Friday to wash the cars. When Winston got the heart, that person had to go.

The more he worked on his new bill-paying program, the more mortified he became at the amount of money they had been spending. Right now, the money was there; Parker had made sure he would be well cared for just as his father had done when he passed. In all of his thirty-two years, he had never been tasked with ensuring there was enough money in an account to do whatever it was he wanted or needed. The money was always there.

His current financial situation seemed okay by the numbers he was looking at in the different accounts they had. However, for the first time in his life, he realized that staying clueless was no longer an option.

Lost in his work, Winston was startled when the groomer let Lucy back into the house and yelled that she was finished.

"Okay, thank you!" he yelled back from his chair. There was no need for an in-person goodbye, which would only prolong her stay.

He waited for the sound of the front door closing, before spinning in his chair to watch her from the window. He watched as she climbed into the van and crept down the driveway. *Could she drive any slower?*

It was after one-thirty when the clatter of the front gate caught his attention. He watched Diego's truck and trailer pull around the circular driveway, coming to a stop exactly where the groomer's van had been an hour ago.

Uneasiness filled his stomach. Shifting in his chair, he forced himself to stay put. He tapped the desk with his fingers, trying to rid them of the tingling sensation that amplified his anxiety.

The idea of letting Diego work before going outside to talk to him was stupid. Winston had to try now. "Lucy, come!" He would use Lucy as his excuse for being outside.

Diego, still at the back of his trailer, didn't see him coming. "How are you?" Winston asked, trying to get a read on him.

"Good." Diego removed his gloves, and tucked them into his back pocket. "And you?" he asked.

"Thank you for last night. I know I probably talked too much about Parker. Sorry about that."

"It's okay. You loved him, no?"

Winston smiled at the fact that Diego sometimes finished his sentences with the word no, turning them into questions. "I do . . . I did," he sputtered. "Look, I was a really bad date, and I'm so sorry and embarrassed! I want you to know me, and I want to know you, but . . . I'm really rusty at all this."

The two stood smiling at one another. Silently, Winston scrambled for something to say. His mouth working separately from his brain; the words just came out. "Would you like to go out again?"

Diego's face, a second ago unreadable, relaxed as a tiny smile pressed his lips upward. "Tonight?" he asked.

"No . . . Yes . . . No, whenever. If you're free sometime this week, or the weekend." It sounded as if he was begging, but he didn't care.

Diego's smile intensified to a full-blown grin. "Okay, but no Mexican food. That place was horrible, no?"

Winston finally took a breath. "You mean you didn't like Molina's Cantina?"

"No, not really."

"Okay, you pick the restaurant this time. We can go anywhere you like. Name a place."

"How about . . . Do you like pizza?" Diego asked.

"I love pizza. I haven't had a good pizza in forever. There are no good pizza places around here. How about I drive into the city and let you pick it?"

"Today?" Diego scratched his chin as if thinking.

"Whenever. If you're free again tonight, I'm game."

"I have things I do later. We meet after eight? I might have to take my brother—" Diego stopped mid-sentence.

"That's fine. Text me where to meet you." Winston couldn't contain the adrenaline that was shaking his entire body.

10

I t was ten-to-eight by the time Diego dropped Rafael off at work. The restaurant was a couple of blocks away. He had plenty of time to get there.

As he pulled into the parking lot, he saw Winston's silver Maserati parked in the front row of the large shopping center, about three stores down from the restaurant. He was sure it was Winston's. Who else drove a Maserati in this neighborhood? Parking a few spaces from it, Diego rushed from his truck towards the restaurant. He was about to open the door when he heard his name. Turning, he saw Winston exiting the beautiful sedan.

"I thought that was your car. I not see you in there. Your windows are tinted. No Jeep tonight?" Diego ogled the vehicle.

Winston approached, adjusting his tie. "No, not tonight."

Diego noticed that he hadn't locked the car. This wasn't a good neighborhood to leave it unlocked. "You not lock it?"

"Oh, it locks itself." Winston held the restaurant door open and waited for Diego to step in.

"Mmm, I love the smell of pizza." The aromas of yeast, garlic, and oregano greeted them. Looking around the dark dining room, Diego trailed behind Winston as they stepped up to the ordering counter.

"What can I get you guys?" a hard-looking older woman asked.

Diego's eyes shifted from a young man in the kitchen, who was sliding a pizza into the giant wood-burning oven, to the older woman. Other than these two employees, the restaurant was empty.

"Can we have a second?" Winston asked, as he squinted at the chalkboard. "What do you like?"

"It doesn't matter. I can eat anything." Diego scanned the board, looking at all the varieties of pizza with their funny titles.

"How about anchovies?" Winston smiled.

"Yep. You?"

"No! I hate 'em." Winston took a step closer to the counter. "Okay, can we have a large combination with extra cheese, no onions?"

The woman barely made eye contact with either of them. "Anything to drink?"

Winston turned to Diego. "Cola?"

"Um, no, I have beer tonight." He needed the alcohol to relax him a bit. He had been forcing himself not to bite his nails.

"Really? Okay. We'll take a pitcher of Bud Light."

The woman rang them up and offered to bring their beer out as soon as she placed their order.

Finding a booth towards the back, they slid onto the wooden benches. "Do you come here often?" Winston asked.

"Not really. A few times. I not live too far from here." Diego's eyes darted about the room, taking in the decorative olive oil cans and dusty packages of pasta that sat on shelves along the walls. He couldn't believe they were seeing each other two nights in a row. He was more nervous than he had been the night before.

Tonight, he wouldn't ask so many stupid questions. Wanting no barriers between them, he slid the Lazy Susan full of condiments to the side of the table. He knew this didn't make sense—the table still separated them—but he felt better with it out of the way.

The old woman approached the table with their pitcher and two frosty beer steins. She stared at Diego as she put the beer and glasses down on the table. "I'm sure you're old enough, but can I see your ID?"

She wanted to see *his* ID. Even though he'd had a real driver's license for five years, being asked for ID always made him nervous. When he and his brothers first arrived from Mexico, they all had fake IDs. No one had ever called him on it, but the fear had never gone away. Diego pulled out his wallet and held up his license so she could see his date of birth.

"Thanks. Your pizza should be right out." She wiped her hands on her apron before walking away.

As Diego started to tuck the wallet into his back pocket, Winston grabbed it. "I want to see!"

Diego wondered why—not that he would have objected.

"Oh my God! You look like a baby!" Amused by the old picture on the license, Winston studied it for a second or two. "How old are you here?"

Diego leaned over the table and looked at the photo. "I not know." He hated that picture. He looked like he was twelve. "That's from my first license. I think I was eighteen or nineteen, I not know." Watching Winston scrutinize his picture, he wanted to die.

"You were adorable. I can't believe how young you looked." Still laughing, Winston handed the wallet back.

Embarrassed, Diego quickly tucked it away so they could move on.

"She was actually kind of bitchy about seeing your ID," Winston joked.

"Do you think she knows that we're—?" He didn't want to say the word aloud.

"On a date?" Winston reached across and took hold of the pitcher. He slowly filled the frosty glass, leaving a thin layer of foam at the top. Sliding it towards Diego, he began filling the second mug.

"No . . . *gay*?" Diego grabbed the mug of beer Winston had poured for him. "Thank you." Taking a gulp, he licked the foam from his top lip.

Winston held the mug to his mouth and then lowered it without taking a sip. "I could care less. What I do care about is giving my money to someone who doesn't appreciate it." He gave a bitter laugh as he finally took a drink.

"So, it not bother you if people know you're gay?"

"I've never been in the closet. For Christ sakes, I grew up in Beverly Hills—everyone's queer."

"I hate that word." Diego looked around for the woman and saw her go behind the counter.

"What word? Queer?"

"Yeah, it's mean," Diego replied. "It's an ugly word."

"I'm proud to be queer."

"Really? It sounds funny to hear someone who is gay say it about himself. I . . ." Diego folded his arms across his chest and leaned against the high back of the wooden bench.

"So, I take it you're not out to your brothers or family."

"Francisco would disown me, have a meltdown. He would tell *Papa*, and it would kill him." His brown eyes, expressive, conveyed panic at the idea.

"Really? You don't have any uncles, aunts, or cousins who are gay?"

Diego was sure of it, as he shook his head no.

"You know that's not possible, right?" Winston took another sip of his beer.

"I'm telling you, there's nobody gay in my family." Diego was sure of it. "How about yours?"

"Gosh, yes. I have an uncle and two younger cousins. In high school, I had a math teacher that was gay."

"How did you know he was gay? Your teacher?"

"He facilitated our gay–straight alliance group on campus. I can't count the number of gay people I know."

"What's a gay–straight alliance?" Diego couldn't help but admire the flawless skin on Winston's face. He wasn't sure if he preferred clean-shaven look or the five-o'clock shadow that he had come to know. He tried to remember if Winston had been clean-shaven yesterday too. His steel-grey eyes, his golden skin tone—it was like sitting across the table from a movie star.

"What do you mean, 'What's a gay–straight alliance?'"

"I never heard of it." Diego wasn't sure he knew the word *alliance*.

"A gay–straight alliance is a group, kind of like a club, on high school and college campuses that is run by students, gay and straight. It's supposed to be a safe place for LGBTQ youth."

"Really, in high school?"

"Yeah. You mean you didn't have one on campus? What high school did you go to?"

Diego's jaw clenched. The question caused him to stumble in his thoughts. "I—I didn't go to high school. I . . ." He struggled over what to say.

"Are you kidding me? Did you graduate early, or take the GED or something?"

"No . . . I not go. We came to America when I was seventeen. With no papers, my uncle and Francisco said I not go. I not speak English. We had to work."

"You guys didn't cross legally?"

Diego shook his head. There was no mistaking the tiny grimace on Winston's face. It spoke volumes. This was precisely why Diego avoided people. Winston didn't have to say any more; Diego knew what kind of a person he was. *Build that wall! Round those Mexicans up and ship them back to their own country! They're taking our jobs!* He'd heard it a million times.

The silence was broken by the cook arriving with their order. "Here you guys go. Combination, no onions. Can I get you any ranch dressing, parmesan, or hot chili flakes?"

"Yeah, ranch," Diego murmured. "And jalapenos, please."

"Okay, I'll be right back."

Without looking up at Diego, Winston reached over and broke a slice of pizza from the pan. He gave it to Diego. "It's hot. Be careful."

Several minutes passed before Winston looked up at Diego. After the cook dropped off their dressing and Diego's jalapenos, Winston wiped his mouth with his napkin. "Why are you so quiet?" he asked.

"No reason." Diego tried to shake his self-doubt. To act as if nothing was wrong.

"Are you okay?" Winston asked. His eyebrows furrowed as he studied Diego.

Diego tried to guess what Winston was thinking. Had hearing that he hadn't gone to school, and was here illegally been too much for Winston?

"I love looking at you. I can't believe I'm here." Winston's eyes softened as a smirk emerged.

Self-conscious by Winston's compliment, Diego squirmed in his chair. "In a pizza parlor?" he joked, trying to dismiss the compliment.

"No . . . With you." Winston's eyes held steadfast on him. "You are so shy, aren't you?"

Diego had never thought of himself as shy. Quiet, yes, but not shy. A flutter stirred in his gut as he was about to prove Winston wrong. He gently brushed his hand across Winston's index finger as if by accident. The slight touch sent a tingle through him. The two smiled at each other, noting the touch for what it was.

Winston brought a slice of pizza to his mouth but stopped short of taking a bite. "I wasn't sure you would agree to a second date. Not after last night." His eyes widened, calling for a response from Diego.

"I had fun." Diego's brows drew closer together, as he cocked his head to one side. "You not have fun?"

"I did. I think I talked about Parker too much, though." Winston's phone chimed from the inside pocket of his jacket.

Seeing that Winston was ignoring the phone, Diego continued. "It means you loved him. It says a lot about you . . . no?"

Winston smiled. "You're pretty amazing."

"If you want to talk about Parker, we can talk about Parker. I not mind." Diego shoved the last of a large piece of pizza into his mouth.

"Thank you, but no. I want to know more about you. So, tell me about your childhood. You said you were born in Mezcala?"

"Yes. Outside of Mexico City. We not have much money. I go to school with my brothers. My *mama* and *papa* worked, my *abuela*—"

"Grandma, right?" Winston asked.

"Yes. My grandma mostly took care of us." Diego grabbed another piece of pizza. "I not know what you want to hear . . ." He wanted to be careful not to say the wrong thing again.

"Were you close to your mom or grandma?"

"My *abuela* is old. I miss them."

Winston nodded. His face took on a somber look. "My grand-mother died years ago. When I was a little kid. I only remember bits and pieces of her. It was my dad's mom, and they didn't get along."

Over the next two hours, they sat and talked, laughed, and trad-ed stories of their childhoods. It wasn't until the server approached their table that Diego remembered they weren't alone. "We're getting ready to close up," the woman said. "Is there anything else I can get you guys before the kitchen closes?"

They both looked up at her, but it was Winston who answered. "No. I think we're good. Thank you." He watched her as she walked away, waiting for her to be far enough away from their table before laughing. "Well, I think that was our clue to leave."

"Okay, I'm ready," Diego lied. He was anything but ready to call an end to their date.

Within minutes, the two walked outside to the nearly empty park-ing lot. "I had a good time tonight." Winston slowed his step. "Thank you."

"For what?" Diego asked.

"For showing me that I can still have a good time. That it's okay. That I shouldn't feel guilty about being out with . . . you." Winston raked his fingers through the front of his hair, lifting it out of his face.

They had reached the back end of Winston's Maserati, when he reached out and grabbed Diego's forearm. "Do you want to humor me for a minute?"

"What do you mean, 'humor me'?" Diego's eyes followed Winston's towards the strip mall's mattress store. A churning in his stomach caused him to gently pull his arm away from Winston.

"I mean, make me laugh . . . Oh, never mind. Come with me." Winston charged in the direction of the store. "Come on!"

When they entered, the sales clerk looked at her watch and greeted them.

"We'll only be a minute. I want to see something." Winston whispered to Diego, "I think they're about to close." He stopped in front of a queen size mattress.

"What can I help you two with? Are you guys looking for a new bed?" The sales clerk was treating them as if they were a couple.

Diego took a step away from Winston. "No, not me!" He waved his hands in front of him.

"I think I need one." Winston lay down on the mattress and stretched across it. "Can you give me a minute? I want to check this one out."

"Sure. Let me know if you have any questions." The woman looked at her watch and walked away.

Patting the mattress, Winston invited Diego to join him. "Tell me what you think. I believe I need a new bed."

Diego bent down and ran his hand across the mattress. "This is nice."

"Come here. Lie next to me." Winston patted the mattress again.

Warily, Diego sank onto the bed.

Winston let out a giggle as his mouth formed into a great big smile. "She thinks we're a couple."

Diego wanted to get up. They shouldn't be acting this way.

"That wouldn't be so bad, would it?" Winston asked. "I think it's time for a new bed."

Several minutes of silence passed as the two lay side-by-side, looking up at the fluorescent lighting. "Someday," Winston murmured, "I want to hear about how you came here. I want to know everything about you."

Winston shifted slightly. Their shoulders were now touching. For an instant, Diego nearly fled. He wanted to pull away, sit up, but his heart held his body firmly down next to Winston. Energy pulsed through him, sending tiny tremors up his spine. He didn't know what to say. *What does he want to know? What should I share?*

"Are you ready?" Winston reached out and touched Diego's hand.

Diego jerked his hand away from Winston and sat up. "Um—yeah, yes." The public touching was too much for him.

His heart was racing as he followed in behind Winston towards the front door. With his eyes focused down, he avoided eye contact with the sales clerk standing at the door. In silence, they walked across the parking lot, reaching Winston's car first. "Do you have a minute?" Winston asked, as the dome light and exterior lights on his car automatically turned on.

"Yeah." Diego looked at the beautiful silver Maserati and then at his truck, which was parked four empty stalls over.

"Get in." Winston held the passenger door open.

Diego's head tilted as his eyes shifted between the car and Winston. Was the date not over? Winston shut the door behind him and made his way around to the other side of the car, sliding in behind the steering wheel.

Diego caught only a glimpse of Winston's beautiful face before the dome light faded out. His breathing accelerated.

Winston grabbed his hand, which was on the armrest. "Last night . . . while we were standing out by my car, I wanted to kiss you. I wasn't sure it was okay, so I didn't. But I want to—kiss you."

Inhaling the scent of Winston's cologne, Diego's tongue instinctively moistened his lips.

"Can I? Can I kiss you?" Winston murmured. He didn't wait for Diego to answer. He leaned in slightly, and their lips met.

The warmth of Winston's breath ignited a fire. Diego's jaw opened, inviting Winston further in. His eyes drew closed. Winston's hands gently touched his face, his fingers sliding over Diego's cheek and coming to rest on his chin. With a single finger, Winston held his face as their kiss deepened, drawing Diego in completely.

Winston pulled back. "Mmm," he mumbled as he wiped his lips with his tongue.

Diego's breathing was heavy, his eyes glistening in the darkness of the car. Their faces were so close that their breath mingled. Diego gave a half smile before turning his head to look out the window.

"They can't see in." Winston said, as he took a firm hold of Diego's hand.

"Are you sure?" Diego pulled his hand away as he leaned back into the soft leather. "I should go." He didn't want to.

"Are you okay?" Winston asked.

"Yes." Diego paused to gather his thoughts, his words. "I like you. I not make out with you in your car."

Winston took his hand back. "Then will you go out with me again?"

It was everything Diego had wanted without knowing he wanted it. "Yes . . . but not tomorrow. Is that alright?"

"Yes—of course. You tell me. But do I have to wait a whole week, until next Monday?"

In a moment of euphoria, Diego smirked. "No. I not wait that long either. Goodnight." He leaned in for one more kiss, before stepping out of the car.

As the dome light in the cabin went dim, Winston disappeared behind the dark, tinted windows.

11

For the last hour, Diego had been replaying the evening in his head. He could still taste Winston and feel the hand that had touched his chin. He still couldn't believe he had kissed Mr. Makena. Lying in bed, he kicked off the thin blanket and sheet. The apartment was too warm tonight to have anything touching his skin. He shifted and tossed about, too excited to go to sleep. He didn't want to put the day behind him, not yet.

Thankfully, Rafael wasn't home to pull his attention elsewhere. He wanted to relish tonight as long as he could. How would he ever forget the moment when Winston's shoulder lightly touched his in the mattress store? He snickered, remembering that the sales clerk had assumed they were together, a couple.

He thought about what Winston had said in the car, that he couldn't wait a whole week. *He asked me not to make him wait.* Diego hammered his fists into his mattress as he kicked his feet up and down, releasing an almost-silent scream.

Then he slowed his breathing. He needed to chill. If Rafael walked in right now, there would be no hiding his excitement. It was like the night before Christmas, except he had just gotten what he wanted. They had been on two dates, and Winston wanted a third. Diego rolled over and looked at the clock on his phone. There was no chance of drifting off to sleep any time soon.

With a deep breath, he tried again to calm himself. Then he smelled it—Winston's cologne. He tried to pinpoint where the aroma was coming from. Was it in his nose, on his skin? Where was it hiding? He had to smell it again.

He cupped a hand over his mouth and released a muffled shriek. He was acting bat-shit crazy, and he loved it.

"Diego, are you asleep?"

It took him a second to realize that Mayra was on the other side of the door, talking to him.

"Diego?"

"Yes?" Diego sat up as she opened the door.

"Can I come in?"

"Sure." Pulling himself together, Diego tried to remove any trace of excitement from his face. "What's up?"

"I wanted to check on you. You've missed dinner the last two nights. Is everything okay?"

Diego knew what she was asking. Where had he been? He didn't want to lie to her, but there was no way he could tell her the truth either. "Um, um—I was with a friend." He had to look away from her if he was going to lie. "I met a friend for dinner."

"Oh?" Mayra's eyes lit up. "That's nice." She sat down at the foot of his bed, and silence fell between them.

Diego couldn't maintain eye contact. He focused on a pair of tennis shoes between the two beds. Would she keep pressing? What was he supposed to say? His heart raced. He decided to change the subject. "Is Francisco awake?"

"Yes, watching his stupid show." Mayra stood up and walked to the door. "I made *mole* if you're hungry. There's a lot left. Rafael hasn't eaten yet though. I can make you a plate."

Without thinking, Diego met her eyes. "No. I'm okay, but thanks."

Mayra stopped at the door and looked back at him. "She's a lucky girl."

Her words stabbed into him. There was now a lie between them. Diego squirmed. "It's not like that."

"Okay." Her tone said more than her words.

Diego's heart had a question, a question he could only ask her. "How did you know you were in love with Francisco? When did you know?"

Mayra leaned against the door. "So, you're in love?"

"I don't know. I might be."

She released the door handle and crossed her arms in front of her chest. "I don't know. I think, the first time I saw your brother, maybe I fell in love with him then. I knew I would be with him someday. Deep within me, I knew he was the one. I remember that I couldn't stop staring at him. He was so handsome. When he talked to me, I would go shy. I couldn't think."

"Had you loved anybody before him?"

"I thought I had. I had a boyfriend when I met Francisco. You know Arturo, the butcher at Nena's Market? I had been with him since we were in the eighth grade."

Diego sat up. "Isn't he married to . . . Leticia? They have, like, four kids."

Mayra laughed. "Yeah. About a month after I met your brother, I found out that Leticia was pregnant, and Arturo was the baby's daddy. He left me for her."

"I never knew you and Arturo were together."

"I thought I was going to marry him, until your brother came along."

"So what happened with Arturo? How did you end up with dipshit?" Winston's scent crossed Diego's nose. He tried to inhale it again, but it was gone.

"Francisco was there for me when I found out about Leticia. Your brother would come into the store every day for lunch. One day, he asked me why I was so sad. I was so embarrassed; I ran back into the storage room and hid until he was gone. The next day, he came back. He said he knew why I was sad. He said I would never be hurt again like that by anyone. Your brother is a good man." Mayra walked back over to the bed and sat down. "It's funny how things go. I knew I was going to be with him, and it happened. I couldn't have planned it, but it worked out the way it was supposed to."

Diego thought about his brother and Mayra, then about Winston and Parker. Was there such a thing as destiny? Did Parker die in order for him to find love—he was mortified at the thought.

Having slept for only a couple of hours, Diego rolled over and grabbed for his phone. Even in the dark, he knew where it would be on the nightstand. Relieved that it wasn't quite five a.m., he pulled his sheet up around his neck, giving himself another fifteen minutes to sleep.

He had been dreaming of Winston all night. It was hard to distinguish between their kiss in the car last night and his own dreams. The biggest difference was that, in real life, they had been sitting in a parking lot. In his dream, they were in the car, and it was moving.

Diego racked his brain, trying to remember where they were going in that dream. In the dream, he knew where they were going. Why couldn't he remember now?

Turning over, he noticed that Rafael's bed was empty. Why was it that Rafael could stay out as much as he wanted, yet *he* went out for two nights, Francisco sent Mayra in to talk to him? Diego had no doubt that Francisco was behind Mayra's visit.

He checked the time again. He had wasted his fifteen minutes by overthinking. It was time to get up and start his morning. It was Wednesday, his busiest day of the week. He hated Wednesdays: nine houses, nine tiny lawns to cut, edge, and blow. No imagination needed, nothing to create; it was about keeping things tidy.

Throwing the thin sheet off, Diego rose out of the bed and stretched. He adjusted his semi-morning erection down in his tighty whities before taking his first step. He made his way across the hall, wanting to get into the bathroom before anyone else. A glance at Francisco's door told him that he and Mayra weren't up yet.

Inside the bathroom, Diego turned on the shower to let the water warm up. With a slight turn, he stood in front of the toilet and began brushing his teeth as he released his bladder. Not completely awake, he swayed back and forth over the toilet. Staring into the tiny mirror above the sink, he cocked his head to one side as he studied his face and upper torso. He was searching for what other people might see; he had never thought of himself as attractive.

Obviously, there was something. His hair, maybe? Looking closer, he had to admit that he did have great hair. Not as thick and long as Rafael's, but nice. His face vanished as the condensation fogged the mirror.

His shower took less than five minutes. That was all the time he had before someone would start knocking, wanting their turn.

With a quick dry, he wrapped himself in his towel and then grabbed his underwear off the floor. When he opened the door, Rafael was standing there, about to knock. Startled, Diego stammered, "Hey, you're home?"

"Yeah, are you done?" Rafael didn't wait for an answer as he pushed past him.

"It's yours." Diego glanced at Francisco's door, which was now open. He heard Mayra in the kitchen. The house worked like a well-oiled machine in the morning. Mayra had breakfast on the table for them to grab and eat, and had them out the door on time every morning.

Just as Diego turned to face Rafael, the bathroom door slammed in his face. "Hey! Are you riding with me this morning or with Francisco?" Diego had no problem asking his question through the door.

"I don't have class until noon," a muffled voice responded.

Diego stepped back into his room in time to hear his phone chime. Snatching it from the nightstand, he saw that it was a text from Winston: *Good morning.*

Diego typed back, *Good morning.*

Within seconds, his phone chimed again. *Had a good time last night. Thank U.*

Me too. Diego inserted a happy face, and then erased it, thinking that it seemed too immature. Winston was different from anyone he had ever been around—maybe too different.

He held his phone, waiting for a response. He thought about his dream again. Where was Winston taking him in that damn dream? When his phone's screen faded to black, Diego gave up hope and returned it to the nightstand. He had to get going; the day was full.

12

Winston had slept better the previous night than he had in months. His date couldn't have gone any better. There was a tenderness about Diego that he couldn't put his finger on. Still, his emotions were mixed. His thoughts drifted back and forth from Diego to Parker. Why did it feel like he was cheating? If he wasn't ready to date, then what was he doing? He couldn't use Diego to make himself feel better.

He ran his hand across the mattress. There was no denying he'd had fun last night for the first time in a long time. They had kissed. The corners of his mouth slowly curled into a full-blown smile as he admitted that the kiss had felt good.

But it had also caused him anguish. Was he supposed to abandon something as precious as his love for Parker? How could it be that simple? If it was, he could never do it.

Turning onto his side, he touched the fitted Egyptian cotton sheet with his fingers. This bed belonged to him and Parker, and Parker was no longer here. He was never coming back. The thought of Diego, or anyone, lying next to him on Parker's pillow was wrong. Winston picked up this phone and saw that he had another text from Diego. *Me too.*

He wasn't surprised that Diego was up at this god-forsaken hour. He would have rather called, heard his voice, but he wasn't sure how long one was supposed to wait after a date before calling. He had told Diego to call *him*, so he had to wait.

Winston lowered the phone to his side, resting it on the bed as he closed his eyes. There was no reason to get up at this hour. His mind drifted back to sitting in the car with Diego. His heart skipped a beat as he remembered their lips touching for the first time—the smell of Diego's breath as he drew in a breath of his own. He had no idea where this was going, or even where he wanted it to go. *What if I'm not ready?* Did he owe Diego some kind of forewarning that this might not go anywhere?

The thought occurred to him: what if Diego didn't feel the same about him? Maybe Diego thought he was too old. But there were only seven years between them; it wasn't as if Winston was fifty.

But twenty-five was young. He could barely remember what twenty-five looked like. He and Parker had already been together, sharing a house. Both were starting their careers. Late nights, lots of friends, dinner parties, pool parties, travel. So much had changed in such a short time. He laughed at himself. Twenty-five seemed like a lifetime ago.

Somehow, for all of Diego's innocence, he seemed more mature, more grounded, and more solid in many ways. Winston got the feeling that Diego's life had not been easy. That might have matured him more quickly.

Rolling onto Parker's pillow, he buried his face into the soft fabric covering the feathery stuffing. Then he sat up in the bed. "Parker?"

He listened and waited as if a voice was going to answer. If not a voice, then a sign that Parker was here. Afraid to move, he drew Parker's pillow up into his chest. "Baby? Tell me what to do. I miss you so much." He tried to dislodge the lump in his throat. "Why did you have to die? We always said I was supposed to go first. I can't do this—not without you. Fix this. Do this one last thing—tell me what I am supposed to do." He buried his face in the pillow as the tears began to flow. It was a mistake to think that a pillow could stop the grief that once again took over.

The clock on Winston's nightstand showed that it was almost noon. Exhausted, he propped himself up with his arm. He had to take care of Lucy. The poor thing must be dying to go to the bathroom. Winston's eyes moved about the room looking for her. She wasn't in her bed, nor was she lying in the chair. "Christ." As if raising a sunken boat from the bottom of the ocean, he pulled himself out the bed.

Find Lucy, and make coffee. If he could get through those two items, he could begin thinking about the rest of the day. As suspected, Lucy was lying in the kitchen at the backdoor. He let her out before making his coffee. Bent over the counter, he rested his elbows on the cool granite as he waited for enough coffee to brew to fill a cup. Maybe he should go to Montana. It was a depressing thought, but he needed to do something other than lie up in this house day after day.

With his first cup of coffee in hand, he headed to his office down the hall. Comfortable in his chair, he released a yawn as his mind drifted back to last night. Diego was so different from anybody else he knew. Their conversation had felt relaxed as they discovered each other. They were as different as night and day. Diego was here, in this country, illegally. His mind tried to discern how he felt about it. It was Diego and not an imaginary person crossing the desert into his country.

Instead of searching for flights to Montana, he jiggled the mouse to wake up his computer. He wanted to search out the little town of Mezcala. Within seconds, photos of dilapidated buildings, dirt roads, and brown faces filled his screen. His eyes scanned each of the pictures as he pictured Diego there. *Is this the house where he lived? Is this the bridge where he and his* abuelo *fished? Are any of the people in these pictures related to him?*

He was looking at Diego's life, right there on his screen. A poor village, surrounded by mountains and desert terrain. Houses that looked like cardboard boxes, women washing clothes in the river. A lifeless place. No wonder Diego and his brothers had left; there was no reason to stay.

It wasn't until the house phone rang that Winston realized he had spent an hour looking at pictures of Mexico, reading stories of life in a third-world country. Reaching for the phone, he clicked on yet another site. "Hello."

"Hey!" Ann's voice boomed, sounding not at all like someone who had only been up for an hour.

"Good morn—afternoon." Winston leaned back in his chair and mentally prepared himself for conversation.

"I hadn't heard from you in a few days. Thought I would check in and make sure you're okay."

"Well, I thought I was better than okay until this morning."

"What's going on?" The concern in Ann's voice was clear.

"Not sure where to start, but I asked Diego out on Monday, and—"

"—and you're just telling me now!" Ann reprimanded him.

Winston pulled the phone from his ear to save his eardrum. "It happened so fast. We went out first on Monday . . . and then again last night."

"Are you shitting me? Two nights in a row, and I'm just hearing about it! I want details. What happened?"

Winston thought for a minute about where to begin. Should he start with the date or with his mental breakdown this morning; the thought of Diego replacing his Parker? Choosing the date, he related everything he could think of that he and Diego had shared, including the kiss in the car.

"So he's closeted, illegal, and uneducated, and you're on pins and needles waiting for him to call. I love it!"

Hearing this, Winston held back the rest, not telling her about this morning. "No, I'm not in love! Don't say that."

"I didn't say you were in love. I said I loved it."

The phone went silent. Winston thought about the possibility of being in love. Of course he wasn't. They had only had two dates. "Well, I'm glad you love it."

"Okay, I have to run. But you need to stop overthinking all of this and call him. I'll call you later for the details," Ann said.

"I'll be here." Winston rolled his eyes as he hung up the phone.

Without skipping a beat, Winston returned to his computer and clicked on several more sites that took him back to Mexico. He envisioned Diego and his brothers and what their lives must have been like.

A sense of loneliness squeezed at his chest forcing him to inhale a deep breath. He wanted to be with Diego. Before he could talk himself out of it, Winston grabbed his cell phone and sent Diego a simple text. *Thinking of you.*

His phone rang within seconds. It was Diego. Winston swiped his screen before the call went to voicemail. "Hello?"

"Hey." The voice was soft.

"Hey." Winston listened as white noise from the other end filled his ear. "Where are you? Driving?"

"Yeah. On my way to my next job."

"Oh . . . Well. I wanted to let you know I was thinking of you. I had a good time last night." Winston stopped there, hoping Diego would respond in kind.

"Me too." The voice was a little louder.

Damn it, it was like pulling teeth with him. "So, I was thinking, when did you want to go out? Remember, you promised that I wouldn't have to wait until Monday to see you."

Silence filled the phone for a moment, then Diego said, "I not know. You want to do something Saturday? We go out?" The voice now sounded normal—like the Diego whom Winston had come to know.

Winston smiled, enamored with his accent. "Saturday sounds like a long time away, but I'll take it."

"Okay, then, how do you say—it's a date?"

"Yes, that's correct, it's a date." Winston was giddy. "So what would you like to do on Saturday? I can cook dinner for us. We can hang out here, or we can go out again. Whatever you like."

"Um, I think . . . do you play putt-putt?" Diego asked.

"Putt-putt? I don't think I know what that is."

"Putt-putt," Diego repeated. Sounding unsure, his voice squeaked, "How do you say . . . mini-golf?"

"Oh, miniature golf! For a minute there, I thought you were talking about a car or something." Winston chuckled under his breath. "I haven't played in a while, but yes, that sounds fun."

"Are you sure? It's alright?"

Winston didn't care what they did. He wanted to see Diego. "I would love to play putt-putt with you." He held back a laugh as the words fell from his lips.

13

The miniature golf course was a lot smaller than Winston remembered it from childhood. Watching Diego sink his bright orange ball into the third hole, this ingenuous game was going to be more of a challenge than he thought. "I swear, I remember being better at this. You're killing me, Smalls."

Diego frowned as he reached down and picked up his ball. "I sometimes not know what you say. What is 'smalls'?"

Winston lined his club up with his aqua-blue ball and eyed the hole two feet away. Diego instructed him, "Hit it slowly. A little tap, not too hard."

Winston tapped the ball. It stopped halfway to the hole.

"Okay," said Diego, "maybe a little harder."

With another tap, Winston sent the ball past the hole. It stopped on the other side. Frustrated, he walked over and used his club to scoot the ball into the hole.

"I think that's cheating." Diego's voice bordered on laughter.

"Hey, you putt-putt your way, I'll putt-putt my way," Winston jokingly barked. It had been years since he'd had this much fun doing something as simple as playing putt-putt. Under the bright lights, Diego had never looked so beautiful.

Diego retrieved Winston's ball from the hole, and the two walked down a tiny bridge onto an island.

"So, I'm getting the feeling you've played this game a lot." Winston desperately wanted to touch him, kiss those beautiful lips again, but he restrained himself. The adrenaline bubbled inside him, and he couldn't focus on the game.

"Many times. My brother Rafael used to work here. We played for free until he got fired." Diego raked his fingers through his hair, trying to keep it out of his face.

"Fired? What did he do?" Winston watched as Diego's hair fell back in front of his eyes.

"You have to know my brother. He is bad." With a grin on his face, Diego surveyed his next shot, toward a windmill on the tiny island.

"Okay, now you have to tell me. What happened?"

Diego pointed to a large grey cave nearby. "He got caught in there . . ." He appeared to search for the right words. "How do you say, *sexo?*"

"He was having sex in there?" Winston's head turned towards the cave. "You're kidding."

"Nope. His boss caught him and a customer. Inside. My brother—he is nasty." Diego stepped up to his marker and looked again at the windmill, which was around a slight bend in the course.

Winston wanted to take a closer look at the cave. Hearing Diego call his brother nasty had made him even more intrigued. He wasn't past taking Diego in there and doing the same. "So, are you as bad as your brother?"

"Me? No!" With perfect precision, Diego tapped his ball, sending it straight for the corner. It rolled perfectly around the curve, up a small ramp, and into the front door of the windmill.

"No way!" Winston shouted as he watched the ball. But his attention was still on that damn cave. The front of his pants tightened slightly at the mere thought of it. He stared at Diego's small, tight ass in his jeans. Diego was half the size of Parker.

Diego and Parker were complete opposites. Parker, at six-two, was the heaviest he had ever been at the time of his death. Too much work, no time for the gym, and a whole lot of rich, creamy dinners and whiskey.

Winston chuckled to himself. He was out on a Saturday night, playing putt-putt, and drinking a diet soda out of a straw. Stepping up to the marker, he had no desire to be anywhere else in the world. "Okay, so if I make a hole-in-one like you did, can I have anything I want tonight?"

"Anything?" Diego questioned. "What do you want?"

"That's the gamble. But if you don't think I can make this shot, then it doesn't matter, does it?" Winston wanted to turn and look at Diego, but he had to focus on the shot.

"Are you fooling me?" Diego walked up and stood beside Winston. The sparkle in his chocolate brown eyes said that he knew Winston was being naughty.

"If I don't make the shot, then you can have anything you want. Deal?" Winston shifted his attention to the task. There were big stakes involved. With his feet together, he positioned his club behind his ball. "Come on, do we have a deal?"

Diego smiled as he looked at the windmill and then back at Winston. "I think you're tricking me."

"Okay . . . your loss," Winston mumbled as he hit his ball, sending it just short of the corner.

"Augh!" Diego shrieked as they both watched the ball come to a stop.

"Wow, you could have had anything you wanted. See?" Winston couldn't believe he hadn't even come close to making it.

Diego's face gave way to a shy but cocky smile. "I already got what I want."

"Oh really?" He hoped he knew what Diego meant, but he had to ask. "And what exactly is that?"

Diego coyly broke eye contact for a second before looking back at him. "To be here—with you."

A moan involuntarily escaped Winston. Had Parker said that, Winston wouldn't have thought twice about kissing him right here in front of everyone. However, Diego wasn't Parker; he was shy and private. Winston's only concern was Diego.

"So, what would you have asked for?" Diego asked.

"Oh—nothing." Winston regretted missing the shot.

"You're smiling. What was it?"

"It was bad. Forget it." Winston glanced at the cave and then back at Diego. His grin widened even more.

After a dreadful eighteen holes, the two carried their clubs and balls back towards the checkout counter.

"You know, you should have been a pro golfer instead of a gardener. You would have made a killing."

Diego laughed. "But I like being a gardener."

"And a good one you are. Are you hungry?" Winston asked.

"A little. Do you want to eat?"

Winston thought how to frame what he wanted to say. "I was thinking—it's early. How about we drive back to my house? I'll cook something. It's been a long time since I cooked for someone."

Seeing the hesitation on Diego's face, Winston pressed on. "We could talk, relax, and hang out." Still not ready to quit, he added, "It's early."

With a quick glance at his watch, Diego conceded. "Okay, I'll follow you." Laying his club and ball on the counter, he excused himself. "I'll be right back. I have to go to the restroom."

Winston placed his club up on the counter next to Diego's. A dirty thought flashed in his brain. *What if I followed him into the bathroom?* Now that would be bad.

After a couple of minutes, Diego returned, smiling. "Okay, I'm ready." Walking right up to Winston, Diego placed something in his hand.

Caught off guard, Winston looked down. It took a second to register that he was holding Diego's underwear: a pair of the sexiest, smallest red bikini underwear he had ever seen. Excitement surged in him, and the crotch of his pants tightened. As much as he wanted to stare and examine Diego's gift, he balled the underwear in his fist and stuffed them into his pocket. *Did he really just give me his underwear? He's commando right now, completely hanging free.* He looked down at Diego's crotch, and his sexual flame ignited, rendering him speechless. *So there is a little cochino to him.* A smile crossed Winston's face. He had so much to learn about this guy.

14

In no time, the kitchen was a complete mess. Pots and pans that had been collecting dust above the Viking gas stove had finally been put to use. Diego watched from the other side of the granite breakfast bar that housed the six-burner gas stove. It had taken Winston a little over an hour to destroy his kitchen. Spillage covered the stove as well as the counters behind him.

Pleased with his lamb shanks with a drizzled wine reduction and shiitake mushrooms, green beans browned in butter, and roasted baby potatoes, Winston announced that he was more than proud of himself. It had been too long since he cooked to impress someone, and he was pleased that he had not lost his culinary skills.

The two ate at the breakfast bar. Diego savored the bony pieces of meat, working to pull every ounce of meat off the bone. He could have eaten twice as much; he proclaimed it the best piece of meat he had ever had.

Afterwards, to flee the mess, Winston suggested they go out to the back yard. Diego stuck close as Winston led him by the hand through the maze of the house and onto the large, covered patio.

Diego had seen this place a million times before. He eyed the large dining table with its eight heavy wrought-iron chairs sitting next to the stone-covered outdoor kitchen.

Winston guided him to the other side of the patio, where two oversize sofas covered with decorative pillows, along with a couple of cushioned chairs, were arranged around a fire pit.

It was strange to be on the patio as a guest. Taking a seat on the couch, Diego felt as if he was seeing it for the first time. Although cleaning the patio wasn't part of his job, he did blow out scattered leaves and pick up garbage here from time to time.

"I thought we would hang out here for a while. It's pretty at night." Winston moved a pillow out of his way so he could sit next to Diego. After adjusting the pillow behind him, he picked up a remote from the coffee table and pointed it at the light above them. "On or off?"

"Um, off—if that's okay." Diego quietly exhaled a breath that he had been unconsciously holding. There was plenty of light coming from inside the house, and any more might reveal his nervousness.

"I had a good time playing putt-putt tonight." Winston let out a little laugh as he again adjusted the pillow at his back, somehow sliding a little closer to Diego.

"Why are you laughing?" Diego asked.

"I love that word, putt-putt. It sounds funny."

"But that's what it's called, putt-putt. What's so funny about that?" Diego didn't understand the joke. Stars filled the dark sky. The yard was different from the place that he spent every Monday and Tuesday grooming. There was nothing now but silhouettes of everything he knew to be there. Even the pool was reduced to a dimly lit shadow of water. Relaxing into the sofa, he eyed the lights of homes on the hillside.

"Are you comfortable? Not too warm out here, is it?" Winston fretted.

"No, it's nice. All the lights on the hill, they're beautiful." He had thought he knew every inch of this yard, yet in this moment, it was all new.

"You're so quiet. Are you okay?"

Diego nodded.

"Are you good?" Winston asked.

Good? Diego thought that word meant 'okay.' "Yeah, I'm o-kay. It's nice out here." He was lying. He felt anything but okay as he imagined where this was going. Would Winston kiss him again? Was there a chance there could be more than a kiss, that maybe—just maybe— they would be intimate? Was it anticipation or doubt that was causing his stomach to flutter and his thoughts to flee?

"I never come out here at night." Winston put his arm across the back of the sofa.

Diego tried to relax. Although Winston's arm wasn't touching him, he knew it was there. In silence, he waited for Winston to drive the conversation.

"I take it you liked the dinner?" Winston slid his arm down around Diego's neck.

Diego snuggled into Winston's arm. "I did. It was better than your sandwiches." He giggled.

Winston squeezed his arm around Diego's neck in a friendly chokehold. "Whatever. I worked hard on those PB & Js for you."

"You did!" Diego agreed jokingly. "So who cooked, you or Mr. Leblanc?"

With the arm that was draped around Diego's neck, Winston ran his hand lightly across Diego's chest. "Um, at first, Parker did, but towards the end, we mostly ate out."

"Oh." Diego thought about how much Winston had already spent on their first two dates. Having dinner anywhere but home was rarely an option for him, with the exception of buying lunch from the taco trucks. Mayra was an excellent cook; he and his brothers were lucky. Her dishes were almost as good as his mother's and his *abuela*'s. "I think your cooking was good. Thank you."

Winston's hand swept down, brushing Diego's arm. "My mom was a good cook. I think I got it from her."

"Oh, yeah? You cooked with her?"

"Not really, but I watched and ate enough of her meals to see what went with what."

Recalling what Winston had said about his mother at the restaurant the other day, Diego asked, "She lives in Montana, right?"

"Yeah, with her husband. They moved there a couple of years ago. Bought a ton of property. I've never seen it, but I've seen pictures. It looks nice—just not for me."

Diego noted this was the second or third time Winston had said something regarding not visiting his mother. Clearly, there was something there that Winston wasn't saying, but it certainly wasn't his place to ask. "Have you lived in California your whole life?" Diego asked.

"Born and raised. I couldn't imagine living anywhere else." Winston again lightly rubbed his hand across Diego's chest. "So, what made you and your brothers come here?"

"Here? America or California?"

"California."

Diego told himself that he was safe with Winston. "We came to live with my uncle."

"I checked out Mezcala on the internet. You said the other day that you crossed the border illegally. How come you didn't apply to come over legally, the whole family?"

Winston's hand lightly brushed Diego's nipple, causing him to squirm. "Um . . . getting a visa . . ." It took a second to regain his focus. " . . .to come to America is hard if you're a Mexican. My father, he tried and tried, and the government always say no to him. It cost a lot of money, and they say no. They not give him his money back, they just said no. My father, my brother, and my cousins, we all work, every day. We make six dollars a day. Not enough money for all the paperwork your government say it needs." Diego's body tensed, more from the conversation than Winston's touch.

"The photos on the internet made Mezcala look like a dump. I couldn't believe that anybody actually still lived that way."

That way? Unsure that he was translating Winston's comment correctly, Diego repeated it in his head several times. Was he talking about them being poor?

"Would you ever go back . . . to live?" Winston asked.

Diego hesitated for a second as he thought about how best to answer him. "Well, no, I wouldn't because I have to stay here. I make money here. I can help my family with the money I make." Diego squeezed out from under Winston's arm and sat up. A quiver in his stomach caused him to fold his arms tightly across his chest.

"How do you do that?"

"What do you mean? Do what?" Diego asked.

"Help them with the money you're making?"

Something about Winston's tone sounded a bit harsh. "I send them money. Every month, we send money to our parents. " Diego stopped short of explaining how the money was used. It was none of Winston's business.

Sitting up, Winston shifted his weight onto his other butt cheek as he leaned back into Diego. "I didn't mean to irritate you."

"I'm not." Diego leaned away.

"You sound irritated." Winston looked him directly in the eye.

"I'm not irritated, I'm . . ." Diego searched for the right words in English. He knew some Americans believed that immigrants hurt the economy by sending money out of the country rather than spending it here.

"I'm sorry. I didn't mean to piss you off. That wasn't my intent."

As if a switch had been flipped, Diego was ready to leave. If he stayed, he might say something he regretted. "Can we talk about something else?" Diego folded his arms across his chest and leaned back into the sofa. He didn't want to appear mad, but it was time for him to go. He had his job to think about.

"I'm sorry." Winston reached out and laid his hand over Diego's thigh. "Sure . . . Earlier, when you told me about your brother and that cave, all I wanted to do was the same with you. I wanted to take you into that cave and ravish your beautiful body."

Fighting the impulse to move his leg out from under Winston's hand, Diego thought about what the two of them had shared. A minute ago, all he had desired was Winston's touch. Now, he wasn't so sure. One minute, Winston was talking about *those Mexicans*, and the next, he was talking about sex. Diego was wedged between conflicting emotions.

"Then you sent me over the edge with your underwear," Winston jokingly added, as his hand brushed lightly up and down Diego's thigh.

Seeing the naughtiness in Winston's grin and eyes, Diego asked, "So why didn't we?" He had thought of Winston as much more than a hookup. Was that all Diego was to him? A pit sunk into his stomach.

"Well, honestly . . . that's not me." Winston stopped rubbing Diego's thigh. "Right now, there's nothing I want more than to take you down the hall, to make love to you. But . . ." He took a breath. "There's something I have to do first."

What did he have to do? Confused, Diego searched for the answer in Winston's eyes. His belly filled with apprehension.

If Winston had asked him to go into the cave this evening, would he have gone? That would have made Winston like every other guy, and Winston wasn't like every other guy. At least, Diego didn't want him to be. Was the thought of going inside to have sex the reason Diego's belly was in knots?

Winston had used the words *make love*. Even with his lack of understanding of English, Diego recognized the difference in the meaning between "make love" and "have sex." Was Winston saying that he, too, wanted more than just sex?

"What's wrong? You look like you've seen a ghost." Winston's eyebrows dipped as his face softened.

No, it wasn't a ghost, but it was just as frightening. Diego felt completely out of his element. Maybe this was moving too fast for him. He had to pay attention: Winston's words, his body language, his facial expressions. Diego wanted to go, but he was now unsure why. Fixed in his seat, he waited for Winston to make a move, whatever that would be.

"Hello? Did you check out on me?" Winston's voice was faint.

Diego had indeed checked out. His heart and mind were racing.

"Look, about whatever it was that I said, I know you wanted to drop it, and I will, but . . ." Winston leaned in and ran his fingers through Diego's hair, pushing strands of hair out of his face. "I don't know what I'm doing here. I haven't dated in a long time. I'm not sure I should be, but I like you. I really, really like you. I screwed up here, and I'm not smart enough to figure out what I did."

Diego blew out a breath that had been bottled up in his chest. He nodded. Yes, Winston was babbling, but he was trying. He waited for Winston to finish. Then he said, "I not know if I can do this. This is not my world . . . I belong out there, cutting your lawn, not sitting here, hanging out with the owner. I should have never—"

"Don't say that. That's bullshit. It's not about our 'worlds' as you put it. We have a connection . . . something. Am I wrong?"

Diego wanted to say no. Whatever he was feeling, whatever Winston might be feeling, it wasn't a *connection*. Their worlds were too different. But, if that was so, why did his heart feel as if it was going to explode every time Winston entered his mind? He felt consumed by thoughts of Winston and the desire to be near him in any way possible.

Winston delicately kissed Diego's bottom lip, pausing for a second as he exhaled. "I like you. I like you a lot. Give me a chance," he mumbled. Their faces were inches apart. "It's me that's in over my head."

"I think I should go." Diego stood up, but an ache in his chest caused him to delay taking that first step. He waited for Winston to say something, anything. He was tormenting himself. "I'll see you on Monday. I should go." He felt for his truck keys in his jeans, relieved that they were there and not in the house.

15

As the two iron gates separated, Diego felt the quiver in his stomach. Since he and Winston had parted the other night, their only interaction had been a brief text yesterday. Winston had asked how he was doing. His reply had been, *Good. I'll be there tomorrow.*

Diego didn't remember the massive gates moving as slowly as they did now. He had little patience this afternoon. He pushed lightly on the accelerator, and his truck and trailer slowly pulled in and around, past the front doors of the house. There was a strange familiarity to the property—not because he had been here two nights ago but because there was no sign of life. No car was in the driveway to indicate that Winston was home. Could it be that both cars were in the garage and Winston was inside? Things were back to the way they had been a month ago, before whatever this was with Mr. Makena.

Shutting the engine off, he hesitated before getting out. He thought about the weekend, he scanned the property. Two nights ago, he had been inside that house, eating dinner, laughing, and staring at a man who openly expressed desire for him. This piece of property, once a sanctuary for him, now pulled at every nerve fiber in his body.

A drink from his water jug settled his nerves, but only for a minute. It was time to get to work, he told himself, as he pulled on the door handle and opened the door. Stepping out of the truck, he couldn't stop himself from looking at the front door. Was Winston inside?

The previous day, he had spent all day before and after church trying to make sense of things. He and Winston, together, a couple. Three dates. He thought much like his mother, a traditionalist. You date, you're a couple, you get married, and you have kids. That's what couples did. That's how relationships worked—unless you were gay.

Father Sandoval's sermon yesterday on not putting expectations on other people had stayed with Diego. After church, when he and his brothers had gone over to the flea market, he avoided their usual banter. He had plenty to think about without listening to their nonsense. He wasn't prepared for his heart to have such a large say in whether being gay was really a sin.

He had tried to convince himself that he and Winston were wrong. Not because it was a sin, but because they were too different. It wasn't until Francisco told him he was moping like a little bitch that he realized he was thinking of nothing other than being with Winston.

For every reason he came up with why they couldn't, he matched it with a reason why they should. He might not be rich like Winston, but he was kind, and he was loyal. Why shouldn't he try, even if it wasn't perfect? Was perfect even real?

Foolishly, he had come here today ready to take that next step. As he looked around the property, he saw no sign of life. His plan to make things right didn't account for Winston not being home.

With his back to the house, he stood on the trailer ramp, thinking of what equipment he needed. Of course, the mower had to come out, the grey trash can, the—

"Hey, there."

Diego knew the voice. As he turned around, his breath caught. Winston stood there, holding a single PB & J on a plate.

"I come in peace. And to say I'm sorry about the other night. I get it now. I'm such an asshole for what I said." Winston's eyes locked onto Diego.

"Which part?" Diego asked. He was willing to risk shooting down the initial apology in exchange for an answer to that question—a question he hadn't had two seconds ago.

"Well, all of it. My friend Ann—you know, my business partner—I called her right after you left." Winston extended the PB & J to Diego. "She called me a bigot, an asshole, and a moron after I told her about our conversation."

"Oh. What did you tell her?" A whiff of the nutty peanut butter led Diego to take the sandwich. "Tell me what you say."

"Well, for starters, I told her about our conversation about you and your brothers coming across the border, about you sending money home—and then . . ." Winston scowled. " . . .Me changing the conversation to sex. I insulted you, and then said I wanted to have sex with you." Winston stepped closer, to the edge of the ramp. "I can't believe I'm such an asshole. I want to say that I'm not, and to ask for another chance, but I think that I am, a real asshole, and I'm sorry."

There was authenticity and sincerity in Winston's apology. The negative energy that had plagued Diego since Saturday evening left his body. As he looked around the property, Diego rubbed the stubble on his chin. He wanted to step off the ramp and into Winston's arms.

"There's no one here, if that's what you're looking for." Winston stepped onto the ramp. He placed his hand on Diego's chest and moved in closer. "Can I kiss you?"

Diego's heart pounded. He wanted that kiss more than anything . . . But they were in public, outside, in the middle of the afternoon. Everything he knew said no, but his heart said yes. Following his heart, he gave Winston what he had asked for.

Winston pulled Diego up into his chest, causing his feet to leave the ground.

The world slowly faded away around them. The sandwich in Diego's hand dropped to the ground as Winston kissed, possessed, and consumed him. Somehow, they ended up in the trailer. Diego's butt pressed against the sheet metal sides as tools fell behind him.

Winston pulled back, giving Diego a chance to catch his breath. There was no mistaking the thickness in Winston's pants pressed against his.

Diego wiped the moisture from his swollen lips. Staring into Winston's eyes, dark as storm clouds, he knew that they were seeing him, all of him.

"I'm sorry," Winston whimpered.

"No. Shhh." Diego placed two fingers against Winston's full lips. He didn't want to lose the energy that was pumping between them.

"Okay, no more," Winston murmured. "Will you come inside with me?"

Diego didn't have to answer. Winston took his hand and led him out of the trailer and to the front door.

"Are you okay?" Winston asked as they entered the house.

Diego drew a breath as he looked around the spacious foyer. This was really happening. His lips were still tingling, and he could hardly breathe. "Um, yeah." His voice was barely audible.

"Are you sure?" Cocking his head to one side, Winston stared into Diego's eyes.

As nervous as he felt, Diego had never been surer in his life. The look in Winston's eyes washed away any doubt he may have had. Although he had no idea how this was to work, he nodded yes.

Winston led him down the long hallway, past several doors, and into the master bedroom. Diego could hear himself breathing, yet he felt as if his lungs were empty. The simple touch of Winston's hand stopped him in his tracks.

Winston turned Diego to face him. "I'm just as nervous. I get it. Are you sure this is okay?"

Diego couldn't speak. He was reduced to a simple nod of approval. The room was a blur to him. The paint on the wall, the furnishings, the vast size of the place, none of it was important. His attention solely on the tall, dark-haired, massive body in front of him.

"Okay," Winston murmured. He took a hold of Diego's hand and walked him over to the large bed.

Diego watched as Winston threw an endless number of pillows from the bed onto the floor. Not one of them made a sound as it landed. Once the bed was clear of pillows, Winston pulled the heavy bedding back to the middle of the mattress.

He kept his eye on Winston as he moved past him and stopped at the edge of the bed. His heart was racing; this was really going to happen. Before he could finish his thought, Winston grabbed him up and pressed their bodies together. Locked together by a kiss, they resumed where they had left off, their lips lightly touching as their body temperatures climbed.

Diego felt the anxiety drain from his body. His brothers, his job, his priest; all were banished to deep recesses of his brain. He took in Winston's smell. Intoxicated, he fought to hold his own head up as his shoulders dropped.

With no resistance, he let himself be piloted onto the bed. He absorbed Winston's weight on top of him; Winston's manhood, pressed against Diego, deepened his dirty thoughts. Releasing a moan, Diego swooned as Winston caressed his neck with tiny kisses.

Winston kissed his way down Diego's neck and back up to his lips. Diego released another whimper, like steam escaping a boiling pot, avoiding an internal explosion.

Winston eased off him slightly. "I want to feel you, your skin, all of you."

Unsure exactly how he was supposed to take his clothes off with Winston on top of him, Diego frantically started with his belt. With his belt undone, he worked to unsnap the button on his jeans and unzipped his fly. His entire body ached to be touched.

Their eyes locked onto each other as they both freed themselves of the only thing between them.

Completely naked, Winston repositioned himself, straddling Diego's small hips. Looking up into Winston's eyes, Diego felt as if he was staring at molten silver, liquefied and about to spill out on top of him.

Diego reached up and laid his hand across Winston's nipple and gently squeezed. He watched as Winston drew a quick breath, his eyes enlarging. Had he just caused that? Diego was unsure, but in the next second, it became irrelevant.

Winston bent down and gently placed a kiss on Diego's chest. The touch of his lips caused Diego to suck in a breath. His lungs were capable only of short, shallow gasps. Winston made his way up to Diego's lips, their bodies melting together as their kiss deepened.

Running his hands delicately across Winston's back, Diego noticed how cool his skin was. When his fingers reached Winston's ass, he traced his hands around the rounded muscles. He had never touched another man's ass. It was different from his, smooth and so much larger. He held on as Winston's kisses caused his body to weaken.

Their naked bodies rubbed together, producing the necessary friction for what Diego knew was to come. As the sensation built, he knew he was close.

Winston moaned softly in his ear, "So beautiful, I'm going to . . ."

Unable to complete his sentence, Winston released a cry as his body tensed and his weight bore down onto Diego. The sheer weight of Winston, his cry—Diego's body responded to it all as he reached a euphoric climax that sent waves throughout his body.

Their spent bodies pressed together. Diego's breathing was labored and weak as he closed his eyes in total ecstasy. With Winston's body covering him, he absorbed the pressure and undeniable weight of what had just happened. The whole thing took less than ten minutes, yet it had been the most important ten minutes of his life. His heart raced as he tried to gain control of his breathing. His body lay weightless, his mind blown at what had occurred. They had made love; Winston had made love to him. Closing his eyes, he blew out a breath in hopes of slowing his pounding heart.

A light brush of his hand against Winston's naked body confirmed what Diego already knew to be true. He opened his eyes slowly, focusing on the heavy crown molding along the ceiling. He was, indeed, lying in Winston's bed.

"Did you fall asleep?" Winston rolled onto his side to face Diego.

Diego had to think for a minute. Had he blacked out or fallen asleep? There was no doubt a loss of time, but was it seconds, minutes, or longer? "What time is it?" Diego stretched his neck to look at the alarm clock, which read two o'clock in the afternoon.

The mattress didn't move as Winston rolled over and left the bed. "I'll get a towel to clean up," he mumbled before walking out of the room.

Diego watched as Winston's tan back and gorgeous, pale ass disappeared into the next room. Trying to wrap his head around what had occurred, he listened to water running and cabinets opening and closing.

Within minutes, Winston returned with a wet hand towel. Still naked, he leaned over Diego and gently ran the warm washcloth over his stomach. "Damn . . . your abs . . . are beautiful." His words in rhythm with each stroke against Diego's skin.

With Winston's naked body next to his face, Diego stared at Winston's manhood as it bobbled freely around. A sudden panic struck Diego, causing him to grab the washcloth from Winston. "I do it." It felt weird, having a man clean him up like a baby.

Clueless, Winston climbed back into bed. Diego felt Winston's eyes on him as he wiped his skin with the damp cloth. Why was he staring? Had it been rude to grab the cloth? It had all happened so fast. He needed to say something, to restore the mood and stop overthinking. "That was nice. Thank you." His voice cracked, and his own words echoed in his head. *It was nice.*

"Thank you." Winston ran his hand across Diego's damp abdomen. The tip of his fingers lightly brushed Diego's bellybutton, sending a charge through Diego's body. "I love your brown skin," said Winston. "It's the color of caramel. Can I get you anything?"

Diego took a large cleansing breath. His eyes followed Winston's fingers as they moved across his belly.

Pulling the sheet over their naked bodies, Winston pulled Diego into his arms. Pressing his face into Winston's side, Diego inhaled his scent and released a long, slow exhale. Every bit of energy left in Diego's body escaped, and he drifted off into a deep sleep in the middle of the afternoon.

The sound of a bark woke Diego. He had slept heavily; the last two restless nights had caught up with him. He opened his eyes to look at the clock on the nightstand, but heavy panting drew his gaze to the floor. Lucy's pink tongue hung out of her mouth as her tail wagged.

"Hi, there. Do you want up?" Diego quietly patted the bed. Lucy remained seated, her eyes fixed on him.

Not wanting to wake Winston, he glanced at the motionless body. The thin sheet draped the curves of Winston's naked physique. He had never done anything like this in his entire life. It was the middle of the day and he was in a strange room, naked with another man.

Diego glanced at the clock before lightly patting the bed again. "What? Am I lying in your spot?"

With zero response from Lucy, Diego decided that he ought to get up, find the bathroom, and then . . . think about returning to work. He scratched at his scalp, before attempting to straighten his hair.

As he entered the bathroom, he found that it was every bit as big as the bedroom itself. It was like nothing he had ever seen. To his right, encased in thick glass, was a tiled shower large enough for his entire family. He counted what he presumed were showerheads: *eleven*. Next to the giant shower, he studied the oval-shaped marble tub with several jet outlets. It must have been some kind of hot tub. His eyes finally turned to a fireplace on the adjacent white marble wall.

The room was immaculate. It was unconceivable to Diego that such a bathroom existed. His eyes scanned for a toilet, stopping long enough to notice matching round glass vessel sinks on top of the sparkling white Carrara marble counters.

Unless he had missed it, there was no toilet. Surely, there had to be one. Opening another door, he found a large closet. *Nope, no toilet in there.*

After searching behind two more doors, he finally found the tiny room that housed the toilet. He couldn't imagine why someone would put a toilet behind a door and in such a tiny space.

After relieving himself, Diego quietly reentered the bedroom. Winston was now sitting up with Lucy in his arms. The clingy sheet lay across his lap, masking nothing.

Startled at seeing Winston up and awake, Diego's eyes were drawn to the small patch of hair between Winston's quarter-sized brown nipples. He wanted to stare, to touch Winston to ensure that he was real. But Diego, too, was naked, and his insecurities about his small frame next to Winston's sent him scurrying under the sheets. His body was no match for Winston's impressive, sculpted physique. Lost for words, Diego smiled.

"Everything okay?" Winston leaned over and tenderly kissed Diego's bare shoulder.

The simple touch from Winston worked to calm him. He said, "I got lost. I not find the toilet."

"What do you mean, you got lost?" Winston cupped the back of Diego's head and brought him in for a real kiss.

"I not find your toilet," Diego murmured through the kiss.

Winston broke into laughter. "So what did you do. Pee in my tub?"

"No!" Diego knew he was being teased. "That's not nice. You kid me. Your bathroom is big." His eyes dropped to the floor, to the pillows he'd had to step over to get back in bed. "How many pillows do you have?"

"Too many," Winston replied as he tried to get another kiss from Diego. "They were on sale."

Diego's eyes scanned the room. This room, that bathroom, this house, it was like a castle.

"You're not going to ask?" Winston finally stole another kiss.

Distracted, Diego used his tongue to retrieve the droplet of moisture Winston's kiss had left on his lips. The salty taste lingered on his tongue. "About what?"

"The bed?" Winston replied.

Diego, confused, looked down at the bed and then back at Winston.

"Do you remember the other night—I know you don't want me to bring it up—but the other night, when I said I wanted to make love to you? I said that there was something I had to do first."

Diego remembered. He had forgotten the statement.

"I needed a new bed. Until I met you, I couldn't give up my bed . . . Parker's bed. It was one of the few places I could still feel his presence, where I could hold on to him. I'm embarrassed to admit this, but . . ." A grin surfaced on Winston's face. "It was during our second date. We were sitting there eating pizza, and it hit me. You are so beautiful. I wanted to sleep with you. Not then, that night, but I knew I wanted to—well, if you asked." Adjusting the sheet across their laps, Winston continued, "It was appropriate that I got a new bed . . . for us."

"So you buy this bed? It's new?" Diego looked at the bed and pile of bedding gathered at their feet.

"Yes. I wanted a new bed, a bed that was just mine and that I would share with you." A smiled grew across Winston's face. "They say you should replace your mattress every ten years anyways."

Diego's heart swooned. Winston had purchased a new bed for him. It was the craziest, sweetest thing anyone had ever done for him. *Unimaginable.* "You're sweet—but you not call me beautiful no more." Diego shook his head. "I am not a *mujer.* I'm a man."

"I wasn't calling you a woman." Winston laughed. "I'm sorry. It's an expression, to say you're attractive." He opened his palms as if to weigh the words.

"You say, *hombre guapo,*" Diego told him.

Winston repeated the words. "*Hom-bre gua-po.* I knew that. *Hombre guapo.*"

"*Si.*" Diego leaned up and kissed Winston.

"Are you hungry?" Winston slid his hands under the sheet and lightly caressed Diego's thigh.

He was. He was starving, but he had to get home. "I go now. I must go home." Diego pulled back the sheet. Ready to get up, he saw that his lower body had responded to Winston's touch.

With the speed of Superman, Winston threw his body over Diego's, pinning him in the bed. "No! Why? Why do you have to leave?"

Diego thought about it for a second. He didn't know why; he just did. After work, he went home every day. This was his life. He ate dinner with his family. He waited around in his bedroom for Rafael. Francisco and Mayra watched TV out in the living room all night. Rafael sometimes came in, and sometimes he didn't. Why was it that nobody cared that Rafael stayed out all night?

Flashing Winston a forged smile, Diego again tried to exit the bed.

Winston clutched his arm. "Let me cook you something. I need the practice, and then you can go. I swear."

The man was begging. Diego couldn't say no to a begging man, especially one who bought a bed just for him. He would at least text his family to let them know he was all right and would be coming home late. Mayra would be the easiest and would ask fewer questions. He didn't know what Francisco would do; he dared not think about it.

"Okay." Diego's voice shook. "I text my brother." That was easier than saying he would text his brother's girlfriend, who practically lived with them and was also kind of his mother; yes, much easier.

The muscles in his jaw tightened. Rafael would have to find a ride to work. Maybe Mayra would take him. When she didn't stay the night, she sometimes offered. That could happen.

He didn't think Francisco would let Rafael take the car. Francisco had been on Rafael's ass for the last month about gas money. With his phone close to his chest, he sent Mayra a text letting her know he was running late. The pit in his stomach grew deeper. He noticed the time at the top of his screen. He couldn't believe it was after five.

16

The two sat at the kitchen bar, facing each other as they ate. Winston could hardly take his eyes off the vision before him. With nothing but a towel around his waist, Diego sat and snacked on the unconventional meal Winston had managed to pull together. Devouring the lunchmeat, cheese, sliced apples, and a can of mixed nuts, the two replenished the nutrients lost during their afternoon workout.

"I feel bad for not cooking you a proper dinner." Winston rolled a piece of lunchmeat around his string cheese. He held his meat roll-up up to his mouth, but the brown shimmer in Diego's eyes stopped him from taking a bite. It was like staring through a jar of warm honey. "Um . . ." Mesmerized by the soft twinkle in Diego's eyes, there was innocence in them. " . . .Um, I guess we could have gone out." Truth was, the last thing Winston wanted was Diego dressed. He had offered Diego his robe earlier and was delighted when Diego declined and opted for the towel.

Winston tried not to stare as Diego sat at the bar. The way Diego chewed his food, looked around the room taking everything in, Winston wanted to pinch himself. Was this happening? The butterflies fluttering in his stomach, his desire to please Diego, his longing to touch him, all said that it was real.

After making love to Diego that afternoon, Winston had plenty of time to stare at him as he lay sleeping. Initially, it was nothing more than a chance to stare at him uninterrupted, no awkwardness in the person staring back, or that perhaps he was staring too long. Slow, shallow breaths, Diego lay perfectly still, childlike. There was a peacefulness to his angelic face. His skin resembled that of smooth caramel that called for Winston to touch it. He restrained himself though, for fear of waking Diego and losing this opportunity, this moment in time that was all his.

For the first time in as long as he could remember, Winston was living in the moment. He had no desire to be anywhere or do anything in this moment in time. Diego had connected him to the present. Since Parker's death, he had been living in the past, almost frightened to move forward. Grief had become the new normal.

Until his and Diego's paths had crossed, he'd had zero desire to meet anyone. How would any other person fill Parker's shoes? Parker was gone, Parker was never coming back, and Parker couldn't be replaced. Now he knew there was room in his heart for Diego. Not to replace Parker, but to have his own space.

"Why are you staring at me?" Diego asked softly.

"I'm sorry," Winston lied. He was anything but sorry. How could he not stare at that face framed in jet-black hair, with thick eyebrows and long eyelashes just as dark? Those full lips challenged anyone not to want to kiss them. There was a man wearing nothing but a towel, sitting at his breakfast bar, and looking at him as if he hung the moon. Of course he was staring.

Diego leaned forward onto the counter as he looked at the platter of food. "I love cheese." He took one slice of cheddar and a slice of the pepper jack. "This is good." He held up the pepper jack before eating it.

"What's your favorite?" Winston finished off his meat roll in three bites. He wanted to know everything about Diego.

"Um . . ." Diego's eyes rolled upward as he thought. "I think probably Manchego or Cotija . . . I think Manchego." His tone gave way to uncertainty.

"I love Manchego!" Winston was surprised that Diego knew of the cheese. "Do you know that there is a sheep in Spain called a Manchega? That's where the milk comes from to make the cheese."

Diego's eyes narrowed. "No . . . we make it with a mixture of cows' and goats' milk."

Winston was surprised again by Diego's knowledge of Manchego. "Does it taste the same?" Winston didn't wait for Diego to finish chewing the cheese in his mouth as he leaned in for a kiss.

"Kind of." Shrugging, Diego obliged Winston's request.

Savoring the kiss, Winston caught the inquisitive look as it swept across Diego's face. Diego didn't know how adorable he was.

"So, why do you like me?" Diego's voice was pensive and vulnerable.

"For one, I think you're adorable. I think you're smart . . ." Stopping, Winston gently kissed Diego's bottom lip. "I like the quietness of your soul . . ." Stopping again, he laid another kiss on Diego's top lip and gently tugged at it as he pulled away. "You intrigue me. There's so much I don't know about you."

Sighing deeply, Winston stared into the flecks of gold in Diego's eyes. They were the most beautiful eyes he had ever seen. Drawing a breath, he said, "You make my heart go pitter-patter. Shall I continue?" He slid his hand onto Diego's thigh and lightly brushed it over the towel. "Did I mention you're sexy as hell?"

Smiling, Diego replied, "I like you too."

"Well, gee, thanks." Winston leaned back on the barstool. It was as if they were twelve. The *I like you* dialogue was so simplistic, but it somehow spoke volumes about Diego's character.

Diego frowned as his head cocked to one side. "Is that not right?" His voice squeaked.

"I'm teasing you. You said it like you like that piece of cheese or something. It was sweet."

"It's not funny. I *like* you . . . but I *love* the cheese." Quickly grabbing another piece, Diego ripped it into two and, without losing his grin, stuffed one half into his month.

"Okay, I have competition. Who knew it was going to be cheese." Just happy to be in the race, Winston couldn't help but stare into Diego's soft eyes.

Swallowing his bite of cheese, Diego licked his lips, his eyes never leaving Winston's. "Your middle name, it's Willow, no?" Diego asked.

"Um, yeah." Winston was unsure how Diego knew this or why he was asking. "Why do you ask?"

"It's different."

"It's English."

"Oh, I was thinking it was like the tree."

Winston's eyes fell down to Diego's towel. "Well, kind-of-sort-of. Back in the day, the willow tree was thought to have magical powers."

"You mean like in Harry Potter?"

Winston couldn't hold back a snicker. "Yes, like Harry Potter." It was more likely that his parents had smoked too much pot and were trying to hold on to their hippy days. That was too much to explain, though, and he was tired of talking. He slid his hand farther under Diego's towel. Diego's soft thighs sent a charge of excitement directly to his brain.

Diego clamped his thighs together. The powerful muscles stopped Winston's hands inches from their destination. "You're bad. *Te gusta?*" Diego relaxed his thighs and smiled.

Yes, indeed, Winston liked it very much. "*Me gusta mucho.*"

Diego raised his chin. "I forget your Spanish is good." He opened his legs wider, giving Winston full access to what he wanted. In Spanish, Diego coyly murmured, "I have to be careful with you."

Winston slid off his stool, moving in between Diego's legs and attempting to undo his towel.

Grabbing his hand, Diego stopped him. "No . . . I have to go." The expression on his face said that he didn't want to. "I have to . . ."

"Come on." Winston made a second attempt at the towel.

"Stop it. *Me gusta mucho!*" His smiled conveyed just how much he enjoyed Winston's hand on his waist. "But I have to go home." There was a plea in Diego's voice this time, as he slid off his stool and wiggled out from between Winston's roaming hands.

"I like you too, and that's why I don't want you to go. Spend the night. Stay here—with me." Winston was now the one pleading.

"All night? No!" Diego shook his head, reinforcing his answer.

"Come on. Give me one good reason why not. Tomorrow's Tuesday. You're coming back anyways, so why not stay? Where are you working in the morning? Isn't the other house, like, down the street? You can drive from here and then come back in the afternoon like you always do. We can have lunch. I promise, I will let you go home tomorrow. I promise."

Winston had no idea what he was asking Diego to do. To stay out all night would garner unwanted attention from Rafael and Francisco. They would drill him until he told them the truth.

"Give me one good reason," Winston pleaded.

Diego sat in silence, shaking his head.

Winston's gut told him that Diego wanted to say yes. Diego's eyes said what his words didn't. "You haven't given me one good reason yet."

"I not have any clothes," Diego mumbled. "No stuff to clean up."

Laughing, Winston grabbed him by the waist and turned his body so they faced each other. "I have a shower, soap, toothpaste, and I bet I could find you deodorant. Try again."

"But—"

"But nothing, I know you want to stay."

"What do I say to my family, my brothers?" Diego's eyes showed his agony.

"The truth: that you're having hot sex with some old big stud!" Winston chuckled.

A smirked formed at the edge of Diego's mouth as he rolled his eyes. "That's not funny!"

Winston stared into the fear in Diego's eyes. "I haven't known you all that long, but I'm thinking you probably don't do a lot for yourself. You want to stay. I know you do. If not for me, do it for yourself. Forget all the reasons you shouldn't, and do it for the one reason you should: because *you* want to." Winston pulled Diego up into his arms, wrapping him tightly against his chest. "It's okay to do something for yourself from time to time."

The energy coming off Diego's body as it pressed against his robe told Winston that Diego was weighing his decision. He knew he had to release Diego in order for him to answer. But what if that answer was still no? That was reason enough to not let go.

"Okay . . . I'll stay." Diego murmured. Then his head turned at the sound of the iron gates out front closing. Pulling away, he took a step backwards. "Is someone here?"

"I dunno." Winston walked over to the kitchen window and peered out. Although he couldn't see his front yard from that window, he saw the tail end of a truck. "Oh, it's the pool guy. He comes late sometimes."

Diego adjusted his towel as he took a step toward the window. "I go outside and close up my trailer. It's still open."

"It's fine. He's not going to touch it. Your stuff will be fine." Winston approached and brushed several strands of hair out of Diego's face. "Your hair is so long." Rubbing his thumbs across Diego's dense eyebrows, he smoothed them out. "Quit frowning. It's fine."

Winston kissed him before releasing him completely. "So I guess I should give you a robe or something to wear for the evening."

As if in a covert operation, Diego moved over to the window to watch as a little old Hispanic man removed a large pole and shower caddie from the rear of his truck. After the man disappeared, Diego turned and looked back at Winston. "I have my clothes. I can wear them." They both turned as they heard Lucy barking at the back kitchen door.

"Does she want out?" Diego asked.

"It's because the pool guy is here. She has a doggy door down the hall, but lately, she has wanted me to take her. I'll take her out, and then I'll get you some sweats to put on."

Winston was outside longer than he intended, having been forced into a conversation about repairs needed for the pool pump. When he finally made it back into the house, Diego was not where Winston had left him.

Passing through the kitchen and dining room, he found Diego standing in the hallway, staring at family pictures lining the wall.

"There you are." Winston walked up and caressed Diego's bare shoulders.

"So you have someone clean your pool too? He is Mexican, no?" Diego glanced at Winston.

"Um, yeah, I guess he's Mexican." Winston's voice trailed off as he tried to figure out why that mattered.

"Who is this?" Diego pointed to an old five-by-seven of a man standing in front of a large stone villa.

"That? That's my grandfather when he was about thirty or so. On our property in France." Winston examined the picture. As a child, he and his parents had visited that house at least four or five times that he could remember. It had been ages since he had been there.

Diego eyed another photograph. "Is this Greece?"

Winston looked at the picture of himself standing in front of the Parthenon many years ago. He smiled at how young he looked. "Yes, that was the summer before I met Parker. I was there with a bunch of friends from school. It was Easter break."

"Hmm. You've been to a lot of places, no?" Diego's eyes moved from picture to picture.

"A few." He had traveled the world, but it was all a blur. No one holiday stood out from the next.

"Where all have you been?" Diego stepped to the side to look at more pictures.

"Wow, I don't know . . . a lot of places," Winston said, blowing off the question.

"Like where?"

Winston knew Diego wasn't going to let him off. "Well, let's see: France, Italy, of course Greece, Monaco, Malta, Brazil, Spain—"

"Mexico?" Diego finally looked at him.

"Um, well, no. I haven't been to Mexico."

"Why not?"

"I don't know. No real reason, I guess. I just haven't." Winston thought for a second. *Brazil and Spain were kind of like Mexico.*

"Why you never go to Mexico? It's right here. Lots of things to see."

Winston thought about it. In truth, the place had never interested him. Diego was right: it was right here, an easy place to visit. Maybe that was one of the reasons. It was too accessible to everyone. *Everybody goes to Mexico.*

Walking away, Diego held onto his towel around his waist. The oversized towel covered his entire lower body and nearly touched the ground. Winston followed him towards the bedroom.

As they entered the bedroom, Diego headed for his clothes, which were on the floor where he had left them.

"Why don't we take a quick shower, get cleaned up?" Winston quickly stepped in front of Diego and snatched his pants and shirt from the floor. He sensed a shift in Diego's mood. Had the pictures upset him? Or was it the fact that Winston had never gone to Mexico? "Come on. Let's get cleaned up, and then I'll show you the rest of the house."

He took Diego's arm and led him into the bathroom. "You want a bath or a shower?"

"Shower."

Winston opened the massive glass door and stepped inside. He began hitting buttons, turning on one shower jet after another. Water came from every direction. Stepping out, Winston let his robe drop to the floor. "Come on."

Diego's eyes moved up and down Winston's naked body. "Together?"

Winston nodded with a mischievous grin.

Diego hesitated before slowly releasing his towel, allowing it to drop to his feet.

Winston had to force himself to draw in a breath. He was eyeing innocence, the beauty of the human form in its unblemished state. He forced his lungs to exhale.

Diego stepped under his arm and into the shower, his shoulders curling upward as the water attacked his body from every angle. "It's too much water!" He moved to one side of the shower, attempting to dodge the streams.

Winston stepped in and shut the glass door behind them. He hit several buttons on the wall, and the brutal attack of water was reduced to a soft rain that cascaded down on them.

"Is that better?" Winston laughed as Diego came off the wall.

Within seconds, the glass fogged, covering them in a cocoon of steam. As Winston begin lathering soap across his chest, he watched as Diego did the same. Their height difference was more pronounced when they stood side by side.

Staring at Diego's youthful body, Winston realized that, despite all of his years of tanning, dieting, hair removal treatments, and hours at the gym, he would never have a twenty-five-year-old's body again.

He tried to get out of his head, attempting to push their differences away. "So, what do you like to do when you're not working?" He turned to rinse the soap off his back. Rolling his head from side to side, he let the warm water run over his hair and then grabbed the shampoo.

Diego laughed. "Not working? I work all the time." He raised his voice to compensate for the water falling around him. Taking the bottle of shampoo that Winston held out, he squeezed a dab onto the palm of his hand.

"What about on the weekends? When you're not helping your brother at the garage, I mean." Winston pressed several buttons on the wall. In addition to the cascade of water from above, water began to flow from a pair of jets on Winston's side of the shower.

Lowering his head, Diego began to rinse the shampoo out of his hair. "I help them every Saturday. On Sundays, we go to church and then to the . . ." He raised his head, letting the water rinse his face and chest before rubbing the water from his eyes and mouth.

Diego opened his eyes as he finished his sentence, " . . .the flea market." To ensure he was soap free, he slid his hands over his glossy chest and arms once more.

"The flea market?" Winston wasn't sure he had understood over the relentless water.

Diego pointed to the soap bottle in the wall basket and nodded.

Winston handed him the bottle. Seeing that Diego wasn't finished, he relaxed and let the soothing jets pummel his back muscles.

"On Sundays." Diego squeezed out another dab of soap and handed the bottle back to Winston. He then took his penis in one hand, and pulled his foreskin back. Without looking up, Diego began washing the head and tip.

Winston's eyes dropped to Diego's penis. He had never been with someone uncut. A part of him said he should look away; this warranted a moment of privacy. He chose the wall to focus on. "So you guys go every Sunday?" *Why am I talking? I shouldn't be talking while he's cleaning himself.* Winston started to read the label on the shampoo bottle in front of him.

"We look for parts for the garage, things Francisco needs to fix his cars." Diego finished cleaning and began rinsing himself.

"Like engine parts?" Winston cleared his throat.

"*Sí.*"

When Diego was done, Winston began shutting down the elaborate shower system. "Do you also work on engines?"

Diego stepped out of the shower, his naked body dripping with water. "*Sí.*"

Following Diego, Winston reached around him to grab a fresh towel from the cabinet.

After drying off, he offered Diego one of his robes to wear. Draped in the white plush robe, Diego followed him into the large family room, which housed an eighty-inch television mounted to the wall. On the opposite wall was a lavishly carved stone fireplace with rocks that ascended to the ceiling. In the middle of the room, the furniture had been arranged to provide views of the TV, patio, and swimming pool.

Winston waited for Diego to sit down and then snuggled in close to him. He wanted to be close, but he didn't want to give the impression of being needy. He hated neediness and never thought of himself that way—until maybe now.

"Do you want something to drink, a glass of wine?" He wanted Diego to say yes. His own nerves could use a little steadying.

"No, I'm okay."

There was uncertainty in Diego's voice. *Was he nervous too?* They had been together for the last six hours, made love, shared a meal, and taken a shower together. That was more than most couples did in a week, so why the sudden nerves?

Diego broke the weird silence in the room. "So . . . what do you do at night?"

"What do you mean?" Winston couldn't help but peer into Diego's eyes. Their intense focus, the long draping eyelashes, commanded his attention.

"At night. Alone in this house." Diego adjusted his small frame on the enormous couch, his shoulders dropping.

"Well . . . I used to get in around six or seven and then work in my office on stuff that I didn't get done during the day."

"Used to? You not work no more?"

"Oh, I do. I'm taking a little time off." He thought of returning to work as he leaned in for a kiss.

"So, tell me again. What you do?" Diego asked.

"We plan big events, parties, ceremonies, galas, any kind of a party you can imagine."

"*El casamiento?*" Diego asked.

"No, not weddings. I can't deal with bridezillas."

"Bride . . . what?"

"It's not important. We take care of everything, from finding the place, to hosting the event, to ordering food, cooks, wait staff, and transportation. Everything you can think of that goes into having a party, we take care of it for the client."

"And Mr. Leblanc, he was . . . an attorney?"

"That's right." Winston reflected on when he and Parker had dinner in the evenings and talked about their day. Then they lay in bed, where Winston watched TV, a lot of TV. Next to him, Parker read and combed over notes and briefs.

"I bet you miss him, no?"

"I do." Those two words were difficult to speak, and a lump formed in his throat. "What about you?" Winston switched the topic. "What did you do before your lawn business?"

"Um, let's see. I do all kinds of things." Diego looked as if he was thinking about his answer. "Many years ago, when I first came to America, I worked in the fields. Picked oranges, peppers, tomatoes . . . everything. Then, I got a job at a car wash, then in a dry cleaner. Then I was a dishwasher. I do a lot."

"What does your dad do in Mexico?"

"My papa, he works in the factory in Xochipala. My *abuelo*, he say that job was no good. He was a fisherman. He teaches me to fish."

"Where the hell did you fish?" Winston remembered seeing a big river in the pictures online.

"The Atoyac River. On the bridge. Many fish in there. We sell to the women in the village. They much loved my *abuelo* . . . My *abuela*, not so much."

Laughing at Diego's cute facial expression when he mentioned his grandma, Winston couldn't help but think of his own grandmother. "How far was the factory?"

"Um, Xochipala, not too far, about thirty kilometers. They take the bus. It stops in the village for all the workers. It takes them to work and then back home at night."

"What did they make?"

"Fireworks. They sell them here, in America, in those little firework stands in July."

"So . . . If you had stayed, would you have been a fisherman like your grandpa or gone to work in the factory?"

"Me?" A look of surprise swept across Diego's face. "I wanted to travel to Mexico City. Go to school. I wanted to be an architect."

"Really?" Winston was flabbergasted. "An architect. Do you still have that desire—to be an architect?" He repeated the word, trying to wrap his brain around it.

"No, no more. If I could do anything, I would be a landscape designer. Design outdoor spaces for people like you, businesses, schools, and other things."

Winston tilted his head at Diego's *people like you* comment. Initially wanting to address it, he opted to ignore it. "I'm assuming you'll have to go to school for that, right?"

"Yes, to university."

"What made you change from buildings to landscapes?"

"Um, I like what I do. Mr. Leblanc, he teach me a lot. I learned a lot about plants, soil, and climate. When you first bought this place, Mr. Leblanc and me, we talked a lot. He took me to a nursery one day and showed me all the different plants, and we studied them. It was fun, and now I make yards nice. Not just cut the grass, but you know . . . more." Diego pointed towards the yard. Some of his shyness had been replaced with an air of confidence.

"Well, you're certainly good at it."

"Yeah?" Diego moved his feet onto the couch as he snuggled in closer to Winston.

"Yes." Winston wrapped his arm around Diego.

Diego's face gleamed. "Maybe one day I'll show you some of my drawings."

"You draw?"

"Yes. I have many drawings of yards and parks. I did a waterpark with lakes."

"I would love for you to show them to me." Winston didn't want to move, but his anxieties had given him dry mouth. "I need a glass of water. Are you sure I can't get you anything?"

"No," Diego answered.

"No, I can't get you anything, or no, you're not sure?"

Diego sat up. "I not want anything. Sorry."

When Winston returned to the family room, Diego had his phone out and appeared to be texting.

"Are your brothers worried about you? Checking up on you?" Winston tried to sound casual but not intrusive.

"Yeah . . ." Diego's voice trailed off. "Do you want to see some of my drawings one day?" He laid his phone down onto the coffee table in front of them.

Claiming his seat next to Diego, Winston again settled in. "I would love to. I can draw a pretty mean looking stickman, and that's about it."

Winston was surprised to see Diego stifle a yawn with his hand. "Are you tired? We can go to bed any time you're ready."

"A little." Diego sat up.

Winston now saw that the poor guy's eyelids were barely open. Clearly, he was tired. "Then let's go." Earlier, he had been hoping for another round, but now, he wanted even more to lie in bed next to Diego, skin to skin, and sleep through the night. Something told him this might be the best night's sleep he'd had in months.

17

It was a little past five when Diego stirred to life. Sliding his hand across the sheets, the smooth, soft fabric told his brain that something was off. His eyes sprung open. It took a second for his brain to start clicking, reminding him of where he was and, more importantly, why he was there.

The only other time in his life that he had awakened in an unfamiliar place was when he and his brothers were waiting to cross the border. Kept in a safe house for seven days, they had bunked eight to a room. They had slept fully clothed to protect themselves from sexual predators and robbers. He would never forget those seven days.

Other than the strange bed, this morning would be like most others. He had to get up; he had to pee; he had to go to work. His natural alarm clock had ensured that he awoke.

He reached out to touch Winston and realized there was no one there. Had Winston gotten up to pee? Diego lay there as yesterday played out in his head. The sex had been incredible. He couldn't believe Winston had asked him to stay the night. As his mind drifted, he reminded himself that he shouldn't overstay his welcome.

Pulling back the heavy bedding, he rolled over and put his feet on the floor. The room was quiet. No one was shouting at him to get up, calling dibs on the bathroom, or crowding the narrow hallway. Diego's mind wandered. What was Rafael doing? Was he up?

After locating his underwear, Diego staggered into the bathroom, looking for Winston. The lights came on automatically. He didn't remember that happening yesterday. Looking at the bottom of the closed door that hid the toilet, he saw that the light was off in there. He gently knocked on the door. "Winston?"

He waited for a few seconds before slowly easing the door open. The room was empty. He recalled seeing at least two other bathrooms: one in the hall and another down by the kitchen. Maybe Winston was in one of those.

Returning to the bedroom, Diego stopped in his tracks. There was an eeriness in the quietness of the house. The only sound was the humming of the ceiling fan motor above the bed. Alone in the room, his eyes scanned over the crystal vase and silk table runner on top of the dresser. Could he ever get used to such extravagance?

When he opened the door to the hallway, a whiff of bacon told him that Winston was cooking. His step picked up as he headed down the hall. He wasn't sure he could find the kitchen. He remembered there were two ways of entering it: from the dining room or from a hall that came off the family room.

Diego stopped at the end of the hall, and looked into a large open room. This was a different living room than the one he was looking for; this one wasn't connected to the patio. If push came to shove, he could always go outside and make his way in from the back yard.

He was about to turn around when he heard faint music playing. Following the sound, he found Winston in the kitchen, dancing and singing as he attempted to harmonize with the music playing out of the Bose speaker on the counter.

Diego was used to walking around his apartment in his underwear, but seeing Winston in his robe, he regretted not getting dressed before leaving the bedroom.

"Good morning," he muttered as he walked up behind Winston.

Winston's eyes widened at the sound of Diego's voice. "Hey! I wasn't sure what time you got up. I was meaning to ask you yesterday, but I kept forgetting. Would you like some coffee?"

Winston stopped what he was doing to give Diego a kiss.

Coffee before a shower was a novel idea. Usually, Diego's mornings were all about getting out the door on time. But this morning, he wasn't competing for the bathroom. "No, I'll wait until after my shower."

"Are you hungry?" Winston didn't wait for him to answer before kissing him again. Diego licked the moisture from his lips as he released a soothing exhale. Maybe he could get used to such extravagance.

It was bacon; of course he was hungry. But first, he had to master that shower. He decided not to ask for help. How hard could it be to turn on?

Winston had piled a mountain of pancakes on a plate and was cooking bacon in a pan.

"You do like pancakes, don't you?"

"Sure, I love 'em. It's been a while since I had 'em." Diego caught Winston's eyes as they peered down at his crotch for the second time.

"Okay, go take your shower and come back. I'll be done by then, and we can eat. What time do you have to leave?"

Diego thought for a second. He didn't need to be up this early; he wasn't driving out here from East LA or dropping Rafael off anywhere. He had at least an hour before he had to leave. "I have plenty of time. I go and take my shower and come back, no?"

"Yes. I'll have everything ready by then. Do you want orange juice?"

Diego looked at several oranges, halved and sitting by a machine of some sort. "Sure, that would be—"

Out of nowhere, Winston grabbed him and aggressively brought him into his arms. "Seeing you in those tiny underwear is making me hungry," he murmured.

Their lips met. The first kiss was slow, yet quick, as if Winston meant to give him only a single kiss. However, Winston didn't let go. Their lips met again, and this time the kiss was deeper, longer. Diego's shoulders dropped, his body succumbing to Winston's touch.

In no time, the crotch of Diego's underwear tightened. Did Winston want to make love . . . right here? Diego attempted to pull away as he mumbled through their kisses, "Do you want me to take a shower or not?"

"Do I have a choice?" Winston eased his hold.

"Yes." Diego was sure they both wanted the same thing.

"No, I want to take you back to bed." Through his robe, Winston pressed his hard erection against Diego's body.

Diego stood on his tippy toes and pressed their bodies together tighter. "We go . . . make love, no?" he whispered, as if someone might hear them.

Winston released his hold completely. With a sense of urgency, he moved the heavy cast-iron skillet off the burner and turned the stove off. "This can wait." Grabbing Diego again, his fingers rolled underneath the waistband of Diego's underwear. "Come on," he mumbled, as he tugged on the front of his underwear. "Come."

Diego barely climbed back into the unmade bed before Winston was on top of him. Winston's massive body hovered over his as he wrapped his long arms around Diego. With one gentle pull, Diego felt his back arch and rise from the bed. Their skin connected. At the warmth of Winston's body, his musky scent, Diego released a slight breath that didn't quite rise to a moan.

Winston's erection pressed into Diego's belly, taking his breath away. He wanted it, and not against his stomach. He had never done it, though he had dreamed of the day. He wanted Winston, all of him.

"Fuck me!" Diego's voice shook as he realized he had mumbled the words aloud.

"What?" Winston eased up. He lifted his head, and their eyes met. "What did you say?"

Nervous and embarrassed, Diego found he couldn't repeat it. He tried to find his voice.

"Really?" Winston asked.

So Winston *had* heard him. It didn't need repeating. A sense of relief washed over him, followed by regret. Maybe he didn't want it.

Maybe it would hurt. All of this overthinking was tampering with his sanity. Had he asked too aggressively? What was Winston thinking? He lay on his back, looking up into Winston's eyes, wanting Winston to kiss him.

To end his embarrassment, Diego grabbed Winston by the back of his neck and pulled him down, their lips meeting once again. He wanted to be lost in the moment, far away from whatever it was that just happened. He wasn't going to say it again.

As their kiss deepened, the two rolled from one side of the bed to the next. They took turns exploring each other. Their lips, their hands, their bodies slowly glided over each other, their hearts beating in unison as their legs entwined.

On his back, Diego found himself on the edge of the bed. His head hung over the side, but Winston held him up securely with his massive hands, which spread to firmly support the small of Diego's back.

Winston kissed and dragged his lips across Diego's chest and neck. Diego's blood surged through his body, igniting every nerve ending. His skin was burning, electrified by every kiss Winston laid on his skin.

Hearing the drawer open next to the bed, Diego realized Winston had taken something out of the nightstand. He watched as Winston sat up and flipped the cap to a tube. Their eyes locked onto one another. Diego knew what was going to happen, and he needed it to happen.

After several minutes of Winston slowly preparing him, murmuring that it would be okay, Diego watched as Winston retrieved a square silver packet from the nightstand on his side of the bed.

Never having had intercourse before, Diego hadn't realized that, of course, Winston would use a condom. There was so much more to sex then Diego knew. A sense of security washed over him at the knowledge that he was with Winston, that Winston would lead the way.

As Winston entered him, the pain shot to his throat. He couldn't breathe as Winston filled him. A cry, a moan, a whimper was all he was capable of as Winston's body bore down onto him.

Just when he was about to beg for Winston to stop, the pain subsided slightly. In that moment of hesitation, the pain converted to a sense of pleasure that washed over him.

Within seconds, another wave hit him, a sensation that continued to grow, a surge of ecstasy that rapidly overtook any pain. Diego's body quivered as yet another whimper escaped him. He relished the rhythm in which Winston's pelvis moved into him, each stroke bringing a ripple of pleasure. He fought the urge to scream.

Winston said something to him, but the words were inaudible. Diego had no control of anything; he was at the complete mercy of his lover. Every nerve in his body had been unchained, and for the first time in his entire life, he climaxed without touching himself. Wave after wave of euphoria consumed him as Winston thrusted faster and breathed more heavily.

Hearing Diego's cry, Winston slammed into him one or two more times before his body stiffened. He released a final roar and then collapsed onto Diego.

The two lay for several minutes before Winston finally rolled onto his side. Diego found himself on the edge of the bed, with no place to go. It didn't matter; he couldn't move a muscle. He just lay there, air oozing from his lungs.

Several minutes passed before his breathing returned to a point at which he could speak or move. With his breathing finally returning to normal, he turned his head slightly towards Winston. "Mmm."

Closing his eyes for a second, Diego for some reason envisioned his jogger, the one he had nicknamed Mr. Legs. His eyes sprang open when his vision of the jogger was replaced with Winston. A flush of adrenaline filled every ounce of Diego's tingling body. His fantasy had just come true.

"Are you ready for breakfast?" Winston asked as he adjusted himself on the bed, giving Diego more room.

"I thought I just ate." Diego stretched his back as he looked up at the clock on the nightstand.

"For bacon, not . . . *salchicha?*" Laughing, Winston cupped Diego's groin with his hand.

Amused at Winston's attempt to say 'sausage' in Spanish, Diego rolled to his side to face him. He couldn't have thought of a better use of time, but now he was running late. "I have to get going," Diego mumbled in Spanish.

It seemed that, after all, this morning would be like every other. He would take a quick shower, grab breakfast on the run, and . . . Diego smiled. *Well, not exactly like every other morning.*

With both feet on the ground, he again stretched his back. Damn, Winston had done a number on him. "I shower now." Diego bent down and gave him a kiss. "And you? What do you do today?"

Winston sat up. "Well, I think I'll give Ann a call. Maybe check in with her. I need to think about getting back to work."

"You're the boss, no?"

"We're equal. Is that what you mean?"

"No. I mean if you don't work, then you not make money, no?" Diego pulled on Winston to get up.

"In theory, yeah, but Ann could run the company all by herself, and the money would still come in."

"But that's not fair. For her to do all the work." Diego turned to walk into the bathroom but slowed, ensuring that Winston was following him.

"I was taking some much needed time off. I like what I do." Winston reached into the shower and turned the jets of water on. "Here, jump in. Let me grab you some breakfast and coffee. I'll be right back."

As Diego stepped into the shower, Winston smacked him on his ass, sending a loud pop throughout the bathroom.

Diego jumped as he released a screech. "Hey! *Bastardo!* That's not nice!" He had rather liked it.

While working in the Bernsteins' yard, his morning with Winston played out in Diego's head. If he'd had any doubt that it happened, his ass was proof that it had. Several times, he cramped up and wondered if something was wrong. Maybe Winston had damaged something inside of him. The pain was not that sharp, nor did it last; it was mostly a dull ache, a reminder of the morning's festivities. He was hyperaware of everything: the warm air as it filled his lungs, his shirt as it clung to the moisture on his back, the number of footsteps it took to travel the length of the yard. Everything was exaggerated.

Most mornings, Diego loved being at the Bernstein estate, but this morning, Winston occupied his every conscious thought. He was also fretting over not getting anything done while at Winston's house yesterday—not that Winston was going to fire him for not working. He would make it all up this afternoon—work as long as it took to ensure the job was done. Yesterday, he had planned to trim the hedges down on the back slope of the property. He had been meaning to do that for weeks.

He knew he was obsessing, but the lines had been blurred. Work was his entire life, and now . . . this morning had been a game changer. Cloud nine was a strange place for him. A flood of emotions, both scary and wonderful, crashed into one another, overflowing and disrupting his ability to be present.

"Good morning, Mr. Castillo," Mrs. Bernstein called to him, as she approached from behind, "I meant to catch you yesterday, but you were gone before I got back. Will you be able to come this Friday? We're having a birthday party for Mr. Bernstein, and I love the way the yard looks right after you've been here. Everything is fresh and clean."

Mrs. Bernstein clasped her hands together as she shrugged her tiny shoulders. She couldn't have been over five feet tall.

"Sure. What time is the party?"

"It starts at four, but I'll have deliveries all morning. The tables, chairs, and caterers will be here around noon. Is there any way you can come early?"

"Okay." Diego mentally processed the things he would need to do to make the yard look clean. This mostly consisted of blowing down the walkways and a quick rake over the planter beds. It should take two hours at most. Factoring in the drive back and forth, he figured it would be a four-hour job. Where he was going to find four hours on a Friday was beyond him. This would be a big disruption to his day. His jaw tightened.

"Oh, thank you, dear. I don't know what we would do without you." Her sweet voice was sincere. It also helped knowing that Mr. Bernstein would more than compensate him for his time. For a couple of extra hours of work, Mr. Bernstein had sometimes doubled the check he gave Diego at the end of the month.

Initially, Diego had thought that the old man had overpaid him by accident, but he soon realized that Mr. Bernstein knew what he was doing and that it was non-negotiable. So of course, he would make sure their yard looked great for the party. It was an honor that they appreciated his work.

"I might need your help setting up the tables and chairs, depending on how many guys show up to deliver them. The last party, it was only the driver, and he said he was only dropping them off—that I hadn't requested setup. One would think that was part of the service. What on earth could I do with fifty tables all folded up at the side of the house?"

Fifty tables, eight chairs at each table . . . That was four hundred folding chairs. Depending on how many people were helping, it could take several hours. "No problem, Mrs. Bernstein. I'll be here on Friday to help." This meant he would most likely have to play catch up on Saturday on the properties he skipped on Friday.

Jockeying properties around in his head, he waited for Mrs. Bernstein to enter her house before opening the trailer and finding the can that held small clippings and leaves.

Through the open window of his truck, Diego reached in and grabbed his cell phone to check his messages. Seeing that he had three, he clicked on the first one. It was from Francisco, reminding him to send the seven hundred and fifty dollars to their parents this week.

The next was from Mayra. Her short message indicated that she was checking on him. Diego replied that he was okay and would be home later.

The third text was from Winston. Butterflies immediately began to flutter in his stomach as he opened it. His eyes studied each word: *Just thinking about U.*

Out of habit, Diego deleted the message, ensuring that no one would find it if his phone fell into the wrong hands, specifically his brothers'. He committed the text to memory, where it would be sequestered and treasured.

Diego gave himself permission to shave a little time off the Bernstein's estate so he could get back to Winston. Maybe they would have sex again. The thought caused a swell in his pants, and his pulse quickened.

He returned to the Leblanc estate shortly after noon. His pulse raced as he impatiently waited for the gate to open.

By the time he had his trailer parked in front of the house, Winston had already emerged and was at his door. "Did you have lunch already?" Winston leaned inside the truck and kissed him.

"I eat on the way over." Caught off guard by the kiss, Diego's eyes scanned the yard. Even behind closed gates, kissing Winston sent a flurry of anxiety through him. Behind it were years of ingrained thinking: men don't kiss each other; men don't have sex with other men. Men were men. Everything about this situation made him nervous. Everything he had ever done with other men up until this point had been one-time, impulsive acts, after which he had always dismissed his attraction to men as a phase. The feel of Winston's kiss told him this was not a phase.

"Okay. But please say you're not going to work out here all day like you usually do. I went to the store while you were gone and picked up something to cook. I was hoping I could talk you into staying for dinner." There was a twinkle in Winston's eye.

Diego fought the impulse to chuck it all and go inside with him right then. He wanted to kiss him again. He wanted to be naked with him, to make love. But he had to get the yard done; Winston paid him to tend to the yard.

He would never want Winston to think that he was taking advantage of him or his money. He could do both, the yard and . . . whatever this thing was between them. "I do your yard, mow, clean up the flowerbeds, no? I'll knock on the door when I'm done."

"Okay," Winston replied, nodding. "I'll be inside." His voice trailed off as he motioned his thumb towards the house.

Every part of Diego wanted to go inside right then. The knot in his stomach had been replaced with uncontrollable flushes of heat down his neck and back. But he was a man of his word, and work came first. His eyes glanced over the yard before looking at Winston. "Maybe a couple of hours. I have a lot to do today. Missing yesterday and—"

"You didn't exactly miss yesterday. You were here, and I diverted your attention to . . . let's say, to more pressing matters."

More pressing matters, Diego thought. *We were certainly pressed together yesterday and this morning.* "Okay, then I start." He motioned for Winston to move out of the way so he could exit the truck. Memories of this morning flashed through his thoughts. What would his family think if they knew what had happened? He tried to push the thought aside. It didn't matter; they wouldn't find out.

Walking to the back of the trailer, he had little doubt that Winston's eyes were following him. Slowly unlocking the tail ramp, he glanced back to where he had left Winston standing. He couldn't believe any of this was real. With a breath, he stepped up into the back of his trailer. He told himself that he had to focus, get the job done, and most importantly, calm himself.

As he immersed himself in his work, it wasn't long before the habitual side of the job kicked in, and he was lost in the music playing in his ears.

He moved to the back of the yard, where a part of him expected to find Winston lying out by the pool. The warm temperature would make this a day for swimming.

He had missed the morning weather report on the radio, but he suspected that it was in the nineties. Wiping his brows with the back of his shirtsleeve, he removed his sunglasses to look at the sun.

Casting a casual glance at the pool, he laughed at the realization that he had never seen anyone in it. The six iron loungers were empty. It occurred to him that perhaps Winston had already been out here and had gone inside.

His eyes dropped again to the water. It was clear and sparkling, yet he could see the tiniest of dust particles floating about. The faint scent of chlorine penetrated his nose. He could hear his own voice and the voices of his brothers as they screamed and played, splashing about in the river under the bridge in their village. They played in that river every summer day as kids. Sometimes, his *abuelo* would sit and fish. He and his brothers would carry the fish home, laughing and joking as they walked up the dirt road to their house, where Diego had been born.

Although his parents had since moved from that house, Diego could still picture it: a tiny two-room flat that he, his brothers, parents, and grandparents all shared since as early as he could remember. The apartment that he now shared with Francisco and Rafael was twice the size of that place.

Mom and Grandma cooked in a makeshift kitchen out back. His entire immediate family slept in one room, and his grandparents in the other. He laughed, thinking of the tiny bathroom that was barely large enough for one person, the tiny shower that only produced cold water. He had no idea they were *that* poor until he came to America.

Diego looked around the gardens and then up towards the house. His chest puffed as a grin surfaced on his face. He would have a house and yard this size one day.

18

Diego had just finished packing up his trailer when Winston called from the front steps that dinner was ready. He wiped down his face, arms, and hands with his handkerchief. There was nothing he could do about his clothes, which he had been wearing since yesterday.

He followed Winston into the house and into the dining room. Unsure where to sit, he stood behind a dining room chair, waiting for Winston to take a seat first. "So, why don't you want to go visit your mom?" he asked.

"In Montana? I have zero interest in going to Montana," Winston replied, before directing Diego with his hand to take a seat. "Be careful. The plates are hot."

Diego looked at the plates. He had thought that only restaurants used plate warmers. "I say your mom. Not Montana."

"But you don't understand. I have to go to Montana in order to see her." Winston moved his body and chair closer to the table. "I have no desire to go to Montana." He removed his napkin from the table and laid it in his lap.

"Not even to visit your mom?" Diego asked. It had been eight years since he'd seen his own parents. With each passing year, the realization set in that he might never see them again, at least not alive. He would give or do anything just to have a moment with them.

Cautiously, out of the corner of his eye, Diego watched Winston's demeanor at the table. Mimicking his actions, Diego pressed his back into his chair to ensure that he wasn't slouching. "Is this rice?" he asked. Whatever it was, it smelled wonderful, and he was starving.

"No. Couscous and roasted portabella."

Diego pushed the couscous around with his fork. It didn't really look like rice up close. Following Winston's lead, he removed his napkin and laid it in his lap. Saying a quick blessing of the meal in his head, he started in on the pork chop. He would begin with that in case the rice-stuff wasn't edible.

"When my mother moved to Montana, we all told her she was crazy, that we weren't coming to visit her. She thought we were kidding."

Diego held the piece of meat dangling from his fork to his mouth. "Who's we?" He asked.

Winston stopped chewing. "We, um, my aunt and uncle. My two cousins. They all live down in Imperial Beach."

"San Diego?"

"Kind-of-sort-of. It's a city outside of San Diego. You've been?"

Thirty minutes from Tijuana, Imperial Beach was a city that many who crossed the border went into. Lots of rich people lived there, oblivious to what was happening under their own noses—yes, he had been there, *once.*

Clearing his throat, Diego changed the subject. "So, it's not that you don't want to visit her, you just don't want to go to Montana, no?"

"Well . . . yes, and no. My mother and I just aren't that close."

Diego thought about his own mother and the last time he'd seen her. Without a doubt, he would give anything to see his mother again. Here was this person that could, and chose not to. It seemed a little disrespectful. She was the person that had given him life.

"Do you ever visit your cousins?" Sensing Winston was not close to his family, he already knew the answer, but he couldn't help but ask.

Winston thought for a minute, "Yeah, I saw my aunt during Parker's service. She was down for the day."

Diego studied Winston, trying to figure out the family dynamics without seeming too nosey. He could not understand why someone would not be with their family when they could choose otherwise.

"So, I take it that you're close to your family?" Winston asked.

Diego nodded. "*Sí*. We're close. My brothers, they are all I have here. No cousins, uncles, or anybody here. Everyone is in Mexico."

"Has any of them ever visited you guys?"

"No. They can't. It's hard to get a visa to come, and expensive." Diego cut the large mushroom into several bite-sized pieces. "Francisco's girlfriend, Mayra, she has papers. She goes to Mexico to stay with her family about once a year. She travels to visit my parents for us and takes many pictures. My mother, she gives Mayra *obleas* to give to me." Diego's eyes brightened as he rolled his tongue over his top lip, savoring the taste of his favorite candy. "And *mazapan* for Rafael, and *mole* powder for Francisco. Well, it's not really for him— it's for Mayra to use when she cooks for us."

"So, I know *obleas* and *mazapan* are candy, right? And I've had chicken *mole*. But what is *mole* powder?" Winston asked.

Diego cocked his head. "You not know what *mole* powder is?"

"I'm guessing it's something you use to make *mole*?"

"*Sí*. It's dried chilies, spices, and cho-co-late. Many spices. My mother, she makes the best. Mayra, hers is good if she uses momma's *mole* powder."

"Well, I can't wait to taste it."

Diego's ear perked. Why would he say that? When would he ever taste Mayra's *mole*?

Winston put down his fork. "Okay, so enough about other people. Can I ask you something?"

Diego froze, waiting for the question. It sounded serious. Serious enough that Winston had to put down his fork.

Winston put his elbows on the table and leaned over his plate. "I like you. I like you a lot. And I want to continue seeing you. I want to take you out again."

Diego's breath caught as Winston spoke. He liked the thought of a relationship. It answered so many of his questions about what they were doing. It would certainly complicate things quite a bit in his life, but love is what he wanted. Could he pull off a full-blown relationship with another man?

A month ago, a relationship with Winston hadn't been on his radar. Any relationship with a man was going to be just sex. Now, he was sitting at the table and sharing a meal with a man who expressed fondness for him. It was mind-blowing how fast things had changed.

Winston cleared his throat as he sat up in his chair. "You know, a month ago, I was in a completely different space and time. I can't believe how much has changed for me in just the last couple of weeks." He paused, his eyes entranced by Diego. "You make me smile."

Diego took what Winston was saying as a sign that, whatever this was, fate had a part in it. Could God really be okay with this? He hoped the answer was yes.

"You're making me nervous. Are you going to say anything?" Winston asked.

"You make me nervous too." The room fell quiet. Diego heard the air rushing from the vent above their heads. "Um, I think that would be good. I like you too." Were they really having this conversation? He was confessing his deepest darkest desire without fear of judgement or consequences.

It was the first time he had told anyone that he was gay. The word rang in his ear, sending a punch to his gut. Could he finally stop telling himself that, one day, he might be different? He was never going to be straight—because he was gay. His chest tightened as he tried to conceal his nerves.

"So, will you go out with me? This Friday or Saturday? I can drive into LA, so you don't have to drive back out here."

"*Si*, I would like that." *Friday or Saturday*, Diego repeated in his head as he fought to hold back a grin. Then, remembering that he would be out this way on Friday at the Bernstein estate, he had a better idea. "Instead of you driving to LA, I come here. Spend the night, if that's okay?" He couldn't believe he was asking to spend the night. He was too excited to process his thoughts. "I come here on Friday. You can cook again, and we stay here. I come here, no?"

Diego felt a tiny bit of guilt brewing. He wasn't being totally on the up-and-up with his plan. Being out in public with Winston made him nervous. He couldn't anticipate what Winston would do or say in public. It would be much safer here.

"O-kay!" Winston rubbed his hands together, signifying that he was pleased with the idea. "I would love to cook for you. You can stay the whole weekend if you like."

The whole weekend? The words hit Diego like a bus. He couldn't stay the whole weekend. He had never stayed anywhere away from his family for more than a night. Staying the whole weekend was impossible.

Drawing a deep breath, he thought about not being there to help Francisco at the garage on Saturday. He would have to tell Francisco he was busy with the extra work at the Bernstein estate. He would have to lie.

There was a weight in his chest. Sunday—what about church on Sunday, and the flea market? He would need to lie again. Diego exhaled. One lie at a time, he told himself. He would figure out what to do about Sunday later.

"Thank you for this morning. It was a nice surprise." A naughty smirk flashed across Winston's face.

Diego bowed his head, shunning eye contact. As much as he had enjoyed himself that morning, it wasn't something he wanted to sit around and discuss over dinner. What had happened that morning had ripped at his manhood. Topping off the chaos inside him was his embarrassment that he liked another man taking him in that way.

A minute ago, he had wanted nothing more than to drag Winston back down that hall and make love to him again, but he hadn't wanted to talk about it.

"I should go." Diego stood up. The room was spinning as he searched for words that would not make him sound crazy. "Thank you for dinner. It's getting late, I go." If he didn't go now, he would lose the last bit of manhood he had. This was much harder than he had thought it would be.

"Really, you have to go . . . now?" Winston stood up, tossing his napkin next to his plate. His face showed confusion as he, too, stumbled over his words. "Um, okay . . ."

The two stood a foot from each other in silence. The sound of the air rushing from the vent sounded like a roar. Diego's eyes rose slowly to find that Winston was staring at him.

Their eyes locked onto one another. Diego finally broke the stare, his eyes shifting to Winston's large Adam's apple as it gently bobbed in his neck.

Everything about this man threw Diego for a loop, pushing him further and further away from his comfort zone. This was never going to work.

19

"I don't know. I don't get it. I keep getting the feeling that I'm screwing it up and that I don't know what I'm doing. It goes from warm to cold, and then he's gone." Winston had Ann on speaker and his phone perched in the windowsill while he rinsed the soap off the last of the pots from this evening's dinner. "Ann, it's eerie how fast the mood changes with him."

"So, is he crazy?" Ann asked.

He wasn't sure if she was joking or not. "I don't know how to answer that . . . I mean, no, he's not crazy." Winston thought about how fast Diego had left the house not more than an hour before. Winston was sure he had said something wrong. He had driven Diego to leave abruptly. "Last night was great; this morning was even better. He completely caught me off guard with wanting to be fucked." Winston looked down at the wine fridge as he debated on opening a bottle. He hadn't had a drink in over a week, nor had he missed it, but suddenly he wanted one.

"You guys had sex this morning for the first time. And everything was okay just after that, right?" Ann asked.

"Yeah. We lay in bed afterwards until he . . ." Winston remembered how quickly Diego had jumped out of bed, something about being late. "He left right after. Took a shower, and we talked about him coming back. I think he was okay when he left."

"So, how was he when he came back this afternoon? Maybe it was too much too soon. Maybe he was having second thoughts."

Winston ran through the afternoon in his head. "He was fine. We kissed, stood out front and talked for a minute, and then he went to work. I came in and started cooking dinner. When dinner was ready, I called him in."

"And then?"

"And then we went into the dining room and ate. We were talking and laughing, and everything was going fine, until all of a sudden, he stood up and said he had to go."

"Um," Ann sniffled. "I don't know what to say."

Winston thought about his conversation with Diego at dinner. What had he said that could have caused Diego to take offense? He racked his brain but came up with nothing. Ann was no help either. "Look," he said, "I didn't call you for your Dear Abby advice, but to let you know I will be in the office next week."

"Okay." Her voice dipped.

"Yeah, it's time. I'm feeling better, missing the work." He largely attributed his wellbeing to Diego. The thought that he could mess up with Diego and be right back where he had started scared him.

"So Montana's out?" Ann questioned.

"Montana . . .What's with everyone trying to get me to go to Montana?" Winston barked. "I miss seeing you every day, the work, staying busy."

"That's fine. I'm ready for you to come back too, if you're truly ready. The Harper Gala is a little over two months away, and things are beginning to get a little crazy. I could use the help."

"I'll be there on Monday. I'll log in sometime this weekend and get up to speed on everything."

"Okay, baby. If you think of anything else that might have sent your boy running, call me."

"I will." Winston tapped the *call end* button and glanced at the time. It was only seven o'clock, way too early to think about going to bed—at least, by himself.

Diego's apartment felt a hundred times smaller than it had yesterday morning. So much had happened in a short time. Immediately, Francisco stood up to meet him. "Ah, you came home," Francisco teased. "The little puppy has found his way home. Or are you a man now? Mayra tells me you have a girlfriend, ah?"

Diego glanced at Mayra, who remained seated on the small couch. Stretching out across where Francisco had been sitting, she said, "Cut it out, Francisco. I didn't say that! I said he was seeing someone."

"My boy does have some balls in them pants of his." Francisco attempted to grab Diego by the balls.

Diego was too quick, slapping his hand away. "Get off me!" Diego took a half step back, ready to turn on his heels, but Francisco caught him, grabbing him in a massive face-to-face bear hug. Diego squirmed to escape from his brother's iron grip, but Francisco was much too strong for him.

"Cut it out. Let me go!" Diego yelled, as Francisco finally freed him.

Playfully, Francisco tried to grab him again. "Come on, let me smell you. Do you smell like perfume or pussy?"

"Franky!" Mayra screeched. "Why do you have to be so nasty all the time? Stop it!" She grabbed the dirty bowl that was sitting on the coffee table and stomped into the kitchen. "Diego, are you hungry? I saved you some dinner. It's on the stove."

Diego slipped and answered her in English. "No, I ate already." Switching back to Spanish, he asked if Rafael was home.

From where he stood, their entire apartment was visible, from the living room, down the hall, and into Francisco and Mayra's room.

The bathroom door was open, meaning it was empty, and his bedroom door was closed.

Francisco wasn't finished teasing him. "Did she feed you, or are you eating at her mommy's house? Have you already met Mommy? Mayra, the boy works fast. Next thing you know, he'll be wanting to marry her. If she's giving it up already, there's no need to rush, *chico*. Just ride it." Francisco moved his hand as if it was going over waves.

Mayra answered Diego's question. "No. He left about a half hour ago."

Shaking his head in disgust, Diego knew it was better to ignore his brother's stupid comments. The more he responded, the longer the teasing would continue. Flipping his brother off, he headed down the short hall to his room.

Refuge behind closed doors. It had been like walking across hot coals to get in here. He should have known Mayra would say something to his brother. Did Rafael know as well? That could be bad—since he shared this tiny box of a room, there would be nowhere for Diego to run. Why did everything look so small all of a sudden? There was less than a foot between the two twin beds. Even the beds looked shorter, half the length of Winston's. Diego smiled as he remembered that Winston's bed was new.

Diego kicked off his shoes before grabbing one of his drawings from a stack on the nightstand. He'd been working on this one for months: the design of an outdoor play area for the Boy's and Girl's Club they were building downtown.

He had thought it would be cool to sketch out his plans as if he was the architect on site. As he started working on it again, his mind drifted to the last twenty-four hours. He regretted getting up and leaving as fast as he had this evening. He had freaked out. The walls had been closing in on him, and he had needed a minute to think. The hour's drive gave him enough time to realize he had messed up and shouldn't have left.

Coming from a country were more than two-thirds of the population was Roman Catholic, Diego had never doubted as a child that being gay was a sin. When he had left Mexico at seventeen, he already felt attracted to boys but had no one his own age with whom to experiment. Hell, he wouldn't have had time for that anyways.

Since he could walk, he had worked. Whether it was carrying fresh water to houses that didn't have any or collecting cans from the side of the road, he was always with his brothers.

That evening, sitting at the table with Winston and talking about dating one another, the conversation had been so direct. Diego knew, always had known, that he was gay. However, a small voice in the back of his brain had told him that maybe, one day, he would meet a girl that did something for him.

That evening, there had been no denying that he was choosing Winston. Another man. He wanted to be with Winston, right now, tomorrow, and the next day. Winston was all he thought about. From day one, it had never been about having sex with Winston; it was about being in his presence, next to him, no matter how nervous the man made him.

There was no denying that Diego was falling in love. Heat tingled in his cheeks, and a lump formed in his throat as he tried to dismiss his anxiety. But there was no dismissing it. The floodgates were open. He said it again to himself: *I'm falling in love with him.*

His body shivered from the adrenaline pumping through his blood. Filled with emotion, he had no idea how he was going to keep this from his brothers. Why should his family know every little detail of his life anyways? His uncle Paul had not remarried after his wife died a couple of years ago. No one said anything about it. He had a cousin on his mother's side who was his mother's age and who had never been married. *Anything's possible*, Diego thought.

Hearing his phone vibrate on the nightstand, Diego grabbed it, hoping it was Winston. It was. He swiped his finger across the screen. "Hello?"

"Hey . . . it's Winston. Can you talk?"

"Yeah." Maybe Winston was calling to say he couldn't deal with his silliness, that he was too young, too stupid . . . too Mexican.

"I wanted to make sure you were okay. You left so fast. Did I say something again that pissed you off? I'm sorry if I did. I swear, sometimes—"

"No . . . it wasn't you." Diego couldn't let him continue to beg needlessly for forgiveness. "I shouldn't have left."

Silence fell between them. Diego knew he owed Winston an explanation. He heard Winston's breathing on the other end, giving him the opportunity to talk. "I . . ."

Winston broke in. "Are you okay with us, with me? If you're not sure, tell me. I'm—"

"It's not you. It's me. I not do this before, dated anyone that is." Diego paused to listen for any sounds from the living room. He heard the television and knew they were still up. That meant they weren't lying in bed on the other side of the wall, hearing everything. He lowered his voice anyways. "I never dated. I not know what to do, what to say, or anything."

There was a moment of silence before Winston chuckled. "There's nothing for you to do or say. I'm not sure I completely understand, so let me ask you this: do you like me? Just a yes or no."

Diego rolled his eyes at the simplicity of the question. "Yes." There was much more he wanted to say, but he gave Winston what he had asked for.

"Okay, now that we've established that, let me go on record once again, and tell you how much I am attracted to you. Am I moving too fast for you? Are you okay with what happened this morning? Talk to me."

Diego couldn't answer those questions without considering years of ingrained thinking about masculinity. It wasn't as simple as a yes or no. His stomach churned as he thought how to answer Winston's question.

"I will sit here with the phone as long as I need to." Winston's words expressed nothing but kindness and patience.

Resting his forehead in his hand, Diego knew the answer. "If you're asking me if I liked it . . . Yes, I liked it." He swallowed, as he gathered his next words. "I've never done it before, that's all."

"Oh my God. Why didn't you tell me before we did it? I had no idea, I just assumed."

The pitch in Winston's voice caused Diego to lift the phone from his ear. "It's alright . . . At the table, you started talking about it, and I wasn't ready to talk about it." His breathing rushed as he tried to stay ahead of his words. "I not know what to do or say." He stared at the cream-colored wall that separated him from the world.

"So, how are you? Can I ask?" Winston murmured.

Diego thought about how to answer, "Better . . . I want to see you too. I want to go out with you." *I want to be your boyfriend* is what he wanted to say.

"I'm blown away at the fact that you were a virgin. Where the hell have your brothers been keeping you?"

Winston's voice said that he was joking, but that was odd given the seriousness of the conversation. "Well . . ." Diego didn't know how to answer Winston's question. "So, do you still want me to come on Friday? Is that okay?"

"Of course I want you to. We can take it slow, at your speed. I'll be a gentleman . . . But do I have to wait until Friday for our next date?"

As he released the breath that he must have been holding, Diego felt the heaviness in his chest subside as air rushed to his brain. He could breathe again. He wasn't sure which of Winston's questions he should answer first, so he chose the last one. "I have much to do tomorrow and Thursday." His brain scrambled to figure out if he could change his schedule in any way.

"Okay, then. Friday it is. What time do you think you'll be done at the other house?"

"Not sure." Diego didn't know how much additional work Mrs. Bernstein would give him. "Can I text you when I'm on my way? She only lives about ten minutes from you."

"Okay. I can't wait."

"Me too," Diego replied before saying goodnight. Hanging up the phone, he took a second to listen for the television, ensuring that they were still out there and not listening.

20

For the next two days, they stayed in constant communication, texting each other first thing in the morning, exchanging simple descriptions of how well they had slept, how much they missed each other, and their plans for the day. Their morning conversations ate up thirty minutes of time that Diego didn't have but somehow found.

At night, Diego carried his dinner plate into his room, and the two ate dinner together via the phone. Winston listened as Diego talked about his childhood and the place where he used to live. Every night, they talked into the late hours. The only interruptions were when Diego had to run his brother to work or when Francisco or Mayra knocked on his door.

When Friday finally came, Winston was thrilled. He checked the time every ten minutes, waiting for Diego's text indicating he was done at the Bernstein estate.

He had chewed off the tip of most of his fingernails when he thought he ought to check his phone one more time. Surprisingly, somehow he had missed that Diego had texted him almost five minutes ago. Diego would be here any minute.

Winston checked his meatloaf on the counter, ensuring it hadn't cooled too much, and then checked for the third time that he had put a liter of soda in the refrigerator for his guest.

Walking to the front door, he changed his mind: He shouldn't wait there—too needy. With a quick glance in the mirror by the door, he checked his hair. His office would be a better place to sit; he would watch the front from there.

As he took a seat behind his desk, he caught the gates beginning to open. His heart raced as he watched Diego's truck and trailer pull in. He stood, but then immediately forced himself to sit. He decided he would let Diego ring the doorbell. That's what a non-crazy person would do.

He watched as Diego grabbed a bright orange and black duffel bag from the back seat of his truck. Diego was even more beautiful than Winston remembered. Diego swung the duffel bag onto his small back and made his way towards the front door. He was in work clothes, of course; he had just come from the Bernstein estate. Dinner might have to wait. Winston would ask whether he wanted to shower first or eat first.

With the sound of the doorbell, Winston and Lucy both took off towards the door. Lucy reached it first, the nub of her short tail swishing as she waited for Winston to open it. "Girl, you need to calm down. He's here to see me, not you." Opening the door, Winston used his foot to hold Lucy back until Diego could get in.

"Hey, there." Diego smiled, but his eyes conveyed his nervousness.

Winston swallowed as he tried to control his breathing. "Come in."

Diego stepped in and stopped in the foyer. With Lucy between their feet, the two stood smiling at each other. They both knew it was coming. The shy look on Diego's face told Winston that he had to make the first move. Diego was waiting for him. Softly, Winston kissed him, absorbing the peppermint lip balm from Diego's lips. The kiss obliterated all of Winston's anxiety that had been building for the last two days. All the fussing and worrying faded from his thoughts.

"Mmm, I've been dreaming of those lips. Come in." Winston's tongue absorbed the moisture from the edges of his mouth. Shutting the door behind Diego, he spotted the sales tag on the outside of Diego's duffel bag.

The two stood facing each other. Winston noticed Diego rubbing his palms on his pants. He broke the silence. "How are you?"

"Good. It smells good in here."

"That's your dinner. I hope you'll like it."

Diego's stomach growled loud enough for the both of them to hear. "I should wash up. Mrs. Bernstein had me up in her attic moving boxes."

Winston leaned in for another kiss. As their lips touched, he wanted more. He wanted to pull Diego up for a full, deeper kiss, but he had promised not to rush.

An elusive scent of perspiration and earth crossed Winston's nose as Diego eased away. The two scents worked as an aphrodisiac, leaving Winston wanting more. "You can put your bag in the bedroom." He pointed down the hall, as if Diego didn't know the way. "I cooked a meatloaf. It can wait until you're cleaned up. Go ahead and shower if you like. There're fresh towels in the cabinet next to the . . ." Winston realized he was rambling. *Stop it*, he told himself. *You're all over him . . . Relax.*

"Yeah, if that's okay, I take shower." Diego held up the bag. "I brought clothes . . . for the weekend."

Again, Winston noticed the tag. "Do you need me to show you how to turn the shower on?"

"No, I remember." Slinging the vibrant-colored bag over his shoulder, Diego flipped his hair out of his face and then pulled it back with his hand.

"I'll let you get cleaned up, and by the time you're done, I should have dinner ready to go. Are you hungry?"

"*Sí.*" Diego held his nose in the air, his eyes widening as they glanced towards the kitchen.

Watching Diego move down the hall, Winston's heart paused and then started again. *What is this guy doing to me?*

Winston had just finished re-heating the gravy on the stove when Diego appeared in the doorway.

"I hope this is okay." Wearing a pair of grey sweat bottoms and a white tee shirt, Diego lifted his arms from his sides.

"Of course. You look adorable." Winston couldn't help but notice the outline of Diego's penis through his thin sweatpants. *Dear God,* he mumbled to himself, as he forgot what he was doing and went to Diego. Taking him by his narrow hips, he drew him up into a kiss, arms wrapping around the man. The smell of lavender shower soap had permeated Diego's skin.

As their kiss deepened, Winston's arms pulled Diego in even tighter. With no room left between them, Diego's erection pressed through his sweats. Winston reached down, brushing his hand lightly across the front of Diego's thin pants.

Diego pulled back, flashing him a naughty grin. "We eat first." He took a step out of Winston's reach and pulled out the stool that he now considered his.

Winston couldn't take his eyes off Diego as he prepared his plate and slid it onto the bar. He had this man for the entire weekend. God help him not to mess it up. His heart pounded with excitement at what was yet to come.

"Why do you keep looking at me?"

Winston's mouth curved, making a tiny grin. "Because you're so handsome." He remembered not to use the word 'beautiful.' "I can't believe you're here, and that we have the whole weekend. I've kind of missed you the last two days."

Winston fixed his own plate and joined Diego at the bar. Before starting in on his dinner, he thought, *How could I be this close and not ask for a kiss?* Leaning in, he waited until Diego finished chewing to pucker his lips.

Diego cocked his head slightly, facing Winston. The brown and gold hues in his eyes flickered, revealing an innocence. He had been quiet since arriving.

Winston thought that maybe Diego wasn't as excited as he was about the evening. *Is something wrong?* Winston lightly brushed the front of Diego's wet hair. He loved that thick, black hair, especially when it was wet and slicked straight back. "You're quiet," he said.

"I am?" Diego took a bite of his meatloaf.

"Yeah." His quietness this evening was contrary to the borderline sexting they had been exchanging the last two nights. "Are you okay?"

Diego nodded and pointed to his mouth, indicating that he had food in there.

Winston waited and waited, beginning to wonder if Diego was ever going to swallow.

Diego laid his fork down and took a sip of his soda. Again, he nodded that he was almost done. Finally, he said, "Will I ever meet your mother?"

The question caught Winston off guard. "You want to meet my mom?" He wasn't sure he understood the question, and he had no idea how to answer it.

"Um, no . . ." Diego took another quick sip of his drink. "It's not that I want to meet her. I mean, would you ever introduce me to her?"

"You mean, like, if she was here?" Winston still didn't understand.

"*Sí.* You say she liked Mr. Leblanc. Would she like me?" His demeanor turned a little somber.

"Of course she would like you. What's not to like? You're smart, polite, ambitious, and gorgeous. She would be all over you." Staring directly into his eyes, Winston rubbed Diego's shoulders. "I'm not sure if you would like her though."

"Why?"

"Well, for starters, she can be a bit of a pill."

"A what?" Diego's face was puzzled.

"Someone who is kind of a nuisance. You know, like a pill that's hard to swallow."

Diego's brows narrowed as he shook his head. He still didn't understand.

"She's loud, very busy, going in a million directions but never finishing anything."

"Is that why you not like her?" Diego straightened his back, leaning away from Winston.

"Um . . ." Winston was again caught off guard by Diego's frankness. "It's not that I don't like her." He was unsure how to explain their relationship. Deciding just to put it out there, he inhaled a large breath first. "Okay, so . . . I was around seventeen when my dad died. It seemed that almost immediately after we buried him, my mom started going out with her friends more. It started out just on Fridays and Saturdays, and then it was Thursday through Sunday. From there, I realized that she was actually meeting men, dating." Winston questioned how much he wanted to divulge.

Trying to moisten his dry mouth by swallowing several times, Winston continued. "As a kid, um, teenager, I was basically raising myself. She was never there. The drinking, it was constant."

"So was she, like, partying and you not like that, or was it about the men?" Diego asked.

Winston knew the answer; however, he hesitated before answering. "Both. It was as if my dad didn't matter. We started fighting, fighting a lot, and then, one day—I guess it was my senior year in high school—she announced that she was getting married. I had never even met the dude, and she was marrying him. It was such bullshit. When I did finally meet the guy, it was like a week before they were leaving for St Croix. They were going to have a beach wedding and I wasn't even invited! She said she didn't want me to miss my prom, the prom I had no intentions on even going to. But she didn't know that, because we hadn't been talking for weeks."

Diego's head raised up, his eyes burning with compassion. "Wow. I'm sorry."

Winston wiggled his fingers trying to relieve his tension. "It is what it is. She flew off and married this dude. I graduated and moved into the dorms at USC. It must have been my second year there when

I got the call that this dude had died. Massive heart attack when they were in London."

"So, was he older than your mom?" Diego asked.

"Yeah, he was in his sixties . . . maybe." Winston slid his hand over Diego's and clasped their fingers together. "It was weird. The call actually came from the manager at the hotel where they had been staying. I dropped everything and immediately caught a flight to London. I wasn't sure what I would find, but I knew she couldn't be alone. We were there for a couple of days before they released the body, and then I brought the two of them home. Bringing her back to the house—that was weird, too. I hadn't been in the house for months. Although the same, it was like a different house. Cold, with nothing but the memories of the time since my father had passed away. Everything before that had somehow been wiped away. My mother was in a walking drunken coma. After we buried her husband, I tried to rekindle our relationship, thinking she needed me."

"So, then she met the guy that she lives with in Montana?" Diego asked.

"No . . . not right away. At first, things seemed good. Parker and I were spending a lot of time at the house. We noticed that her drinking hadn't lightened up, but at least we were having conversations. Within about three or four months, '*The Real Housewives of Beverly Hills*' slowly crept back into her life. She took to her old ways, and I cut my losses. I was done with her. Parker tried, but I was done." Winston released Diego's hand and crossed his arms tightly across his chest, as if hugging himself.

After a second or two of silence, Winston guffawed. "She married Cal just a couple of years ago." Wanting to lighten the mood, Winston tried to think of something nice to say about her. He didn't want to paint too ugly of a picture of her. "Norma Desmond from *Sunset Boulevard*? That's my mom! 'Mr. DeMille, I'm ready for my close-up.'"

Diego looked even more confused.

"Oh, please don't tell me you've never seen *Sunset Boulevard*—the movie?" The answer was obvious by the hollow look in Diego's eyes. "Oh my God, we have to watch it! It's an old black and white. It's supposed to be serious, but it's as funny as hell. The actress Gloria Swanson plays this faded silent film actress whose dream is to make a comeback on the big screen. She was never a big star, but in her head she was."

Diego's left eyebrow rose, as his nose wrinkled. "I not think I want to meet her."

"So, why would you ask me that question? Where did it come from?" Winston was curious now.

Diego shrugged. "I was wondering . . ." He paused.

Winston took a bite of his dinner as he waited for Diego to answer.

"Sometimes, I think a lot," Diego said. "Today, I was talking and looking at Mrs. Bernstein, and I wondered if that is how your mom is. *Mi mama* is very different."

"How so?"

"We not have much money. My *mama* worked. She worked all the time. She not have friends. There was no time for that. I guess I asked because . . . the other day, you say something about tasting Mayra's *mole*." Diego paused again, and his eyes filled with emotion. "I not introduce you to my family. They—"

"I didn't mean I really wanted to try it." Winston leaned back and laughed. "It's just something . . . something that you say to be nice." Wow! What a conversation they had just to get here. Winston took ahold of Diego's hands and threaded their fingers together, hoping to set him at ease. "I get that you're not out to your family. I don't expect you to introduce me to your brothers. I respect that. Just because my family is okay with the fact that I'm gay doesn't mean it's that way for most people." He saw the muscles soften in Diego's jaw. "I don't have to meet your family, and if you don't want to, you don't have to meet mine either."

Diego poked his fork into his meatloaf and carved off a small piece. Dipping it into his mashed potatoes and gravy, he brought the fork up to his mouth and stopped. "Okay, then I ask you another question?"

"Anything—I want you to feel like you can ask me anything." Winston laid down his fork and listened carefully.

"What do you do all day, since you're not working?"

Winston fought back a smile at Diego's adorable emphasis on each word. He knew Diego was trying to ask a serious question. "Well, mostly, working on myself . . . trying to understand life." He folded his arms tightly across his chest. "I—" He stopped. He had to admit that the question was harder than he had thought. How much did he want to share with Diego about how mentally screwed up he was?

He thought about how much life had changed for him in just the short time that he had known Diego. "I was pretty bad emotionally after Parker died. I thought I would keep working, fill my days with work, and things would somehow get better. But they never did."

Their eyes locked onto one another. Winston smiled first, trying to keep the mood up. "Things didn't get better until I met you. I know it's only been a couple of weeks, but . . ." It was too early to use the L-word. "I think Parker would be okay with this, with me seeing you. It's almost like he set it up." Winston knew that he was sounding almost creepy. "If it wasn't for Parker's death, we wouldn't have met."

Diego's entire face softened. "You're right."

Staring down at his plate, Winston cleared his throat. "Okay, so it's time for me to ask you some questions." They were questions Winston was dying to have answered. Over the last several days, he had begun questioning his views on illegals that came across the border. How could he have been so wrong in his thinking? He tried to justify his feelings by thinking of the law; this was a country of laws, and illegals couldn't do what they wanted just because it benefited them.

He had spent hours on the internet, reading stories of those that had crossed illegally. The amount of paperwork, money, and bureaucracy involved in getting a visa to work in the United States was shocking. Shamefully, he had been one of the many Americans who always said that immigrants needed to get in line and wait their turn. Now, he was starting to think that it wasn't that simple.

"Seriously, if you don't feel comfortable answering, it's okay." he added, as he pushed his empty plate away.

Diego's eyes narrowed in a look of concern. His eyes probed Winston's.

"Tell me about your trip, how you guys came over. I mean . . . when you left Mexico to come to the United States." He immediately sensed discomfort in Diego. "No—you don't have to answer that. It's really none of my business." Filled with guilt, he had put Diego in the uncomfortable position of disclosing illegal activity.

Diego sat up. "You want to know? I tell you . . . No?" The innocence in his eyes conveyed his trust in Winston.

Winston placed his hand on the side of Diego's face and gently rubbed his cheek. "I don't want you to ever do anything you don't want to, just for me. But . . . I do want to know everything about you: where you came from—how you became this beautiful soul." He knew Diego didn't like the word beautiful, but no other word seemed to fit.

"Okay, I tell you." Diego leaned his head away from Winston's hand and drew a breath. "I start . . . I told you about my *papa* trying to come, and the government keep saying no. How we had to take a bus to Mexico City first, no?"

Diego stared at Winston, his head slightly cocked, his forehead furrowed.

"Oh, are you asking me?" Winston had gotten so used to Diego ending his sentences with "no" that he didn't realized the man was actually asking a question. "Yeah, yeah, you told me about that."

Quickly scraping up a heap of mash potatoes, Diego stuffed them into his mouth. Placing a hand across his mouth, he continued to chew as he talked. "Okay, then I start when we were in Nogales."

"What's Nog-ales?" Winston didn't mean to interrupt, but he wasn't sure he had heard the word correctly. He already felt lost.

The corner of Diego's left brow raised. "It's a city close to the U.S. border. It's where we were supposed to meet the *coyotes*."

"Oh, I've never heard of it," Winston said.

"No? It's very big city." Diego sneaked another bite.

Winston shook his head, his eyes cast down. Diego's plate held only a tiny bit of the meatloaf and potatoes, but almost all his broccoli remained. "Not a fan of broccoli?" Winston asked.

Diego's forehead and eyes narrowed as he puckered his lips and shook his head. "Sorry."

"No. It's okay. I want to know what you like. Go on, finish your story." Winston rested his elbows on the counter, as he shifted his body weight in his stool.

"Um, um, so there was this lady. I not know who she is. She picked us up at the bus station and drove us to this house. There was a family living there, but in the bedrooms, there were a lot of peoples. Peoples waiting to cross the border like us. We had to stay in that room. I only came out to use the bathroom that was across the hall."

"So who were these people, the people that were living there?" Winston asked.

"I not know. But there was this man, I think he was the boss. I hear him talking to the family when I go out into the hall. I hear him talking, like they were making plans. Inside our room were five older men. They were going to North Carolina to find work. They have family there. I know there were lots of other people in the other rooms. I hear them. Some up all night."

"So did you get to know the other guys in your room? How long were you there?" Winston thought it was all starting to sound like a movie—a horror movie. But he wanted the details.

Diego slowly shook his head. "No . . . they were from Nicaragua and spoke Miskito, not Spanish."

Winston was surprised to hear this. He had assumed they would all speak Spanish.

Diego continued. "I not think they were nice men. I never asked Francisco, but I think something happened. I remember waking up in the middle of the night, and Francisco and Rafael had this man up against the wall. The other men were trying to pull my brothers off him. After that, Francisco made me sleep with my shoes and jacket on, and he put me between him and Rafael at night."

Winston had a good idea what might have happened. He remained silent, not wanting to interrupt Diego's story.

"They were not coming with us. I hear they not have enough money. They were waiting for their family to send more money to the *coyotes*."

"So, how much does it cost?" Winston asked.

"Well, now, it's very, very expensive. Your government has spent a lot of money to make it harder for us. Back then, it cost us nine thousand dollars."

"Nine thousand dollars!" Winston howled, sitting up. He was positive Diego had the numbers confused.

Diego nodded. "Now, it is way more."

"But, nine thousand dollars. If you guys were poor, and your father didn't have the money to pay the government for him to come, where did you guys get nine thousand dollars?" He wasn't sure he believed Diego.

"My uncle. He do good in construction. Had his own business. The money came from him, and when we got here, the plan was to live with him. We would do construction, work for him until we paid the money back."

"But you said he died after you guys got here, right?" Winston was slowly putting together the pieces of this amazing puzzle called Diego.

"That was sad. His wife, she go back to Mexico after this." Diego paused to finish the last of his potatoes. Laying his fork down, he blew out a puff of air, leaned back, and stretched his back against his stool.

Winston watched as the front of Diego's tee shirt rose, exposing his delectable belly button and his tiny happy trail. Wanting to stay focused, he looked away. "Um . . . so how did you guys actually come across the border?"

Clasping his hands behind his head, Diego stretched his back again. This time, he sheepishly smiled as his brown eyes followed Winston's down to his stomach. "We were at the safe house for around seven days, waiting. Then, one morning, a coyote came into our room and say we were leaving. We gathered up what little stuff we had and were out the door. He drove us to a truck stop and around to the back. We were told to get in the trailer. They rushed us very fast. It was so fast I not remember much, but we crawled through a bunch of boxes to the front of the trailer and down into a hole. Within seconds, the entire hole went dark. We couldn't see anything, but there were others already in there." Diego stopped to take a drink of his soda.

Winston watched Diego's Adam's apple bob as he conquered his thirst. Anxiously, he waited for Diego to continue.

"I felt the truck moving. I not know how long it was, but then we came to a stop. The truck kept jerking forward and then stopping for what seemed like forever. We must have been in traffic, close to the border. There was no air inside there. The muscles in my legs had cramped, and now I not feel my legs at all. We heard the engine roaring every time it jerked forward. Then, all of a sudden, we were moving again. The engine, the road noise, it was a constant humming. We rode like that for a while. Not long though. Then the truck stopped again. This made me nervous; I not know what was happening."

Diego's voice shook as he drew a breath. "Then we heard a noise, a loud noise. Followed by light—it wasn't much, but it was light. Then everyone started moving and pushing. Someone pushed me through the hole. I saw more light, and I knew it was America. I knew I had made it. We all jumped out of the back of the trailer; there must have been about twenty of us. Everyone was rushing, moving fast. I had to find Francisco and Rafael; they were behind me. Francisco pushed me away from the crowd, and we went off in a different direction. We made our way down to a Taco Bell. There, Francisco asked a woman if he could use her phone. He had my uncle's number on a piece of paper. He called my uncle. We had to wait about . . . not long, then my uncle showed up."

Hearing the details of something so life altering, Winston's heart was broken. The desperation, the determination to find something better. He wanted to hug Diego, hold him, and comfort him. It was a testament to the love of Diego's father that he had been willing to put his boys on a bus, knowing they might never see each other again, in order to give them a better life. Winston released a deep sigh. "Thank you for telling me that." He needed a kiss. He wasn't sure why, but he did. The closeness that he felt at this moment came with a realization.

Diego smiled, his eyes locked onto Winston's. "Why you look at me like this?" he murmured, before looking away. His eyes darted about the kitchen before returning to Winston.

Winston wiped a tear from his eye. Reaching out, he took Diego's hands and clasped them between his. They were cool to the touch and so much smaller than his. Raising Diego's hands to his mouth, Winston kissed them and stared into Diego's eyes. The man's small size was deceiving. He was bigger than anyone Winston knew. Diego was a man of strength and integrity, and he had a heart of gold. He filled the emptiness in Winston's heart and made it flutter and dance. It was something uncontrollable.

As if reading his mind, Diego softly kissed him. Biting down, Diego tugged lightly on his bottom lip.

Diego's breath filled Winston's lungs, speeding up his heart. Winston leaned in and deepened the kiss. His body was flooded with warmth, his fingers aching with the need to touch Diego. "I want to make love to you. I want to hold you. I want all of you." His voice faltered.

"Yes," Diego murmured. "Yes."

21

Between their several lovemaking sessions that weekend, they watched *Sunset Boulevard*. This was followed by several other classic black-and-white films filled with dramatic dialogue and acts of heroism.

Lying in bed in the middle of the afternoon, snuggling with Winston, joking, laughing, and being silly, Diego felt safe. He had also fallen in love.

They had unplugged completely in those three days, which was why the sound of Diego's phone alarm startled him so much. It was time to get up and return to the real world.

Monday morning had come—more specifically, six a.m. Diego ran his hand across the bed. It didn't go far before it reached Winston's arm. Lightly rubbing the fine hairs on Winston's arm caused Diego's pulse to quicken. He slowly reached out to silence his phone before returning his fingers to Winston's soft skin. He could barely remember his previous life. This now felt like him: his life, his happiness.

"What time is it?" Winston mumbled, as his body stirred under the comforter.

"Six. I have to get up." Doing the opposite, he pressed his backside against Winston's warm body. A sense of peace washed over him as Winston's arm draped around him, pulling him in tighter.

"Why?" Winston asked in a sleepy, gruff tone.

"Because I have to work." Diego's internal alarm clock had failed him this morning. He couldn't believe their time was over. The daily tasks of being a gardener crept into his thoughts. No doubt, tables and chairs would be scattered across the Bernsteins' yard after their big party. He would spend hours re-stacking them before he could work on the lawn. He wouldn't know how bad the mess was until he got there.

"No . . . I don't want you to," said Winston. "I want you to stay in bed with me. The weekend went too fast. I want to rewind back to Friday night."

The thought of Friday night sent a charge through Diego. They hadn't even finished dinner before the fire was ignited. After stripping away half their clothes right there in the kitchen, they had bounced off the walls in the hall as they made their way to the bedroom.

Without question, the last two days had been a dream. Winston had swept him off his feet, done everything right, and treated him like a king. Cinderella also came to mind; Diego had to move quickly before his carriage turned back into a pumpkin.

The previous night, before drifting off to sleep in Winston's arms, Diego had proclaimed his happiness to Winston. He was happier than he had ever been, happier than he had known possible. With a couple of savoring breaths, he then attempted to quiet his soul as he closed his eyes and nestled closer into Winston's side.

Nervousness, conflict, and insecurity had been replaced with excitement, confidence, and desire. He questioned if he was indeed in love, but his heart already knew the answer. He wanted nothing more than to stay in bed with Winston, make love, and continue the beautiful weekend that Winston had given him. But that was not his reality. He had to get up. "I have to go to the Bernsteins'. I do her yard, then I'll be back to do you."

Winston laughed.

Diego was getting good at recognizing when Winston was being playful. "No, I have to do *your yard*."

"Can we have dinner tonight?" Winston asked.

Diego didn't want to overstay his welcome. He needed to go home. But how could he say no when his heart was screaming yes? He decided that it would be rude to take more from Winston. "You do too much already. I shouldn't." He was lying to himself.

"I promise to let you work. Then when you're done, come in, and we can have dinner. Something easy, I promise."

It was only dinner. Winston would have dinner whether he was there or not, so there was no harm in sharing a meal, right? "Okay."

A calm entered Diego's body. The weekend wasn't over. Rolling over, he scooted his backside up against Winston, bringing their bodies together tighter. His heart surged when he realized that Winston's erection was pressed against his back.

Aroused, Diego flipped over, knowing there was time for one last one before he hit the road. Climbing on top of Winston, he heard what he thought was the front door. He pulled back, his ears focused on the noise. "Someone's here. The front door!" Frozen, he continued to listen.

Winston rolled Diego off him as he too listened. "Oh shit, it's Araceli." They both looked at the bedroom door, which was open.

"Who?"

"Araceli. She cleans on Mondays."

"Hello? Mr. Makena? Mr. Makena?" The sound of footsteps coming down the hall grew louder.

Jumping out of bed, Winston bolted to the door. "I'm here! Just waking up!" He shut the door silencing her steps. "I'll be out in a minute." Winston leaned back against the door. "It's my housekeeper," he whispered.

The reality set in that they were both naked. As if caught, Diego jumped up. He had to get dressed. It was definitely time to go. Not wanting to talk for fear that she would hear him, he ran into the bathroom for cover.

Winston followed him. "It's okay. She's not coming in here. Go, take your shower and get dressed. I'll go out and put some coffee on."

Winston was right; he had to take a shower to clean the sex off him. There was no way he would go anywhere without cleaning up first. "What will you say to her?" He had lost his erection, as well as any desire for morning sex.

"About what? You? It will be all right. She's fine. Trust me, she's not going to care. But you do have to put some clothes on. I'm thinking that seeing you naked might be a bit much." Winston reached into the shower and turned the water on. "Take your shower, get dressed, and come out. It's okay."

Diego couldn't imagine showing his face to her. She would know. He was in Mr. Leblanc's house, sleeping with Mr. Leblanc's husband. Mortified, he stepped into the shower. He watched as Winston grabbed the robe that was hanging on the back of the door and walked out.

Within minutes, Diego finished his shower and dressed. He sat on the edge of the bed and waited until Winston walked in with a cup of coffee and Lucy at his feet. "What are you doing? Are you coming out?"

"Where is she?" Diego thought he might avoid her all together and make a run for his truck.

"She's in the kitchen." Handing Diego his coffee, Winston grinned. "Why?"

Diego took a sip of his coffee and then put the cup on the nightstand. "I go." He stood, ready to bolt.

"You don't have to hide. Araceli's not going to care. I forgot she cleans on Mondays. She's usually gone before you get here in the afternoons."

Diego's heart pounded against his chest. "I not want to meet her. Araceli—is she Mexican?"

"Yeah." Winston's brow wrinkled. "Why?"

"No reason." He thought of Mayra for the first time in days. She often talked about the lives her clients led, the things she pretended not to see. The secrets she pretended not to know. In his head, Araceli *was* Mayra, and if Mayra knew, she wouldn't keep it from Francisco. He could bet his life on that.

"Why are you freaking out?" Winston softly stroked his shoulder. "She doesn't care." There was teasing in his voice.

Winston didn't get it, and Diego couldn't explain it. The flood of thoughts running through his mind were irrational yet very real. Diego stood and moved towards the door. "I see you this afternoon, no?"

Diego cracked the door opened and listened for a second. With a half wave saying good-bye, he bolted down the hall, making it to the front door without being detected. He didn't stop until he was safely seated in his truck. His carriage had most definitely turned into a pumpkin this morning.

22

With a fresh cup of coffee and the phone to his ear, Winston returned to his bedroom in an attempt to stay out of Araceli's way. He had been talking to Ann for the last thirty minutes. Starting with Friday evening, he had brought her up to date on the entire weekend.

"Is it too soon to be in love? Am I being silly?" Winston acknowledged the fluttering in his stomach and the excitement in his voice. He was hyper-aware, rejuvenated; he was already planning the next time he would be with Diego. This afternoon couldn't come quick enough.

Ann's laughter in the phone made him smile. "I'm absolutely hearing something in your voice," she said. "I haven't heard you this excited in forever."

Forever . . . that would include Parker. There was a quiver in Winston's stomach. Consciously, he tried to shut down the feeling, a mixture of guilt and denial. Staring at the closed door of the bedroom, he heard the vacuum cleaner running in the hall. With Parker, everything about his life had been on autopilot. It had rolled on, day after day, weeks into months, and they had all looked the same.

Winston's mouth went dry when he realized what he was about to tell her. "You know—" He debated whether he should continue. His mind made the therapeutic choice. "Before Parker died, we hadn't made love in over a year. As much as I loved him, it was like we had become just best friends."

Winston didn't know exactly what he wanted to reveal to her . . . or to himself. "I'm falling for this guy. Shit, I don't remember being this giddy and clumsy in the beginning with Parker."

He heard Ann breathing in the phone. His own breathing accelerated as he said, "I miss Parker so much. I can't shake the guilt, because if he hadn't died, I wouldn't have what I have with Diego. I *want* what I have with Diego. I would have never left Parker." Listening to the vacuum, Winston swallowed. "I never thought about leaving him. I was content. At least, I thought I was."

"Wow, I would have never guessed any of that. I'm your best friend. Why haven't you ever said any of that to me?" Her question was forgiving, without admonishment.

Winston thought about it. There was no single answer. At the time, it had been his life. There was nothing big or secretive about any of it. Okay, the "no sex" part had worried him from time to time, but he would always blame it on their schedules. They were both crazy busy, and as soon as things slowed down, it would come. Days turned to weeks, then months . . . and then Parker had died.

There was self-blame there, a lot of it. His chest tightened as the words formed in the back of his throat. "I always thought I had tomorrow, that life would be different tomorrow. Magically, it would fix itself. Yet I denied that it was broken." Winston fell back onto the mattress. Collecting his thoughts, he exhaled a deep, cleansing breath.

"You shouldn't feel guilty about falling in love. It wasn't your fault. It's not anybody's fault how things came to be," Ann said.

Her words did little to remove the guilt that consumed his heart. As he stared at the ceiling fan that whirled above his head, pieces began to come together. "You know, Ann . . ." Winston sat up. "Right after Parker died, my life felt like riding a horse through the forest in pitch darkness. I was going full speed, like I was on a racehorse, and I couldn't see anything. The wind was hitting me in the face so hard that I couldn't breathe. I sat in this house day after day. Even the days that I was in the office were all a blur. I was waiting for the crash. I was barely holding on."

Resting his elbow on his thigh, he continued. "I used to love life. The world was full of bright lights. Dance music played in my head constantly. I was often dumbfounded that no one else heard it. Until the crash."

"You mean the accident?" Ann interrupted.

"Yeah. No. Yeah, I mean the horse, my world. Until I met Diego, every day was pretty much a bad day. In that forest, I had moments of light, when I could breathe, normalcies, and then *bam*, darkness again. That was until I met Diego." Winston had shared all he could for now.

After a long pause, Ann spoke. "When do I get to meet this thief, the man who stole your heart?"

Winston thought for a second. Would it really be possible to introduce Diego to Ann? To his mother, to the people in his life? If this was the real deal, if they were a couple, if he was indeed in love, then of course, Diego would be involved in every aspect of his life. He would move in and be here every day. Winston couldn't contain his smile.

The darkness that had surrounded him for the last year had been missing ever since he and Diego met. He had forgotten what a sense of normalcy was like. It had only been two months, and a couple of dates, and their first weekend together, but he was alive again.

"Why don't you bring him as your date to the Harper Gala? Introduce your new boo to the world?"

That was two weeks away. He couldn't think past this evening, let alone two weeks down the road. "Yeah, I guess I could." It would be fun to share his world with Diego: the bright lights and glitter of an impressive event like the Harper Gala. Champagne, the food, men in black tuxedos and women draped in expensive jewelry and designer gowns. He quickly embraced the idea.

"So, speaking of the Gala, are you still planning on coming in today? I have a meeting at one o'clock with the team so we can nail down some of the final details," Ann stated.

It hit him like a ton of bricks. He had told her last week that he was coming back today. Caught up in the indulgences of the weekend, it had completely slipped his mind.

How could he have forgotten that he had a business to run? Being with Diego the past two months had taken him completely out of the business mode. It had also given him a reason to want to get up in the morning. Nevertheless, the business waited. "Yes, I'll be there by nine."

He looked at the clock on the nightstand. If he jumped in the shower now, he would be there in plenty of time. *Shit*—he remembered that Diego was coming back this afternoon, expecting him to be here.

He had to text Diego to explain that he wouldn't be at the house when he arrived. Would Diego wait for him after finishing the yard? The last thing he wanted was to go into the office today. It had seemed like such a good idea last week. He wanted to be here when Diego returned; he wanted to be *with* Diego. The reality set in that his plans for this afternoon had vanished in the blink of an eye.

After ending his call with Ann, Winston glanced at the clock again, figuring out how much time he had and what he needed to do. He would call Diego on his way into the office. If he couldn't see him until this evening, he would at least hear his voice.

Winston knew there was no telling exactly when he would get home. He could only hope to be back by six. Would Diego wait around the house all day? If so, Winston certainly didn't want to waste time this evening cooking. He would pick something up on the way home. Quick and simple.

He couldn't shut his brain off as he picked through his closet, matching a shirt and tie with his navy blue suit.

In less than forty-five minutes, he was saying goodbye to Araceli and Lucy and backing the Jeep out of the garage.

The idea of going to the office sent a burst of adrenaline through him. Despite the disruption of his afternoon plans, he was looking forward to being back in the thick of things. Negotiating prices and shopping for outlandish requests from each client was what he did. Ensuring that their evening stood out from all other parties was what he loved.

As he waited for the front gates to open, Winston struggled with the audio system in the Jeep before realizing Diego's number hadn't been downloaded into the system's phonebook. He loved the Jeep's ruggedness, but the communication system was no match for his Maserati's.

He glanced back and forth between the road and his phone as he manually called Diego on his phone. The phone rang four times before rolling over to his outgoing message. *"Bueno, te encuentras con el telefono de Diego. Por favor deje su mensaje después del tono."* His beautiful, sexy voice was followed by a long beep.

"Um, hey Diego, it's me. I had to go into the office today. Call me back . . . Oh, um, I want to see you tonight. Please call me back." After ending the call, Winston pictured Diego's phone sitting on the front seat of his truck. Diego might not get the message for hours.

Winston had just pulled into the underground parking garage when his phone pinged. It was a text from Diego. *Just got your message. It's okay, I have a lot to do here. What time do u think u will be home?*

Winston had no idea. He replied, *Maybe five thirty.*

He parked his car in his assigned spot, and waited a few minutes for a response. What if he didn't want to wait? After a minute or so, he exited his car and headed towards the elevator.

When he arrived on the twelfth floor, Winston still had his phone in one hand. He and Ann shared this floor with only one other business, some sort of call center with a handful of employees. Since neither business generated much foot traffic, the long hallway looked like it belonged in an abandoned building.

The sound from his shoes' heels echoed off the plain, ivory-colored tile as he made his way to the other end of the hall. He thought, not for the first time, that he should spend the money to spruce up this shared area.

As he reached the metal door marked *A Night to Remember,* his phone pinged. His heart raced as he cautiously held the screen up and read the message: *Okay.*

Diego's message was simple. He would wait. But for how long? The thought of turning around and going home pulled at Winston. He had seen Ann's car when he pulled in, so he knew she was there.

Tucking his phone into his jacket's inside pocket, he reached for the brass knob. His life lay on the other side of this door. He knew it would be unlocked, alarm off, lights on, coffee made, copy machine on—all the things that the second person coming in didn't have to do.

The plain metal door gave way to a large room with floor-to-ceiling windows that provided views of downtown Los Angeles. Behind glass walls were his and Ann's private offices.

Debra, their shared secretary, receptionist, and office manager, greeted him with her *million-dollar-you're-special* smile. "Good morning, Mr. Makena, and welcome back."

"Good morning, Deb. How are you?"

"Good, sir. Can I get you a cup of coffee?"

Winston cut his eyes over towards Ann's office, seeing that she was on the phone. "Yes. I could use one more cup this morning."

"I'll meet you in your office with it." Debra went one way, while Winston went the other. Waving to Ann, he stepped into his office. His oversized mahogany desk sat unusually empty: a phone, an empty in-basket, a leather notebook, and a framed photograph of Parker standing at the base of the Eiffel Tower four years ago. Behind his chair was a low bookshelf and a single print—an oil painting of a vase of flowers by Vincent van Gogh.

Debra arrived with his coffee, followed by Ann. "Good to see you," Ann said, smiling from ear to ear as she waited for Debra to exit so she could enter the small space.

"Shall I close your door?" Debra asked, as she skirted around Ann.

"Thank you." Winston replied. Reaching for the warm handle of his beloved coffee mug, which was imprinted with pictures of Parker, he waited until the door clicked. "Oh my God!" he exclaimed. "So, since I talked to you—what, two hours ago?—I've been thinking . . . overthinking, actually. I want to ask him to the gala, sort of a coming-out party."

"Newsflash, everybody knows you're gay. No news there." She laughed.

"No, not that kind of coming out. I'm talking about letting people know I'm okay. I'm dating, I'm happy, I'm back!" He picked up his phone and looked at the screen before continuing. "So they can stop asking me how I'm doing. Looking at me with those sorrowful eyes."

"Come on, now. It's because we care. I was worried about you. I wasn't sure you were progressing through . . . what do they call it? . . . The stages of grief."

"Oh, there's a name for it?" This was more of Ann's psychoanalyst bullshit.

"No, it's real! It's actually called the Five Stages of Grief!" Ann leaned forward in her chair as she counted them on her fingers. "Denial, Anger, Bargaining, Depression, and Acceptance. You, my friend, were bouncing back and forth between anger and depression."

Winston waited. *It's best to let her talk. I'll pretend I'm listening and agree, or else she'll continue.*

"I'm telling you. Some of that is normal, but you weren't moving."

"Well, okay then. Maybe you were right about me taking the time off."

"I know I was. You needed the time for clarity. To move into acceptance."

Winston laughed. "No. I meant that if I hadn't taken the time off, I would have never met Diego."

"Well, yeah, that too." Leaning back into her chair, she smiled at him. "You look happy."

"I am." Winston repeated his words to himself.

"Actually, you look like a man that's getting a lot of hot sex . . . Well?" She folded her arms.

"Well, what?" He knew damned well what she was asking. Once upon a time, many years ago, they had shared some of the nastiest details of their sex lives with each other. This morning, however, Winston wanted to keep it between him and Diego. The fact that it was mind-blowing monkey sex had nothing to do with it. Diego was a private person; it was the responsible thing to do.

"Come on! Let me live through you! You gays have way better sex than we do. It doesn't matter if you just buried your mama, y'all be stalking each other for sex."

This girl just went black on me! Winston looked down at his desk for something to throw at her. Damn, why was his desk so clean? "I'm not telling you!"

"For real? You're not going to tell me?" Her face went cold.

"Maybe later." Winston changed the subject. "So catch me up with what all is going on. What does our calendar look like?"

The two dropped into work as if Winston had never left. Soon, it was time for their one o'clock meeting. They greeted the team in the outer office. It included all the people who were working behind the scenes on the gala. There were several faces Winston didn't know.

As the chef talked over her final plans for meal preparation, Winston glanced down at his phone, hoping for a text or message from Diego. Nothing. Had Diego even made it to the house yet? Was he in the front yard or the back? His mind drifted as the chef finished up. The florist took the floor to discuss the final selection of flowers for the centerpieces and stage.

Winston looked at his watch. Ann had told him they had a meeting at the Beverly Hills Hilton for a fiftieth anniversary. That meeting was at three-thirty. If it went for an hour, he would hit traffic on the way home. He wouldn't get to the house earlier than six-thirty or seven o'clock. Winston released a deep sigh.

Ordinarily, that would have never been a concern. He got home when he got home. Parker was home, Lucy was fed, and dinner . . . came from somewhere. He thought about texting Diego to let him know it was okay to leave. It wouldn't be fair to ask him to wait for that long. The thought of not seeing Diego caused his body to ache. He was being selfish, but he couldn't tell Diego to leave. He couldn't.

"Winston? Winston? Are you listening? It's your call. You're the expert when it comes to that." Ann and the rest of the group were staring at him. Obviously, he had missed something. "What? Say it again," he asked, as nonchalantly as he could.

"Using the apricot-colored roses instead of the overused hydrangeas?" Ann asked.

He didn't need to know the question after all. He hated hydrangea arrangements. "Of course, let's go with the roses. Can we get enough for that big of a room?"

"If that's what you *want*, I can get them." The florist made a steeple with his fingers as he smiled into Winston's eyes.

Winston ignored the florist's overt focus on him by choosing to look at the screen on his phone. *Nothing.*

He needed to text Diego and be honest with him. He would say it was okay not to wait. He would put it out there: he *might* be late. He would leave it up to Diego. He was powerless over what Diego would do.

23

The cleanup earlier this morning at the Bernstein Estate had gone as he expected. The yard had looked like a tornado had hit it. Chairs and trash lay everywhere. Half-eaten desserts had sat on some of the tables; at least, he assumed they had been desserts at one time.

Only after stacking the tables and chairs was he able to begin his actual job—working on the lawn. Receiving the text from Winston had been a blessing. He hadn't made it back to the house until almost three o'clock.

The property was quiet, like old times, not a soul around. Unsure exactly when Winston was going to be home, he had plugged his earbuds in and worked for a couple of hours. Stopping to quench his thirst, he checked his phone for any messages. He had two, neither from Winston. They were from Mayra. Usually, a text from her was nothing out of the ordinary, but today, they caused a hitch in his breath.

Your brother is going to need a ride this evening to work.

His throat tightened as he rolled his eyes and moved on to her second text.

I made pozole for dinner yesterday. I saved you a big bowl.
You can have it tonight. Missed you at church.

Really? Was she trying to lure him home with food and guilt trip him over missing church? Both texts had Francisco's name all over them. It was Francisco who wanted him to come home. There was no reason one of them couldn't take Rafael to work, or give him the car to take, or make him ride the bus. Have him call one of his friends, or better yet, one of his girlfriends. Diego ran down the list of options, as if it mattered.

His body temperature rose the more he thought about it. Her second text was her expressing her guilt for submitting to Francisco's manipulation.

Diego refused to be treated like a ten-year-old who had stayed out after curfew. His immediate inclination to agree and come home pissed him off even more. Hell, he was already planning to go home after dinner. He didn't need to be told to come home.

Diego knew this had nothing to do with Rafael. Francisco hadn't liked him being away since Friday. This was a reaction to him being gone for three days.

It was almost six o'clock. Even if Winston pulled in right now, if Diego stayed for dinner and did what he wanted to do, that would take them easily into this evening. By the time he drove all the way home, it would be well past the time Rafael supposedly needed a ride. He would have to leave right away to get Rafael to work on time.

The burden of always being the obedient and responsible one weighed heavily on him. He was twenty-five years old and had no life of his own. Rafael never asked for permission to do anything. Francisco never bothered to clear anything that he was doing with anyone either. It angered Diego that he used Mayra to do his dirty work. As much as he wanted to shoot a text back telling them to go to hell, Mayra didn't deserve that.

The clang of the metal gates opening stopped his internal rant. His mood changed at the sight of Winston's black Jeep pulling in. He breathed a sigh of relief as he tucked his phone into the front pocket of his jeans. Energized, he swung the blower off his back, laid it on the ground, and walked towards the garage.

Opening the car door, Winston made a pouty face. "I'm so sorry that I'm late." Stepping out of the Jeep, he kissed Diego.

A single kiss was all that it took for the stresses of the day to lift from Diego's body. Francisco no longer held his attention. Licking his lips, he felt star-struck in Winston's presence. Winston was beautifully dressed in his tailored suit, and his steel-grey eyes stood out against his shirt and tie. There was no question the decision to stay had been the right one.

Diego felt a tad embarrassed by his own appearance. He had been working all day in the heat and sun. His work clothes were beyond dirty, and he could only imagine what he smelled like. But when he saw the way Winston was looking at him, it didn't matter.

"Have you been waiting long?" Winston shut the car door.

"No," was all Diego was able to say before Winston kissed him again.

The two walked to the back of the Jeep. "Since I'm late, I picked up dinner for us."

Diego watched as he opened the rear hatch and pulled out two plastic bags containing several cartons. Handing Diego one of the bags, Winston shut the hatch of the Jeep.

"Chinese food. I didn't know what you liked, so I picked up a little of everything."

"Good." Diego caught the distinctive aroma of Chinese food. He didn't eat it much, but he loved it.

"Good." Winston smiled as he took Diego's free hand and locked their fingers together.

From the garage, they walked into the kitchen where Lucy greeted them. Her tail, which controlled her butt, was wagging a hundred miles an hour. "Has she been let out?" Winston asked as he tried to move past her without tripping over her.

Diego's mouth turned downward. It had never occurred to him to let her out to pee. He hoped she hadn't peed in the house. "No. I not try to come in. I not know if an alarm was on or not." Was Winston saying that it would have been okay that he let himself in? Was he saying that he trusted him, or was it really about the dog?

"Okay, girl. Let's go pee first." Winston laid his bag on the counter and kissed Diego again. "Gosh, I missed you. I hated not being here when you got here. I'm so sorry. I had forgotten that I told Ann I was coming in this morning." Winston walked over to the back door. "Come on, girl!" he called for Lucy to follow him.

Diego and Lucy followed Winston out the back door. Stepping into the yard, Diego experienced a sense of déjà vu. So many times, he had been working in the back yard when Winston and Lucy stepped out of that door. Now, he was stepping outside with them. He was living in a dream.

"Hey . . . I wanted to ask you, um . . . if you wanted to go to the Harper Gala?" The emotions of a puppy emanated from Winston's eyes.

It took Diego a second to remember what the Harper Gala was. *Go with him? To do what?* Diego was unsure of the question. The look on his face must have said so.

"You don't have to." Anguish appeared in Winston's eyes. "I thought it would be fun." He scratched the side of his head, his lips curling downward. "I think I get it. I hadn't thought about it being such a public date and all. Forget that I—"

A date? Of course he meant a date. Stupid me. Winston wasn't asking him to work it. "Wait . . ." A nervous laughter trapped in his throat, Diego managed to push his words past the lump. "You want *me* as your date?"

"Of course I want to take you as my date." Winston's chin rose. His brows furrowed as if he was trying to read Diego.

"I not embarrass you?" Breaking eye contact, Diego looked for Lucy in the yard as he sorted out his emotions. This could be a problem. He would be in the company of a room full of Winston's friends as well as strangers—wealthy strangers. He knew well what that kind of party looked like. He had worked enough of them, setting up, busing tables, parking cars. He knew all too well what the Harper Gala would be. "I'm not like you—hell, I'm your gardener."

Lucy ran past them without slowing and continued into the house. Winston took Diego by the waist and drew his body into his. "You're also my boyfriend, and I think you're amazing. I want to show you off to the world." Winston moistened his bottom lip before gently kissing him.

Diego pulled back, his head shrinking into his neck. "I'm your boyfriend?"

"Oh, I guess I should have asked. I'm such a fool sometimes . . . I'm falling for you. I don't want anyone but you. Diego Jose Ramirez Castillo, will you please be my boyfriend?"

Unsure if his smile came from the fact that Winston remembered his full name or that Winston had just asked him to be his boyfriend, Diego slapped a hand over his mouth to hold in a giggle.

As they ate dinner, Diego asked questions about the gala. With enough information, he assured himself, he could get through the night.

Trading cartons, Diego swapped his pork fried rice for Winston's carton of ginger beef. "This is good," he admitted, as the tangy ginger sizzled on his tongue.

"Yeah, I love this place. A little hole in the wall downtown, on Hill Ranch Drive."

Diego had been through downtown Thousand Oaks several times and had never gotten a good vibe from it. To him, it seemed a little snooty. Its residents were clearly not his people.

The vibration of his phone in his jeans couldn't have come at a worse time. He ignored the repeated pulsation against his thigh. It was either Rafael or Mayra, and he refused to let them question him about his whereabouts in front of Winston.

With this decision came a sense of independence, but he couldn't deny that he felt anxiety as well. It wasn't how his parents had raised him. Was he being selfish? Was this a bad decision?

24

O ver the next two weeks, Diego arrived at Winston's house every Saturday evening after working in the shop with his brothers. They spent their weekends and Monday nights together. Winston had thought of the arrangement, saying that it was perfect since Diego was in the area every Monday and Tuesday anyways.

Francisco and Rafael were pushing to reestablish their dominance over Diego, but Winston's doting on him made it bearable. He found that the less he talked to his brothers, the easier it was.

The trickiest day was Saturday, when the three of them worked closely together all day in the tiny shop. Diego sidestepped their comments and probing. He had his bags packed and in his truck, ready to flee. He cut out as soon as he could.

There was no mistaking Francisco's opposition to Diego's assertiveness. Their relationship became more contentious by the day, the two sparring over everything and anything.

Rafael was another story. He badgered Diego constantly, begging for the identity of the girl who was taking up his brother's time. The goading kept Diego in a constant state of anxiety. He had to stay on guard with everything he said and did, to ensure that he didn't slip up and reveal something. Rafael was smart, too smart.

The night before the gala, Diego waited until Rafael had gone to work before reaching into the back of the closet to retrieve the black garment bag. The bag contained his brand new suit. It was navy blue, the same color as the one in Winston's closet. Diego had picked it up earlier that day, and now he wanted to look at it again. It was by far the nicest thing he had ever purchased or owned.

Initially, he had only intended to buy the pants and jacket that the store advertised for ninety-nine dollars, but the sales clerk had convinced him that he needed a new shirt and tie to go with it. By the time he added the shirt, tie, tee shirt, shoes, socks, and belt, he had spent over three hundred dollars.

The money he spent had come out of the fund for his new truck. It was his money, and although the suit had cost a lot, it had been well worth it. He was going to the Harper Gala as Winston Makena's boyfriend, and he had to look every bit as sharp as everyone else. He repeated the word *boyfriend* in his head. It still sounded strange.

Unzipping the bag, Diego rubbed the lapel of his new jacket. He would never forget being fitted for it—the tailor pinching back the extra fabric on the coat as she moved about, sticking pins and chalking marks all over it. He looked in the bag to be sure his white shirt wasn't being wrinkled. Carefully zipping up the bag, he placed it in the back of the closet.

Only Mayra had noticed his haircut, or at least commented on it. It was probably the shortest he had worn it in years. It was nice and tight on the sides, and he had the stylist put a part on one side. He had seen the cut in a copy of *GQ* magazine and torn out the page to show her what he wanted.

Pushing down his guilt about all the money he had spent, he told himself that he deserved it. It was his own money, money never intended for anything other than his new truck. He could take care of his family and still have something for himself. If there was one thing he had realized over the last couple of months of dating Winston, it was that he liked nice things.

He had no expectation that Winston was going to provide for him. He could do that all by himself. He had lived in poverty all of his life. Diego knew that possessions weren't important, but he certainly couldn't deny that they were nice.

At the sound of a knock on the door, Diego's heart jumped. He slammed the closet door closed. "Yes?"

The door opened, and Francisco stepped in. "Here's my money for *Mama* and *Papa*. Here's Rafael's too. He'll pay me back when he gets paid."

Diego stepped away from the closet as he took the cash from his brother. He stuffed the money in the nightstand between the two beds and took a seat on his mattress. Francisco sat across from him on Rafael's bed. The tension loomed between them.

Somehow, over time, Francisco had become his father. There was little doubt that he was here to talk, but that was the last thing Diego wanted. He certainly didn't want to talk about his relationship to someone who, in a million years, would never understand. He knew how Francisco felt about homosexuals. He would bring God into it. The fact that he was having unwed sex with Mayra was, somehow, not the same.

"So, how've you been?" Francisco leaned back, resting his elbows on the bed.

The fact that Francisco was speaking English to him struck him as odd. It was just the two of them in the room.

Francisco hesitated. Clearly, something was on his mind. "Rafael and I were talking the other day. I don't know if he told you, but he's got a kid on the way."

Diego had not been expecting that. Mixed emotions filled his head. It was just like Rafael to get some girl pregnant.

"Who is she?" Rafael's supervisor at the coffee shop popped into Diego's head. Would Rafael marry who ever she was, stand by her, and do right? Diego laughed under his breath at the notion that they had to marry like their *abuelos*—to marry a girl because she was pregnant, to do the "right thing." She would be a fool to marry his brother. Hell, she was already a fool for sleeping with him.

"He said her name. It's not Silvia. I know that wasn't it. It's a white girl."

Diego tried not to roll his eyes at Francisco's stupid comment. He knew that Rafael hadn't been with Silvia in months. The only white girl was Rafael's boss. "When's the baby coming?"

"Don't know." Francisco gave a half shrug. Then he switched back to Spanish. "So what about you?"

"What about me?" What was Francisco asking?

"You're hardly here anymore. You're out all night. You barely speak to me. When I do see you, you act like a bitch. I asked Mayra. I know she knows something, but she won't say." Francisco's eyes were locked onto Diego.

Any reaction to Francisco's probing would confirm that he was hiding something. He had to break eye contact before it was too late. Bowing his head, he focused on their feet and the chestnut-colored carpet.

"Well, where are you these days?" Francisco's voice took on a domineering tone that Diego knew all too well.

Francisco's direct question, coupled with his intense stare, made it almost impossible for Diego to lie. Stalling to come up with something, anything, he avoided eye contact.

There was no way on earth he would answer honestly. In a million years, he could never tell Francisco the truth. The truth lodged in his throat; he swallowed several times, trying to push it down. "Been busy."

"With who?"

Diego couldn't hold back a groan. His eyes bounced about the room, everywhere but Francisco. "I don't want to talk about it!" He jumped up from the bed. He was in flight mode, but there was nowhere to go in the tiny room.

Francisco stood up as well. "Not sure why you're being so secretive. What's the big deal? Who is she?"

Spinning around, he faced Francisco. "Can we just leave it?"

"No . . . We can't. What are you doing?" The question was accusatory.

"I'm not doing anything. I'm twenty-five years old. I'm not a kid. I'm not your child . . . It's none of your business what I'm doing!" He had to escape this conversation. "I'm going to the bathroom."

"Diego!"

Ignoring Francisco, he escaped across the hall and into the bathroom. The closed door gave him security, time to think. His heart was racing. *I need to move out*, he thought. If his relationship with Winston was to stand a chance, he would have to be out on his own. He had to make a choice: his family or Winston. The two couldn't co-exist in the same space.

He remembered that his phone was on his nightstand. Francisco was still in this room. Panic struck him. What if Francisco looked in his phone? There were hundreds of texts between him and Winston. One look and anyone would know they were lovers.

If the texts weren't bad enough, there were also the pictures Winston had sent, showing how much he was thinking of Diego at that particular moment. *Shit! What if Francisco goes through my photos?* Why had he stopped erasing his messages? He was a fool to have kept them.

He couldn't go back into that room, but he couldn't leave his phone in there either. Frustration turned to anger as he flung the door open and raced back into his room to retrieve the phone. It was right where he had left it. Francisco and Mayra were now fighting out front. Quietly closing the door, Diego felt the acid in his stomach gurgle. Why couldn't he be straight? That situation, whatever that was with Francisco, it was too close to the truth. A truth Francisco could never understand or accept.

25

The gala was everything Diego had imagined it would be. The grand ballroom was adorned in fresh floral arrangements, glittering lights, and a sea of dark suits, black tuxedos, and women in fabulous gowns.

The horns and strings of a small orchestra sounded from the far corner of the room. Several people were dancing on the glossy hardwood floor in front of the orchestra. He and Winston had arrived long before the guests, so Diego had watched the room change from an elegant, empty space to a full-blown party. It didn't matter that he didn't know anybody here. This actually worked in his favor, as the guests didn't know him either.

Although the crowd was much older than Diego, Winston went out of his way to ensure that he was comfortable, introducing him to the host and several other business associates as they showed up. Diego wasn't sure if being introduced as his *dear friend* was Winston's way of being private or if it was code for boyfriend. Either way, everyone responded warmly, smiling and using words such as *it's a pleasure, welcome,* and *thank you for coming.*

Diego had listened as Winston made polite conversation with the guests, who stood in line for the chance to talk to his date. Although the evening was about raising money, clearly Winston was the star.

Winston had left Diego about an hour ago to attend to a glitch of some sort. Wandering about the room by himself, Diego seized another champagne flute from one of the wait staff, who were circulating in the crowd. With a nod, Diego thanked the young Caucasian waiter before continuing. He moved through the crowd of cologne and perfume, the murmur of voices all blending in his ear. This was by far the most spectacular night of his life.

He knew that he looked good in his new suit. Although it wasn't a tuxedo, it was money well spent. He felt many eyes on him, including men who gave him the *do-you-see-me* stare.

When he returned to their table, a young African American couple whom he hadn't met yet was sitting there. The man immediately stood, rising about six inches taller than Diego, and offered his hand, introducing himself and his wife as William and Val.

"We saw the names on the table, but we don't know anyone except Ann and Winston," the man said.

"Do you guys work with them?" Diego asked as he glanced at his name card, ensuring he was at the right table.

"Oh, no. I'm Ann's stepson. I'm in IT . . . And you?" The man studied him.

"I'm—" He didn't know what to call himself. "Gardener" sounded inadequate and somewhat pitiful given the crowd. Pulling out his chair, Diego took his seat. "I'm, um, own a landscaping company." He wasn't sure where that came from, but it wasn't a lie. The sign on his truck door said so.

"Oh, that's cool." The man looked at his wife. "We were talking last week about ripping out all the grass in our front yard. Maybe getting that fake stuff. But shit, that stuff's expensive."

Diego pictured the synthetic lawn that had been popping up everywhere. He hated the look of it and couldn't understand why people were buying it. "Yeah, it's expensive." He reached for his champagne; the alcohol had worked to calm his nerves throughout the evening.

He was surprised to find his glass empty. He certainly didn't remember finishing it. Fidgeting, he grabbed the ends of his shirt cuffs and pulled them out from under the sleeves of his coat, revealing about an inch of his shirt like the model in his *GQ* magazine.

He had succeeded all evening at dodging people, content to people-watch and move about the gala. Now he had been forced into conversation with two strangers. They appeared nice, but they were strangers nonetheless.

Val gently patted her husband's shoulder. "Yes, he almost had a heart attack when he found out the price of that stuff. Now he's talking about bark. Cheap, like his daddy."

Smiling back at his wife, William's eyes shifted between her and Diego. "You dry?"

"Sorry?"

William grabbed his wife's empty glass and pointed it towards Diego's. "You ready for another?"

It clicked; he was talking about his drink. "Sure." Diego handed William his glass. As William stood up, Diego again noticed that he was a big guy. His biceps pressed firmly against the fabric of his suit jacket. Diego's eyes scanned his body as he buttoned the top of his jacket.

"Watch my lady." William smiled as he turned and disappeared into the crowd.

Val turned to Diego. "So, how long have you and Winston been seeing each other?"

Diego released an inaudible gasp. Had she really asked him that? There were people standing all around them. Many were in earshot. "Um." He reached for his champagne glass, which wasn't there. He was speechless. He had nothing.

"My mother-in-law said he came back to work a new man. We all loved Parker, but we're also happy he's smiling again." Val's eyes softened.

His mouth still dry, Diego swallowed. His knees bounced uncontrollably under the table. "A couple of months." His voice cracked as he confessed his secret to a total stranger.

Val's face continued to soften. "Oh, you're still honeymooners. William and I have been married three years this December. I worked for William Sr. as a clerk back in college. Jr. and his dad are so much alike. How did you and Winston meet?"

He tried to piece together how she knew about him and Winston. Deep into his own thoughts, Diego didn't completely catch Val's question. He was fairly sure she had asked how they met. Drumming his fingers on the table, he wasn't sure where to begin. Or had she meant to ask how they became . . . His thoughts scattered, as he bit at his thumbnail. "I take care of his yard." His mind continued to race trying to connect the dots on how these two people were connected to Winston. Finally, he remembered that she referred to Ann as her mother-in-law. He exhaled a sigh of relief, trusting that he could talk to her safely.

"So, did you know Parker?" she asked.

"I did." The mention of Parker's name made him smile. Not only had he known Parker, he had liked him. He even missed him. The truth was, if Parker hadn't died, he wouldn't be sitting here having this conversation. Looking around the room, Diego realized that he was now on the other side of the fence. He was the guest, not the help. People wanted to talk to him.

Val started to speak. "He was a sweet man. I—"

"Hey, honey!"

Diego's eyes turned to the sound of Winston's voice. He was relieved to see the most handsome man in the room closing in on their table. Two men were with him. One was William Jr. and since the other man looked a lot like William Jr., Diego deduced that the other guy must be Ann's husband.

"You've met Val." Winston laid his hands on the back of his chair as he leaned towards Diego. "How are you doing?" The question was only slightly louder than a whisper.

Diego nodded. "Good." He forced a smile as the other two men took seats at the table. William Jr. slid another glass of champagne over to Diego.

"Thank you." Diego held his smile a second longer.

"William, have you met Diego Castillo?" Winston asked.

William Sr. stood and extended his hand across the table. "No, I haven't." William Sr.'s eyes narrowed as they shook hands. His grip was firm, and his bulging eyes were penetrating.

As hard as Diego tried not to, he broke eye contact with William and retracted his hand.

"So you're the Diego Ann has been doting about?" William Sr. asked.

Diego looked at Winston. He wasn't sure what *doting* meant. His pulse quickened as he tried to make sense of William Sr.'s statement.

"Yes." Winston interjected, as he laid his hand on Diego's shoulder and lightly caressed him.

Diego wanted to say something, but he was at a loss. He watched for a reaction from anyone at the table. Obviously, William Sr. knew of their relationship too.

Sitting back down, William Sr. reached for the pitcher of water and poured himself a glass. "Diego, is your family here in the States?" he asked in Spanish.

Taken aback by the man's perfect Spanish, Diego automatically responded in kind. "They are in Mexico."

Francisco had told them never to speak Spanish in front of Americans. He had made the rule when they first started to learn English—by speaking English in public, they would avoid standing out.

"*¿Qué parte?*" William Sr. asked.

Switching to English, Diego directed his answer to everyone at the table. "What part? Um. I was born in Mezcala, Guerrero." The tinkering of flatware hitting glass echoed from the front of the room. The entire table turned their focus to the front as the orchestra's music faded out.

"Can I have everyone's attention, please?" In a beautiful robin-egg blue dress, Ann addressed the crowd from the makeshift stage.

She talked for several minutes before thanking everyone for attending and turning the mic over to the two hosts of the Gala.

After half an hour of speeches and another forty minutes of raffling off an abundance of extravagant prizes, the wait staff served the first course of dinner. Diego was starving, and he was relieved to see that their table was one of the first to be served. He was examining his plate when he heard someone call out to Winston.

Two women appeared at the side of their table. "You and Ann have done a fabulous job this evening. It's been a wonderful evening." The woman who was speaking bent over and presented both of her cheeks for Winston to kiss.

Although Diego couldn't recall their names, he remembered that they were past clients whom Winston had introduced him to earlier. Full of compliments, the two women conversed with Winston and Ann for several minutes before leaving.

Diego waited for the table to resume eating before returning his attention back to his own plate. He examined the small display of mustard greens and butter lettuce that made up the salad. He hated kumquats and cranberries, so he pushed them aside, leaving little else to eat.

Winston, Ann, and William Jr. ranted about the latest woes coming out of the White House while William Sr. single-handedly defended the president.

Offering nothing to the heated dialog, Diego munched on a sourdough roll as he pretended to listen. A mixture of excitement and wariness filled his gut. He knew he didn't measure up to anyone in the room, yet people accepted him because he was with Winston.

"May I take your plate, sir?"

Diego's ear caught the accent before realizing the server next to him was asking if he was finished with his salad. Attempting to clear some of the plates from the table, the young Hispanic woman balanced two of them on her arm.

"Yes. Thank you." Diego answered as he leaned to one side, giving her room to remove his plate.

"*De nada*." The server gave him a half smile before removing his plate. From the corner of his eye, Diego watched as she continued around the table, stacking more plates across her arm.

As chatter continued around the table, the wait staff began serving the main course. Diego and Winston were served first, but following Winston's lead, Diego didn't eat until the entire table had been served. He was more than content with the three rolls he had already eaten.

The table grew quiet as everyone started in on their dinner. Relieved that the duck ravioli over a tart cherry braised cabbage was actually good, Diego slowed his eating so he wouldn't finish twice as fast as the rest of the table.

"Winston tells me you're the youngest of three boys. What do the others do?" Val asked.

Diego got the sense she was only asking to include him in their conversation. He carefully chose his words. "My brother Rafael goes to college . . . Francisco, he's the oldest, he owns a garage." Pleased with his answer, he continued. "He specializes in rebuilding old cars, classics, but he works on everything."

Val nodded as if interested.

William Sr. jumped in. "Really? In college, I had a '66 Chevrolet Chevelle. Three-speed automatic with a V8-454. Damn, was she fast."

"It was a piece of junk," Ann whispered loud enough for the table to hear.

William Sr. shot his wife a stink eye. "Come on, now. Why you want to talk about my girl like that?"

Turning to Winston and Diego, Ann chuckled. "I guess you don't forget your first."

Not understanding the joke, Diego laughed with the rest of the table. He enjoyed the way Ann and her family teased each other. They were funny and affectionate. They were the exact opposite of his family . . . or what was left of it.

With the evening dying down, the crowd had shrunken by about half. People had finished dinner and returned to mingling. The band was back in full swing with a hand full of people on the dance floor.

"Shall we walk?" Winston tossed his napkin on the table as he pushed his chair away from the table.

"Sure." Diego followed Winston's lead, tossing his napkin on the table as well.

"We'll be back. I just want to walk the room. Check in with everybody." Winston announced to the rest of the table.

"You want me to go with you?" Ann asked.

"No. Relax for minute." Winston held out his hand, signaling for Ann to stay seated.

Diego and Winston talked as they causally strolled through the crowd making their way to the other end of the ballroom.

"Have I told you how handsome you look tonight?" Winston asked.

Diego breathed a deep, quiet sigh. He loved his new suit. Rubbing his hand down the front of his jacket, he felt like a million bucks.

"I absolutely love your haircut. I'm going to miss running my fingers through your long curls, but your short hair makes your eyes really stand out—I love those brown eyes."

Diego rubbed at the part of his neck once covered by his hair. He wasn't sure how he felt about his hair being so short. Winston liking it helped him to like it as well.

They passed the dance floor, where several people had gathered in a cluster, all flapping their arms to a weird tune the orchestra had started playing.

Diego chuckled as he stopped to watch. "What are they doing?"

"The Chicken Dance." Winston laughed. "You've never seen the Chicken Dance?"

With a snort, Diego knew he had probably had too much champagne. "Why are they doing that?"

"It's a dance. It's what we do at every wedding, retirement party, and birthday. If you don't do the Chicken Dance, then you haven't partied," Winston said.

Even though Winston was working the party, Diego was having the time of his life just being with him and watching him smoothly interact with everyone. They walked towards the front of the room.

"Walk with me to the bathroom?" Winston asked.

Not needing to respond verbally, Diego exited the room with Winston and walked down the long hall and around the corner, where the men's restroom was located. As Winston disappeared behind the doors, Diego pulled out his phone and began checking his messages. One missed call from Mayra and forty-eight new posts on his Snapchat account.

Within minutes, Winston reappeared, along with another man. The man smiled at Diego as he passed him and, without a word, continued down the hall.

Looking at the man, Winston smiled, and his nose wrinkled.

"Is everything okay?" Diego sensed the enormous change in Winston's previously playful mood.

"Mike said that he knows you," Winston muttered.

A pit immediately formed in Diego's stomach, as he turned to get another look at the stranger. Seen from behind and halfway down the hall, the man looked like any other person in the ballroom. "No . . . I not think we've ever met." Diego shook his head.

"He says you have." Winston's tone was gruff.

Winston's tone caused Diego to question his own memory. "Where? I swear I not know who that person was."

Winston's face was expressionless. "He says he knows you from the Jolt Café. He was there with a friend." Crossing his arms, Winston took a half step, closing the gap between him and Diego. "Supposedly, you and his friend had sex in the bathroom."

Diego turned to look at the guy again, but he was gone. Hearing the words Jolt Café jarred his memory, and it wasn't good. Last year, sometime, he had let a guy suck him off in the bathroom. The guy had been eyeing him from across the room . . .

It all came flooding back to him. There had been two people sitting at the guy's table. That guy who had spoken to Winston was one of them.

"So is it true?" The whites in Winston's eyes had turned pink.

Embarrassed as the event played out in his head, Diego lowered his eyes. "Yeah, I guess so. But that was way before I met you. We not have sex. His friend sucked me off, that was it."

"That's funny. He was very clear in his narrative that it was sex."

"Well, that's a lie. We not have sex." Diego drew a breath. It seemed unimportant whether they'd had intercourse. It didn't change the fact that he had hooked up with the guy.

"Um." Winston took a large breath. "He said you asked for twenty bucks after the two of you were done. Is that true?"

Diego's heart stopped. Never in his life had he asked for money for something he wanted as much as the other person. He wasn't a prostitute. "That's a lie! I'm no *puto*!" Now, this was something he would defend himself against. "I never asked anybody for money. I not need their money." His body temperature rose. *Why would the man lie like that?*

"Why would he make that up? If everything else is true, why would he lie about that?"

"I not know." Diego shook his head. "I not know."

"Diego, don't lie to me!"

"Are you calling me a liar? What? Do you want to believe him?" Diego's embarrassment turned to anger.

As a group of chattering women approached them, Winston straightened up. "We'll finish this later. I have a party I have to attend to." He turned to walk away.

"Bullshit!" Diego wouldn't allow someone to call him a prostitute and walk away. That was total bullshit. "No . . . We finish it now." Diego took a step into Winston's personal space. "You not going to call me a whore and walk away." He tried to control his voice.

"I never called you that!" Winston hissed.

"Yeah, you did. Do you think I take money from that guy?"

Waiting for the women to pass, Winston lowered his voice. "Look, only you and that guy know what happened. I wasn't there."

"No, you weren't, but I told you what happened!" Diego's voice shook.

Two older men walked out of the restroom, neither paying them any attention.

"I said we'll finish this up later." Winston's tone was low, sharp, and dismissive.

"When it's good for you? When your friends aren't staring at you? God knows, you not want them thinking you're dating a prostitute, now do you?" He wasn't going to stand here and let someone disrespect him. "Fuck you! Fuck you and your friends." His voice rose enough that several people turned their heads.

Seeing the two men's heads turn back toward them, Diego included them in his message as well. "Fuck you!" How he wished he had that champagne glass now—not to drink, but to smash against something.

Diego looked around for the nearest exit. Not seeing an exit, he instead marched back into the ballroom to find the liar. Finally locating him standing with two other men, Diego stepped right into their space.

"Excuse me. I not think we've actually met. I'm Diego." Winding up, he sent a powerful blow to the man's jaw. It was the perfect punch. The man's head spun as his legs collapsed, sending him to the ground.

Shaking the pain from his knuckles, Diego raised his fists, ready to take on either of Mike's friends. As neither of the other two men were interested in fighting, he exhaled as he lowered his hands. "Sorry to interrupt." Diego stepped over the man's body and stormed out of the ballroom.

26

Buried deep under the blanket, Diego couldn't decide if he was coming down with a virus or if he was sick over his fight with Winston two nights ago. He hadn't eaten anything all day yesterday or this morning.

He rolled over and saw that Rafael was still asleep. Taking a deep breath, Diego rolled back over, hoping to go back to sleep himself. He knew there was little chance of it. He had been awake for hours.

It was another hour before Rafael stirred. Diego pretended to be asleep, so he would not attract his brother's attention. He listened as Rafael farted, yawned, and made the noises of an old man. Finally, his brother exited the room and entered the bathroom across the hall.

He couldn't believe this goddamn apartment was so tiny. He heard Rafael peeing in the bathroom, Mayra in the kitchen, and the TV in the living room. The difference between his apartment and Winston's massive house had never seemed so huge. He pulled the pillow over his head, hoping to shut them all out.

When Rafael returned, he shook Diego's shoulders. "Hey, you going to church with us?"

Rafael knew he was awake, but that didn't mean he had to get up. "No . . . I'm sick." Keeping the thin blanket over his head, Diego curled into a ball.

"Yesterday, Francisco and I checked out that new garage. It's got twice the room that we have now." In his boxers, Rafael moved about the room, picking up Diego's clothes from Friday night. "Hey, so where did you go on Friday?"

Diego ignored his question, hoping he would go away.

"This is a pretty nice suit. Where did you get this?" Rafael asked.

Diego remembered that when he took his clothes off the other night, he had thrown the pants and jacket to the floor on the other side of his bed. It had never occurred to him that Rafael would ask about them. That had been stupid. Of course, he would ask.

Diego continued to ignore Rafael's probing questions. Pretending to be asleep again, he tried to breathe as quietly as he could. He wanted to know the time—and how long he would have to wait before everyone left—but he didn't dare peek out from under the blanket.

"You want us to swing by and pick you up after church? Go with us to the flea market?"

Trying to mimic the sound of snoring, Diego lay motionless.

He must have indeed dozed off, as the next thing he remembered was waking up to a quiet apartment. Reassured by the quietness of the apartment, he emerged from his blanket and grabbed his phone from the nightstand. It was a little after eleven. He had nine missed calls and twenty-two text messages. Without looking, he knew they were from Winston.

As his thumb hovered over the envelope icon, Diego realized that Winston might actually be texting him to come pick up the few belongings Diego had left at his house. Winston, pissed off and embarrassed, probably never wanted to see him again. The loss of income from the Leblanc estate would be substantial. Diego would have to pick up several accounts to make up for it. Without a doubt, that account was gone. He didn't have to read the texts to know what they said.

What had made him think that being with Winston was a real possibility? Who had he been trying to fool? Whatever that thing was between them would have never worked. They were from two different worlds. Ensuring that his phone was on mute, he returned it to his nightstand and pulled the covers back over his head. A single tear slipped from his right eye, as he closed his eyelids and heart a little tighter.

After sleeping for another couple of hours, he was forced to get up and pee. Standing over the toilet, he tried to determine if he was mad at himself for hooking up with those strangers or mad at Winston for calling him a *puto*.

His two middle knuckles were slightly bruised. That guy's legs had folded like a rag doll's as he hit the floor. Diego still couldn't believe he had knocked him out. He should have hit Winston as well, for calling him a whore.

Diego heard the front door open. Someone was in the apartment. The sound of footsteps stopped on the other side of the door. "Diego?" Mayra called through the door.

As much as he wanted to ignore her presence, he couldn't. "Hi."

"Your brothers are heading out to the flea market. They're downstairs waiting in the car. Are you going?"

"No. I'm sick." Diego rested his hands on the sink.

"Okay. I'll let them know to go on."

Diego listened as the front door opened and closed. He retreated into his room. As he pulled the covers over his head, it suddenly occurred to him that the guy he'd hit might have called the police. What if the cops were looking for him right now? Shifting in the bed, he couldn't get comfortable.

If he were arrested, would he go to jail? They would know he was an illegal. After jail, would they deport him? He envisioned himself on a prison bus, arriving back in Mexico. He had screwed up. He had put everything and everyone in jeopardy.

Maybe he should tell Francisco that he wanted to go home. Run before they actually caught him, before Francisco, Rafael, and Mayra lost everything because of his stupidity. Could he get a job at the fireworks plant? It was the highest paying job anywhere around the village. He couldn't deny there was a part of him that missed home.

He tried to convince himself that if he had to go back, it wasn't the end of the world. He would see his mother again.

Within minutes, Mayra was back. She knocked gently on his bedroom door before opening it. Her small face poked in. "Do you feel like talking?" She was still wearing the white sack-like rose-print dress that she had worn to church. Not waiting to be invited, she moved over to Diego's bed.

"About what?" Diego felt his mattress sink as she sat down next to him.

"About your heart."

What did she know? Diego scrambled to figure out what she could have learned about his broken heart.

"I know you're upset. I know something happened the other night. I don't know what happened, but . . ." Mayra's voice trailed off.

On many occasions, he had wanted to talk to her about everything that had happened over the past few months. Each time, her loyalty to Francisco had stopped him. Unlike his brother, her religious convictions stemmed way beyond words in the Bible. She was nonjudgmental and forgiving.

After the fight with Winston the other night, when he had run out of the building, he had wanted to talk to Mayra. At some point, she had become his surrogate mother, the calm in his storm.

He remembered running out into the street that night. The traffic had been heavy as he had darted in and out of the slow-moving taxis and buses. It had taken him two hours on the bus to get home. Two hours of replaying that horrible scene in his head. He had been relieved when he had walked into the apartment and found everyone asleep.

Now, with the police looking for him, he would be going to prison. His entire world had been shattered into a million pieces—so many pieces that he didn't know how to start to put it back together.

Mayra pulled the sheets down off his head. "I know you're sad, but whatever happened, it will be better."

How could she say that? She had no idea what had happened. Sitting up in the bed, he propped himself up against the headboard. It was killing him not to be able to talk to her. He wanted to so badly, but she would tell Francisco.

"Have you ever done anything that you regretted?" he asked.

Mayra's eyes softened. "Of course I have."

Diego pushed on. "Anything that you've never told Francisco or your parents?"

"My parents, yes. Your brother, no. We don't have secrets between us."

That confirmed that Diego wasn't going to tell her anything.

Mayra rubbed his arm. "You know those secrets, the secrets we try so hard to hide so the world won't judge us for them? Well, the truth is, most of the time, we make them out to be a bigger issue than they really are."

Diego couldn't help but disagree.

"Diego . . . I know there's a part of you that you're afraid to share with the rest of us. You think we wouldn't understand, or perhaps wouldn't love you as much as we did before. But that's not true. I will always love you, regardless of what it is."

"I'm pretty sure Francisco would blow a gasket if he knew," Diego stated. He had often wondered if Mayra already knew, but there was no doubt Francisco didn't. Was she waiting for him to say it? As much as he wanted to tell her everything, her commitment to Francisco trumped all else. This was something Diego would take to his grave. It would be a lot easier to keep under wraps now that he was no longer seeing Winston.

"Are you hungry? We stopped after church and picked up some tamales. Mrs. Gonzalez and her sisters made them to raise money for her nephew."

"What kind are they?" Diego remembered hearing something about the nephew going into the police academy. He needed money for uniforms, books, and whatever else.

"Cheese and jalapeno. There was a dozen of the cinnamon and raisin, but Rafael and Francisco ate most of them. I think there's a couple left."

All of a sudden, Diego was hungry. The sound of his gut moaning was proof. For two days, he had lain in bed doing nothing but thinking. Eating had been the last thing on his mind.

Mayra stood up and straightened her dress. "I'll heat them up." Giving a sorrowful smile, she stroked the top of his head before walking out.

He thought about what she had said—that no secret was that bad. What if she was right? If he came out and told them the truth, what was the worst that could happen? The worst was that Francisco might disown him, kick him out. No . . . the worst was that he would say something to their parents. His parents would call for him to return to Mexico, thinking they could fix him, turn him into a real man.

He looked at the sketches on his wall. They were much more than drawings; they were his dreams. He used to think that, one day, everything on those walls would be built, that people would look at him as they looked at Winston the other night. Now, his career was over before it had even started.

Could he come out? If he and Winston weren't together, there was nothing to hide from them anymore. Wrapped up in his thoughts, he failed to hear Mayra returning with his lunch until she was right on top of him.

Later that afternoon, when Rafael and Francisco returned from the flea market, Diego had been sitting on his bed drawing for a couple of hours. Rafael's loud cackle echoed as the two burst through the front door. From the back bedroom, it sounded as if they were right next to him.

Damn Winston and his big house. Before Winston, Diego had no idea that their apartment was so small. It was twice the size of their house in Mexico. But now, it was a cage. It was only a matter of time before Rafael came in, and then the badgering would start.

On cue, Rafael walked into the room. "What's up? How are you feeling, *mijo*?" Rafael asked, as he sat on the edge of his bed and kicked his shoes off.

"Like shit." Keeping his focus, Diego continued sketching out a cobblestone walkway that made its way through the park. "You working tonight?"

"I'm closing."

"You need a ride?"

"No, I've been using the car." Rafael slid his belt out from around his waist and unsnapped his jeans. Dropping them to the floor, he flopped down onto his bed. Lying face up, he crossed his arms behind his head. "So, what's going on with you?"

"Nothing." Diego tensed as he waited for the next question to drop.

"Are you really sick?"

Balancing his sketchpad on his lap, Diego said nothing as he brought his knees up closer to his chest, closing the empty space between him and his drawing. He wanted to ask about the pregnant girl, but that would open the door for conversation.

For the next hour, Diego continued to scribble, tuning out his brother's presence as he slept a few feet away. Then he noticed that it was time to wake the beast.

"Dude . . . It's five o'clock." Diego shook Rafael's toes, trying to wake him. "What time do you have to leave?"

Rafael's sleepy eyes stared blankly at him. Diego hated to wake him, but if he didn't, he wouldn't wake up in time. "Get up, dude. You're going to be late."

"What time is it?"

"It's five o'clock." Seeing that Rafael was actually awake, Diego returned to his bed and buried his nose in his drawings.

Within twenty minutes, and minus the twenty bucks that Rafael borrowed right before he left, Diego had the room to himself again. With the exception of the TV from the front room, the apartment was quiet. Too quiet. He could hear himself think, and he couldn't turn it off.

He needed air. Grabbing his phone and keys, he slipped on his shoes and rushed past Francisco and Mayra, not giving either of them a chance to say anything to him. Out the front door and down the metal steps that led up to their apartment, he skipped the last two, springing onto the sidewalk. He reached for his keys in his pocket, and then changed his mind. He felt like he needed to walk.

He hadn't walked his neighborhood in ages. He looked up at the sun and guessed he probably had an hour left of daylight left at best. In deep thought, he began trying to sort everything out as he walked towards the corner. He wondered if Rafael was going to marry his baby's momma. If so, he might move out. Too much thinking over the past forty-eight hours with too little food had given Diego a headache that he hadn't been able to shake.

When he reached the corner, he crossed the street and walked over to the gas station where he usually got his morning coffee. The bell above the door chimed when he entered, causing the petite, dark-haired Middle Eastern woman behind the counter to look up. In all the years he had been coming in here, he had never once had a conversation with her or her husband. She was speaking to an elderly woman sitting on a stool behind her. Diego wondered if that was her mother. The old woman's face was full of deep wrinkles. There was no way of telling what she had looked like in years past.

It was a neighborhood of immigrants. His people lived here, and the middle easterners owned almost everything, except the Mexican dress shop and bakery. None of the faces had changed in years. The old lady in the apartment below them, the family across the hall: nobody had left.

Grabbing a cold soda out of the cooler, Diego eyed the chips, candy bars, and gum as he made his way to the front counter. When he reached the register, the old woman on the stool gave him a warm smile. He wondered if she spoke English. She reminded him of his own grandmother. How he missed his family in Mexico.

As much as he loved America, he missed home. A simpler time, a lifetime ago it seemed. As if it was yesterday, he remembered his father telling Francisco to look after his brothers, to be the man. It had been raining that morning, and Diego didn't have a coat. His father had taken off his own coat and had given it to Diego to wear. The three of them had stood in the parking lot that morning, receiving instructions from their father as they waited for the bus that would take them to Mexico City. It was the last time he had ever seen his parents. Over the years, he had convinced himself that they would be together again someday. Now, he was sure of it, but this didn't bring him comfort.

Diego made his way down the long, narrow street full of parked cars. It was the one thing he hated about this neighborhood: too many cars and not enough parking.

They had been lucky to find their apartment because it came with a small, private parking lot. With his truck and trailer, parking would have been a nightmare in this neighborhood.

Crossing the street, he squeezed between two parked cars and then made his way into the small neighborhood park. When he reached the playground, he took a seat on the bench directly across from the monkey bars and swings. There were several children playing, laughing and screaming as if their lives were truly in danger. The homeless also lived in this park, and this bench would most likely be someone's bed come nightfall.

Diego couldn't help but smile at the little girl screaming her lungs out as she ran from another little boy in and around the tire swings. The only adults were a young couple about fifty feet away, pushing a baby stroller towards him.

Eyeing the couple, Diego recognized the guy. It was Mr. Legs, his morning jogger. He had never actually seen him except in passing. The couple gave him a smile and nod as they walked by, their baby kicking its legs and trying to squirm free of the stroller.

He got his confirmation that the man was straight, that his long-term fantasy boyfriend had a wife and kid. The jogger that once held his attention almost every morning barely caused his pulse to rise now. The man held nothing compared to Winston. Mr. Legs wasn't even cute. He had been nothing but an illusion.

Laughing within, he felt positive energy replacing his negativity. Diego wondered if he and Winston were truly over. He ran through a series of scenarios that would lead to them making up. All of them ended with his family having to know about him. *Would they accept him like Winston's family had accepted him?* What if he moved out, found another apartment?

Diego glanced over at the small apartment complex across the street. He wondered if they had any one-bedroom units for rent. He could maybe afford a one bedroom on his own. It would likely mean less money being set aside for his truck, but the truck could wait. He, on the other hand, couldn't. What if Rafael married his baby's momma? He might move out too.

Would the three amigos finally be separated, going their separate ways? Tired of thinking, he covered his face with his hands. The heaviness in his chest, the lack of energy—he was exhausted.

27

Like clockwork, Diego's body sprung to life at five a.m. When he came in last night from the park, he was so tired that he must have fallen asleep within minutes. He had slept almost nine hours.

He was torn as to what he was going to do about the Leblanc estate this afternoon. How could he show up there as if nothing had ever happened between him and Winston? He had made a complete fool of himself on Friday night and had been ignoring Winston's messages all weekend. There was no way he could show up there that afternoon.

He realized that going to the Bernstein estate wasn't safe either. If Winston was looking for him, he knew he was there every Monday morning. If Winston showed up at the Bernsteins' and made a scene, Diego could lose that account too. It would take him months to recover from the loss of those two big accounts. His dream was to build more of those accounts, not lose them.

Francisco popped his head in the door. "Hey, are you going out this morning?"

His question forced Diego to make a decision. "I'm still feeling pretty shitty. I think I'm going to skip today."

"Really?" Francisco stepped in the room. "You want me and Rafael to handle the route? Rafael knows the route, right?"

He considered it, but he realized he would be sending his brothers right into the fire. What if Winston said something to them? He couldn't take that chance. "No. I can make them up. It's not a problem."

"What's wrong with you?" Francisco held his eyes on Diego.

"Nothing." Diego had no words this morning to describe the emotions that were kicking his ass. Even if he did, he certainly wouldn't be sharing them with his brother. He brushed past Francisco and headed out to the kitchen.

"*Bueno.*" Mayra never made eye contact with him. She spun around in the tiny kitchen and continued packing Francisco's lunch.

He pulled a box of Cheerios down from the cabinet, and then inched around her to the refrigerator to retrieve the milk. Taking everything he needed for his morning meal, he put it on the coffee table and looked around for the remote.

"Are you going out this morning?" Mayra asked.

"No."

"Still sick?" She finished drying the dishes and hung her apron on the refrigerator door.

"Are you ready?" Francisco asked her as he ran back down the hall to his bedroom.

"Yes." Mayra grabbed Francisco's lunch and hers before shutting the kitchen light off. "Go start the car. I'll be right down."

Francisco looked curiously at Mayra and Diego, followed by a scowl on his face. He grabbed the keys without saying a word, and with a shake of his head, he was out the door.

Mayra swung her purse over her arm and walked over towards Diego. "When your brother gets up, let him know not to eat the pork in there. I need it for tacos tonight."

"Okay." Bowl in hand, Diego never looked at her.

"Diego . . ." Her voice trailed off.

He couldn't look her in the eye, but he also couldn't stop himself. "There's something I want to tell you."

Standing over him, Mayra placed her hand on top of his head. "I already know. You don't have to say it."

"And?" His heart begun to pound in his chest.

"And what? It doesn't change anything."

"No?" He forced himself to meet her eyes.

Mayra brushed her hand lightly through his hair. "No. We're family. We're all we have. I don't understand it, and I can't talk about it right now, but it doesn't change the fact that I love you."

"Does Francisco know?"

Mayra drew a breath. The muscles in her face stiffened. "No."

"I feel stuck. Like whatever I do, it's going to be wrong."

Silence hovered between them for a few seconds. "You always do the right thing. This time, you need to trust your instincts. Stop worrying about everyone else, and do something for yourself for a change." Mayra tucked the tag back beneath Diego's tee shirt.

Hearing what she said, he read between the lines.

"Look, I have to go, or we're going to be late. We can talk later, okay?" She rocked the top of his head with her palm before kissing it and walking out the door.

Do the right thing? If only he knew what that was. He could never face Winston again after what had occurred at the party. Why would Winston want to speak to him anyways?

That evening, Diego planned to take to his room as he had the last several nights. Retreating there after dinner, he pulled out his drawings and began working. He hadn't been working long when he thought he heard the doorbell. *Was it on the TV?*

He reached for his earbuds to tune out any further disruptions. He was about to put them on when Mayra called for him.

Surely not. Diego hesitated another minute as he listened.

"Diego!" a faint voice called again.

Pulling himself off his comfortable bed, Diego made his way over to his door and entered the hallway.

"Diego!" Mayra's voice had a sense of panic in it.

"Hold on, I'm coming!" Diego called out to shut her up.

When he reached the living room, he first noticed Mayra and Francisco both standing up. Their backs were towards him as they faced the front door. There was another person standing in front of them, but it wasn't until Mayra stepped aside that he realized it was Winston.

The sight of Winston standing there was like a kick in the gut. Diego felt his legs go weak. "Why you come here?" he asked Winston in English.

"Who is this guy?" Francisco asked in Spanish. His face was stony, his fists tightly balled at his sides as if ready to fight.

Diego's eyes shot over to Francisco and then to Mayra. Had she said something to him? Did he know? Diego didn't have the energy to fight both Francisco and Winston at the same time. He still couldn't believe Winston was standing in his living room. Pushing between Francisco and Mayra, Diego stepped between them and Winston. "I said, why you come here?" he asked again.

Winston stood just inside the door. Dressed in a pair of baggy jeans, a white tee shirt, and flip flops, he was more casual than Diego was used to seeing. Facial hair shadowed his cheeks and jawline, and his hair was tossed. Diego knew he had been rubbing his head and had rubbed all the gel out of it. He looked horrible, yet beautiful.

"We need to talk," Winston said.

"You shouldn't have come here. What you do is not right." Francisco spoke in English. He attempted to move in front of Diego, but Mayra grabbed him by the wrist.

"You need to go!" Francisco repeated.

"How you find me?" Diego looked over his shoulder and shot Francisco and Mayra a look that said, *Stay back.*

Winston took a half step forward. He looked over Diego's shoulder over to Francisco. "Um, um." Winston took a deep breath. "You haven't called me back. I need to talk to you." His eyes again looked at Francisco and Mayra. "Can we please talk? Just a minute, hear me out, and then I'll go. I swear."

"How you know where I live?" Diego tried to divert Winston's question to something less revealing.

"Well . . . I've been driving around for the past five hours trying to figure it out. I knew the general area, or so I thought. Then I saw your trailer behind the fence . . ." Winston again looked over at Francisco. "The old lady downstairs, she was outside watering her plants. She told me you lived up here."

Diego cried, "You shouldn't have come."

"Like I said, you're not answering my calls . . . You're not texting me back. What else was I supposed to do?"

Diego drew a breath as he looked back at Mayra and Francisco. Grabbing Winston by the wrist, he spun him around towards the door. "Outside!"

Diego led Winston outside onto the tiny cement landing, shutting the door behind them. Crossing his arms, he waited. He would at least listen to Winston before he sent him on his way.

"Let me start with: I screwed up. I know I did." Winston's eyes were bloodshot.

Diego leaned back against the door. His eyes darted about, ensuring the old lady downstairs wasn't within earshot of their conversation.

"About what happened between you and that guy in the restroom—I believe you. I believe everything you said. I know you, the real you, and I know you wouldn't have asked anybody for money for any reason, let alone for that. I was embarrassed, stressed about the night, probably had drunk too much, and the whole situation went from zero to sixty too fast. I immediately tried to call you to say I was sorry. I left the party in hopes that you had gone back to the house. When I got home, the house was dark, quieter that it's ever been."

The muscles in Diego's neck tightened as he listened to Winston's apology. Forcing air through his nose, he felt his heart beat a little faster than it had a second ago. He didn't want to hear an apology. He wanted to be mad, mad at Winston for disrespecting him.

Winston kept talking, "That night, I thought it was just a dumb fight. I would say sorry, and things would be okay. But when you didn't come home, and you wouldn't return my calls . . . and then you didn't show up today, something told me that I had lost you. I can't lose you!"

"Okay . . . Are you done?" Diego knew he had to stay strong, but all of a sudden, Winston was larger than life. It was like Diego was standing in front of a twenty-foot wall. There was nowhere for him to go. He couldn't get around what Winston had just said, nor could he argue against it. Nevertheless, he also couldn't be sucked back into the illusion that what they were doing stood a chance. Their worlds were too different.

"No . . . No, I'm not done." Winston frowned. "I have one question for you."

Diego's body withdrew, his chin tucked into his chest. He couldn't find his voice.

"Did you ever love me?" Winston asked.

Diego forcefully inhaled a breath of air. Holding it for a second, he slowly exhaled. He had not expected Winston to be so direct. Of course, he loved him. Diego leaned back against the front door, trying to put a little more distance between them.

"Did you?" Winston repeated.

Diego nodded slowly. "Si."

Winston released a heavy sigh. "Okay."

Giving Winston complete control of the conversation, Diego waited for him to say something, something that would make everything okay. But was there anything that could fix this? The weight of his body, the heaviness of his chest—he was exhausted and just wanted it all to be over.

"Do you still love me?" Winston asked.

With a lump wedged in his throat, Diego turned his head away from Winston. If he were going to cry, he wouldn't do it in front of him.

"Do you still love me, Diego?" Winston's voice was sturdy.

"Maybe you not love me. Maybe . . . you not like me next month." Diego mumbled, as tears started down his face and his vision began to blur. He couldn't look at Winston, or he would lose it. He couldn't fight him off; he was too strong.

"You couldn't be more wrong. I love you, Diego. And if you say you love me, I promise you that I will never hurt you. I know you. I know you want this too."

"No, that's where you're wrong. You not know anything about me." With a surge of emotion, Diego pushed himself off the front door. He could defend himself from Winston if he struck as hard as he could. "You grow up in Beverly Hills. You go to France, England, Italy, as if you go to Disneyland. Hell, I not go to Disneyland, and I live right next to it."

"But—"

"Let me finish! Someday, you want more. More than a gardener. Someone who knows the difference between rice and goose-goose. Me not order a glass of wine off a menu without embarrassing you."

"Can I please say something . . . please!" Winston begged. The ends of his mouth twitched as if he was holding back a smile. "It's couscous . . . Couscous, not goose-goose." Winston couldn't contain it, and a snort escaped him.

Seeing Winston smile at him, the warmth of his face as his eyes melted into him was too much for Diego. Winston had somehow managed to rip the air from his lungs, causing him to stumble in his thoughts.

Winston continued, "You're so adorable. Damn it, I wanna grab you, pull you into my arms, hold you, and protect you from every-thing. To take care of you, to be everything that you need. But I know that's exactly what you don't need or want. You don't need anyone to take care of you. You're a bigger man than I'll ever be. Can't you see? It's me that needs you! Do you remember our first fight? It might have been something like our third date. I'm not sure, but I was running my mouth about something I knew nothing about, and you ended up walking out that night." He stopped and drew a breath, his nostrils flaring.

Winston was breathing hard, but he continued, "Do you remember the peanut butter and jelly sandwich I made for you to say I was sorry? I came out in the yard and said that I was an asshole? Well, guess what? I'm still an asshole, but an asshole who loves you, who wants to be a better person. You make me want to be a better person. There's nothing I can say that would excuse what I did. I have racked my brain trying to come up with something, something that would get me off the hook, but there isn't anything. So, I could take my mistake, learn from it, and never see you again, and that would be mine, mine to own for the rest of my life. But I'm not willing to accept that."

"So?" Diego folded his arms tighter around his chest.

"We're standing here right now because I didn't have the guts to say what needed to be said. But I do now, and damn it, I'm going to say it. I love you. There's a million reasons why we're not meant for each other."

The two stood silent, looking at one another.

"I know you think it would never work—that I'll hurt you or that, somehow, you're not going to be enough for me."

Diego shifted his eyes away as another tear escaped them.

"Yeah, there might be a million reasons why we shouldn't do this, but there's one reason that tells me we should."

"What is it?" Diego swiped at another tear that had formed at the bottom of his eye.

"I love you. And you love me."

"Your friends, your house, your car. We not the same," Diego protested.

"None of that means anything to me."

"And that's the problem. It should! You have more than anybody else. Why you say it means nothing?"

Winston pulled at Diego's arms, causing them to fall to his sides. "Without love in my life, it means nothing! When I lost Parker, I thought my world had ended. None of this shit that you're talking about matters. I know that because I lived it. I would have given it all up for one more day with Parker, all of it. But I never got to make that deal. And here I am again, ready to give all of it up if it means keeping you. I'll take that deal right now!" Winston drove his finger down towards the ground.

"But . . . Sometimes, you say things that are not nice. I love this country, and I'm glad to be here. But not a day goes by that someone doesn't remind me I not welcome. I can't live in your world and feel that way every single day. I live my life, take care of my family—be happy. I not do that living in your world."

Winston leaned closer. "My world? I can't help the circumstances in which I was born any more than you could have controlled yours. We're here, two people who love each other despite all the shit that makes us different. When your father put his boys on that bus, he knew he might never see you again. As hard as that must have been, it didn't stop him from attempting to change your world for the better. You're not stuck in any world unless you tell yourself you are."

Diego knew Winston was right. He had spent the last eight years of his life allowing others to dictate his mood. He hated watching everything he said and did in an effort not to look too Mexican. He was proud to be Mexican, yet every day somebody tried to make him ashamed of it.

"Why it not be easier?" Diego muttered.

"I don't know, baby, but it isn't. What isn't complicated is my love for you."

"So how's your friend?" Diego needed a minute to think.

"Who?"

"The guy I hit?"

"You mean the guy you knocked out? He's a little embarrassed, but he'll live."

"The po-lice. They not look for me?"

"Naw, he was too embarrassed to let anyone call the police for him. You knocked the shit out of his pride as well. Remind me never to piss you off."

"Um, it's too late for that." Diego couldn't hold back his smile, and it felt good.

"Okay, to never piss you off again," Winston added. "I want to kiss you."

Diego knew Francisco and Mayra were on the opposite side of the door, two feet away at most. He shook his head no, as he backed up against the door. "Not a good idea." Diego wanted that kiss just as much, but it could never happen here. "What car did you bring?" He had an idea.

"The Maserati, why?"

Diego laughed. "Probably also not a good idea. They maybe take it by now. Let's hope not." Diego threw his weight into Winston's side, bumping him off balance. It wasn't perfect, but it was contact, enough to sustain him until he got Winston behind those dark, tinted windows.

28

With no shoes on his feet and without his wallet or keys, Diego fled with Winston. On the drive back to Thousand Oaks, the cabin of the sports car was silent. For Winston, just being able to interlock his fingers with Diego's, to touch him, was enough. Winston's heart was overflowing with trepidation and love. He knew loss. How could he have nearly caused himself to lose love again? In that moment, he promised himself that he would never again be so stupid and careless. A tear fell from his eye as he realized everything would be okay.

Diego reached across and wiped the tear from his cheek. Somehow, they communicated their love for each other without anything needing to be said.

Having barely made it into the entrance of the house, Winston pushed Diego up against the door as it shut. "Don't you ever leave me again." Although he was playing, he also meant every word. Softly placing a kiss on Diego's mouth, he allowed their lips to linger less than an inch apart. "I love you," Winston mumbled.

He tried to steady his breathing as a rush of energy pumped through his body. He could say he was sorry a million times, and it wouldn't be enough. The sadness in Diego's eyes when he came out of his bedroom would forever be imprinted in Winston's brain. The hurt he had caused him. Never again, he told himself.

Kissing Diego again, Winston took in the man's breath; the warm sensation of cinnamon from his gum filled the back of his throat. Their eyes, hands, and lips danced harmoniously about each other's bodies. Winston ran his hands down the sides of Diego's ribcage until he came to the small of his back, but Diego's jeans prevented him from going where he wanted to go.

Diego whimpered as Winston pulled him in tighter. Winston kissed him several more times before pulling away. "Come on."

Taking Diego by the hand, Winston led him into the bedroom, the room that had been so cold and empty for the last three nights. His plan was to undress his lover, but Diego was way ahead of him, yanking his sweatshirt and tee shirt over his head in one movement. He tossed them to the ground. He tore off his jeans with the same urgency.

As if time was of the essence, Winston threw the pillows from the bed onto the floor. Every inch of him craved Diego as he watched him crawl up onto the bed, wearing nothing but his white briefs.

Winston tore off the rest of his clothes as he watched Diego's perfectly round ass climb towards the headboard. He was seconds from joining him, when Diego rolled over onto his back and threw his legs up. Performing for him, Diego grabbed the waistband of his underwear and slid them slowly down over his ass, tossing them to the floor.

Watching Diego's performance, Winston's body responded accordingly. All thoughts became insignificant but one. Winston moved onto the bed and climbed up over Diego's body. He nuzzled his nose into the side of Diego's neck and drew a breath. The smell of his skin was intoxicating, sending heat down his spine. Delicately, he kissed his way up and over to Diego's mouth. Their breath mingled as Winston drew him up into his arms. Unable to contain himself, Winston slammed his lips against Diego's, setting off a fire within him. Skin to skin, he wanted more. He wanted all of Diego.

The swirl of emotions forced his breath from him. Lust, desire, and resolution. Diego's hands caressed the small of his back. The warmth of skin-on-skin contact sent a charge through his spine.

Pulling away, Winston reached over into his nightstand and grabbed lube and a condom. It wasn't about having sex; it was about needing to be one with the man he had almost lost.

Diego's dark eyes were like liquid. Winston wanted nothing more than to give all of himself to him.

It was fast and intense. Winston needed urgently to breathe life back into what they had three days ago. He wanted to rid his body of the deep, depressing emotion that was all too close to his mourning. In the end, they had stripped the bed of nearly all of its bedding; the only thing left was the fitted sheet, which had sprung lose from one corner.

Their naked bodies lay tangled as Winston listened to Diego's light breathing. He knew Diego had drifted off; the tremble in his right leg every so often told him so. Caressing Diego's naked body, he nuzzled his nose into Diego's arm. If Diego was dreaming, he hoped it was of him. He had fallen in love again and would do what it took to ensure Diego always felt safe, loved, and respected.

Positioned under Winston's arm, Diego's naked body shifted. Winston lay perfectly still, not wanting to move for fear of waking him. To think that he had lost him, that things could change in the blink of an eye, scared him. Although he had known Diego for only a short time, the man consumed him.

As much as he and Parker had loved each other, he would never let his relationship with Diego become that routine, that systematic. He would do what he had to do to ensure Diego would always be not only his friend, but also his lover, a role bestowed only to him.

How was it that he was blessed with so much, even the chance to find love again, and yet somebody else had so little, despite how hard he had fought for more? Every aspect of his life was wildly extravagant in comparison, and he needed none of it. He would give all of it up for love.

Afraid to move, he wanted to lie there and listen to Diego's breathing—to hold him, to shut his own eyes and experience the moment. Diego stirred after about an hour of being curled up in his arms. Winston had never been so content just to lie there. He would have lain there all night if Diego allowed it.

Stroking Diego's back, he waited a few minutes for Diego to come back to life. "Hey, Sleeping Beauty. Are you waking up?"

"What time is it?" Diego released a roar of a yawn as he stretched his arms and legs out across the bed.

Winston looked at the alarm clock on his nightstand. "Almost nine."

Wiggling as if still trying to wake up, Diego sat up against the headboard. Clearing his throat, he rubbed his face with his hands. "Um . . . um." Diego took a breath. "My truck."

"Huh?" Winston waited for Diego to finish the sentence.

"My truck. I not have my wallet or house keys. Can you take me back to my house?"

"Tonight?" Winston's head tilted. He knew he would. He would do anything Diego asked him to do, but why?

"I left everything when we left. I have to have my truck."

Still, none of what Diego was saying was making sense. "Why do you need your truck tonight?"

Still not awake, Diego rubbed his eyes. "I not go to the Bernstein estate today. I go tomorrow. My trailer is at the house. I not want to go back to the house, but I have to."

"Why can't you have Rafael drive it out here? Then we can take him back. Wouldn't that be easier?"

"I not have my phone either. I can't call him."

"Well, use mine. Call him and have him drive the trailer out here. Or we can meet him halfway. That way, you don't have to go inside." Winston moved his hand onto Diego's knee and then up his massive thigh. "Do you know how much I love you?"

"No." Diego's voice trailed off as he nuzzled back down into Winston's arm. "I go back." Shifting again, he reached down to the floor and grabbed the sheet and comforter to cover himself and Winston.

Winston pushed the heavy comforter down to just above his waist. He couldn't understand how Diego could be underneath all of that and not cook. "Why don't you want to call Rafael? Because of what happened at the apartment? Because of me?"

"He's at work."

"Talk to me." Winston rubbed the comforter that lay over Diego. "If it's going to be a problem, move in here, with me." Winston wasn't sure where that had come from, but hearing it aloud, he didn't regret saying it for one second.

Diego cocked his head as if he wasn't sure he understood.

"Really. Move in with me." Winston repeated. "Don't overthink it. I love you. You love me. Why shouldn't you move in? I want you here, with me. I don't want you an hour away. It's not like I can hang out with you at the apartment." He was begging, but he didn't want to give Diego a chance to say no.

"I not do that."

"Why?" Winston sat up, ready to fight for what he wanted. "Why can't you move in here?" Winston couldn't think of a single reason why Diego would object. It was the perfect solution.

Diego was silent. Although he was staring at Winston, it was as if no one was home.

"Diego . . . talk to me." Winston shook his legs.

"And leave them?" Of course, Diego was thinking of his family. Winston should have known that. He tugged at the covers. "Hear me out. You said you wanted to go to school, right? Move in here, cut out all those little accounts you have. Keep the Bernstein estate, keep this house, which would be more than enough to pay for your school and still have money to send home. You're too good to waste your time mowing lawns. You're a designer, that's what you need to be doing."

Another idea came to Winston. "Let's start our own company. With what you know and with my contacts, why wait for you to finish school?"

"But I want to go to college," Diego cut in.

Winston thought that he might win this one. "That's fine. You should go to school. All I'm saying is that we can do both. We don't have to wait. You know more about landscaping than anybody I know."

"I not know," Diego murmured. The two sat in the bed staring at one another.

Studying Diego's face, Winston's confidence that he was winning his argument began to slip.

Diego wilted down into the bed. "How can people be so nasty? Your friend, I mean."

"What exactly are you referring to?" Winston's heart dropped at the abrupt change in the conversation. He wished they didn't have to talk about the other night, but it wasn't his call.

Diego raised his head to look at Winston. "Why would someone lie about something I not say?"

"First of all, that guy, Mike, he's not my friend. Secondly, gay people, especially men, can be malicious. It's insecurity, a way to make themselves feel better. If I can find fault in you, then I must be better than you. However, to actually say that would be egotistical. So it comes out in a catty, bitchy way. Sometimes they think they're funny, and that makes it okay somehow."

"I not think he was trying to be funny. He lied." Diego sounded more hurt then angry.

Winston tried to think of a better way to explain why the man had lied about him. "I suspect . . . he saw you. He obviously knew you were with me. It was a jab at me. He wasn't trying to hurt you. He never considered your feelings. You were the hottest guy there. I know for a fact that every gay man in that room was checking you out. You have no idea how good looking you are. That's one reason why you're so sexy, because you don't even know it." Winston rubbed Diego's short hair. "That guy was trying to get a rise out of me. And I'm sad to say, it worked. I took the bait. I bit."

Diego kicked the covers off his right leg as he rolled over to face Winston. "So you know he not tell the truth . . . about me, no?"

"I'm not sure why I reacted like I did. It happened so fast. One minute we're talking, and the next minute, you've knocked some dude out and are storming out of the hotel."

"Did it bother you, that I do that in a bathroom? I not do anything like that since we've been together."

"You don't owe me an explanation for what happened before we got together. But if we're to be a couple, we have to talk to one another. So . . . let me ask you. What scares you about moving in with me?"

Diego laid his hands across his lap. Lowering his head, he mumbled, "Losing my family."

Winston crawled up to Diego and kissed him. Pulling back, he playfully scratched the bridge of Diego's nose. "Baby, you've got me. I know you love your family. I can't say what they will or won't do. But I know you also have to be you. You can't live your life by what you think people are going to do if they find out who you really are. The real you is the most wonderful, loving, loyal friend anyone could want. Why would you want to pretend to be anything different?"

"But—" Diego cleared his throat. "There's this thing inside me. All the time, I see how people look at me. I see the news . . . the protests. 'Send those people back to where they came from' . . . They, not nice."

Winston started to speak, but Diego cut him off. "I want my *mama* and *papa* to be proud of me. They not be if they knew I was gay."

"I hear what you're saying, I do. But . . ." Winston rubbed his chin. "You're not the only one here that is afraid. After Parker died . . ."

Winston wasn't sure exactly how to say what he wanted to say. "I remember the first time I ever saw you. I had this huge guilt inside of me that said that I could never look at another man or have a sexual thought about someone without it being disrespectful towards Parker. Like I couldn't let myself love again. So when we started seeing each other, the guilt inside of me was enormous. I was supposed to be sad, but I wasn't; I was walking on the moon thinking about you. The fact that I was crazy about you—did that mean that, somehow, I hadn't loved Parker? That scared the shit out of me. The fact that I was going to be sad the rest of my life, that I was somehow trapped in that perpetual grief. I'm still afraid. Afraid that you will learn who I really am and won't love me as Parker did. Afraid that my nose has been so far up my ass for so long that maybe it's karma. That I will live in that perpetual grief, and there's not a damn thing I can do to change it." Winston got on his knees, bent over, and took Diego's hands. "But if we don't go for what we want, then we'll never know. Now that would be sad."

Winston jumped out the bed and walked over to his dresser. Grabbing his phone, he walked back to Diego. "Here, call or text him. Have him bring your stuff out here. Or we can go right now and get it. I know you're scared, but I'm scared too. Scared that I'm going to lose you. Scared that you won't choose me." Winston held the phone out for Diego to take. Naked, he stood in front of Diego, more exposed then he had ever been. Drained, he was raw. "I love you, and I'm scared I'm not enough for you."

Diego sprung out of bed and wrapped his arms around Winston. With Diego's head buried in his chest, Winston heard it.

"I love you."

29

Standing at the back end of the van, Diego watched as the dog groomer fussed over the bow on the top of Lucy's head. If the groomer stopped talking long enough to pay attention to what she was doing, the poor dog would have been free five minutes ago.

Now Diego understood what Winston meant about avoiding her. He had made the mistake of being curious and peeking in the Mercedes Benz conversion. He couldn't believe someone was driving around in a Mercedes van giving baths to dogs.

Satisfied with the bow, the old woman lightly patted Lucy before putting her on the ground. Lucy sat and waited for her treat before running up to the house to escape.

"Well, I need to get back to work. I guess I'll see you in two weeks." Diego was trying to be polite. In reality, he didn't intend to be anywhere around the next time she showed up.

Fastening her equipment to the wall of the van, the groomer stopped what she was doing. "What did you say your name was?"

"Diego." He wasn't sure if he had ever introduced himself to her.

"Oh, my second husband's name was Diego. He was quite the Latin lover, that Diego." She rolled her eyes up into her eyelids, and her shoulders shivered.

Diego didn't know how to respond to such a statement. Embarrassed, he smiled and said, "Okay, I work now." He hurried away from the van and into the back yard. Pulling his phone out of his pocket, he looked at the time. Rafael had been due thirty minutes ago. In fact, Diego had only walked out front so he could see when Rafael pulled up to the gate.

It had been two weeks since he and Winston had made up. When he had returned to the apartment a couple of days later to tell Francisco he was moving out, Francisco wouldn't even talk to him. For the first time in Diego's entire life, he saw fire in Francisco's eyes, and it had devastated him. When Rafael had said, "Just go," Diego wondered if it was for his own safety. He had never seen that side of Francisco and was a little relieved when Rafael offered to bring his stuff over to Winston's. Of course, it was like Rafael to take a week to do it and to show up late.

Nervously, he thought of the questions that Rafael might ask. Surely, he had put it all together by now. Mayra knew and, clearly, she had told Francisco.

Pacing the yard, Diego thought about everything he and Winston had talked about during the past week. Everything about his life had changed. He would be going to college soon, and his dream of being a landscape designer would come true.

In the back of Diego's mind, he heard the groomer's van leaving, but then there was the sound of a horn. *Was that Rafael coming in?*

He laid down his rake, and walked back towards the front yard. Seeing Rafael standing beside his car, Diego tried to smile.

"*Hola,*" Diego called out.

"*Que paso,* what's going on?" Rafael rushed towards him and wrapped him in his arms.

Diego wiggled lose, his eyes prickling as he tried not to cry. Rafael was not a hugger; his version of affection was to hit you in the arm or chest. That hug spoke volumes.

"Nice place." Rafael looked around. "Kind of far out here. But check you out—my baby brother is living with *los gabachos.*" Rafael shook his head and snapped his fingers.

Diego didn't like hearing Rafael bragging on him. None of this belonged to Diego, and Rafael shouldn't be acting as such. He tried to change the subject. "So what's this about you having a baby? Is it true?"

"Yeah, man. The one time I didn't suit up. You know my shit is potent." Laughing, Rafael reached into his car window and pulled out a shopping bag.

Staring at the bag, Diego asked, "Who is she?"

"This chick that comes into the shop all the time. She and I have been seeing each other for a couple of months. She's alright."

Knowing his brother as well as he did, Diego sensed that Rafael liked her more than he was letting on. "So, what's going to happen?"

"She wants to keep it. I asked if she wanted to get married or something. She said she didn't know."

"Smart girl. I not marry your ass either." Diego chuckled.

Rafael's face took on a stern look. "Hey, do you remember what *Papa* told us the day he put us on that bus?"

It was eight years ago, yet Diego remembered it as if it was yesterday. "He said to be good . . . to look after each other . . ."

"Don't wait for it to happen, make it happen," the two brothers said in unison.

"Look at you, bro. *Papa* would be proud of you." Rafael punched Diego in the arm.

"How's Francisco?" Diego couldn't resist asking.

"Ah, you know him. He's like *Papa*." Rafael shook his head and grinned. "He'll come around. It has to be on his terms. But I know he misses you."

"Oh, yeah? Why you say that?"

Rafael handed Diego the shopping bag he had been holding. "Here. Francisco found these for you on Sunday. He thought you would use them."

Taking the bag, Diego pulled out a box of new Bazic drafting pencils. They were some of the most expensive pencils you could buy. "What's this?"

"He found them on Sunday. He didn't haggle with the woman. He just bought them. I think he paid something like thirty-five dollars for those damn things. Don't you ever say anything about me spending foolish money again."

Diego knew the pencils cost about two hundred and fifty dollars new in the store. There was no sign that the box's seal had been broken.

"You know he would have never asked you to leave. You didn't have to move out."

Diego tried to ignore those words. He was sorry he had brought it up. "It was time. Something tells me he wouldn't have been too cool with it."

Rafael popped the trunk. "Yeah, well, he wasn't the one sharing a room with you."

"What does that mean?"

"You know, you could have told me you were queer. I could care less what other people do in their own beds."

Diego wasn't sure he could get used to people using the word queer lightly. "Really?"

Was his brother saying he didn't care that he was gay? For years, he had listened to Rafael and Francisco talk shit about gay people. "So you don't care that I'm—gay?" The word seemed to hang out there, like a grenade without its pin. Not waiting for the explosion, Diego looked down into the trunk of Rafael's car at three black garbage bags.

Grabbing the first bag, Rafael shoved it into Diego's chest. "Why the hell would I care? I think if Francisco knew half the shit I've done, he would have shipped me back to *Mama* and *Papa's* a long time ago. I bet sleeping with a rich dude wouldn't seem so bad."

"I doubt that. Being gay is probably the worst." Diego couldn't believe all of his stuff fit into only three bags. He would have to look through them later to find out what Rafael had kept for himself.

Rafael snickered. "So, I guess having a three-way with my boss and her husband would be okay?"

"No way!" Diego wasn't sure he had heard correctly.

"Yeah, a couple of times."

"No!" Diego tried to picture it, without actually picturing it. "Please tell me you're bull-shitting."

"It was all right. Not sure why you guys like sucking dick though. Tastes like playdough."

Diego didn't know the person standing in front of him. Speechless, his mouth hung open.

"You know that Mexico City has approved same-sex marriage?" Rafael continued to talk as he grabbed the remaining two bags and closed the trunk. "To be fair, give him some time. He just found out about you. I don't know how long you've known you were gay, but shouldn't he get time to digest it, like you did?"

Rafael, for the first time in a long time, was sounding like a big brother. His words meant something.

"Hey, do you want to come in?" Diego was really asking if Rafael wanted to meet Winston. As much as Rafael would probably embarrass him, they were brothers, family forever. Winston was now his family too. Hearing his *papa*'s voice, Diego knew it was up to him to bring family together, to make it happen.

EPILOGUE

One Year Later

Pacing the floor, Diego stopped long enough to look out the second story window for the hundredth time. The breathtaking panoramic view of Flathead Lake, Montana did little to calm his nerves. He looked out across the expansive lawn and the water, which shimmered like glass. There was Winston standing on the dock with his stepfather, Mr. Richardson. They appeared to be deep in conversation. Both wore black tuxes. Winston's hand was on Mr. Richardson's shoulder, and Mr. Richardson's two adult sons stood nearby.

In the distance, several young men were hurling a football back and forth. He had no idea who the jocks were. Perhaps locals or neighbors.

When Diego had talked Winston into finally visiting his mother, he had never dreamed that visit would be for a wedding. His own.

Winston's moodiness the morning they had flown out had him nervous. At the time, Diego had assumed Winston was being weird because of the ensuing visit with his mother. It hadn't helped that the dog sitter had been late, and the morning rush hour traffic going into the airport had been backed up for miles. It wasn't until they had boarded the plane, and they had accepted the flight attendant's offer of champagne, that Winston finally had given him a smile.

It had all become clear that night at dinner with Winston's mother and Mr. Richardson. At the table, they had been talking about Diego's impending meeting next week with an Immigration Attorney. He had been a good friend of Parker's and was supposedly the best around.

Diego had just looked over at Winston and noticed all the color had drained from his face. He was about to ask if he was okay, when Winston had backed his chair away from the table and stood. Walking over to Diego, Winston had dropped to one knee. In his mother's grand dining room, surrounded by moose heads and Native American Indian memorabilia, he had taken Diego's hand.

The candles about the room, the polished silver cutlery, and the exquisite meal served by her staff had meant nothing to Diego. In front of Winston's mother and Mr. Richardson, his eyes had swelled. He was deeply in love with a man who continuously surprised him and made him feel like the only thing that mattered in the world.

No sooner had Winston finished his proposal, Diego had jumped from his seat and had thrown himself into Winston's arms and wept, 'Yes, yes, I'll marry you."

Winston, Mayra, and his mother had been planning the wedding for quite some time. Thank God Diego had said yes, for unbeknownst to him, Winston had been working to ensure that the wedding included some important Mexican traditions and customs.

Today, Diego was about to marry the man of his dreams, and he was a wreck. Coming away from the window, he exhaled a long breath as he sat on the edge of the rich mahogany Renaissance canopy bed. He had been looking at this view for almost a week now, and it still caused his insides to quiver. It was the most spectacular piece of property he had ever seen. The ten-thousand-square-foot house sat on thirty-seven acres between Flathead Lake and the Mission Mountains, just south of Bigfork, Montana.

He had just gotten used to calling the one-acre parcel back in Thousand Oaks, which had once been his source of revenue, home. Where had the year gone? He had spent months cramming to take his *GED*. Practice test after practice test on line had done little to re-assure him that he would be able to pull it off in the end. But in the end, he had crushed the test, just like Winston said he would. Two weeks ago, when his Economics Professor at Moorpark College had stopped him in the hall, her accolades had restored his confidence. Not only had he been able to handle fourteen units in his first semester, he had loved it.

His heart sped up as he heard the violinist begin to play. The time was near. The music was his cue. He was barely able to breathe. This was really happening.

A light tap sounded at the door. Before he could say come in, Mayra poked her head into the bedroom. "Can I come in?"

He was happy to see her. He needed the distraction, something to keep his nerves from sending him over the edge. "Come in."

Mayra entered the room and moved close to Diego. She had come to get him. Straightening the lime-green bowtie around his neck, she gently kissed his forehead. "I'm so happy for you. You look beautiful. Are you ready to do this?"

Diego couldn't find his voice. He was going to cry. He tried to breathe. He didn't want to cry, not now. They had practiced the whole thing yesterday. He just had to keep himself from passing out.

"We should head downstairs."

"Where's Winston?"

"He's outside. I saw him standing with his mother. We're just waiting on you." Her eyes glowed with adoration for him. Handing him his jacket, she sniffled back a tear.

She was going to make him cry. He couldn't look at her. He went to the window again. Scanning the yard, he saw Winston, his mother, and Ann. Standing next to them was the Unitarian Universalist minister. Dressed in a white and gold robe, the minister was the closest Winston could get to a priest for Diego. The four stood facing the large, seated crowd. Seeing Winston standing with his mother warmed Diego's heart. Mother and son each had been through so much and it appeared they both wanted to rebuild their relationship. Months ago, Diego had been successful in getting the two to talk on the phone, but he was unsure if pushing Winston into this visit had been the right thing to do. Within forty-eight hours of their arrival, he saw the tension released from Winston's body as the four of them laughed and shared stories, stories you shared with friends. He and Winston were relieved to see that she was no longer that person that Winston had separated himself from for so many years. Diego liked her and could see so much of her in his husband-to-be.

Diego mentally counted the crowd below. "There's so many people," he said.

In the front row, Rafael sat holding his son. His new wife sat to his left. On the other side of Rafael were two empty chairs. In each chair sat a framed eight-by-ten photo, one of Diego's mother and the other of his father.

Mayra joined him at the window and lightly rubbed his back. "Perhaps. But right now, there's only one person that matters, and he's standing out there waiting for you to marry him. Come on. It's time to go."

Diego released a heavy, controlled breath. Looking at Winston, he wanted to run to him. He loved him more than he had known was possible.

As Diego came down the steps, Francisco stood at the back door waiting for him. Over the past year, Diego had seen his brother maybe five times. Each time had gone better than the last, but it was a complete surprise when Diego learned that both his brothers and Mayra were planning to attend the wedding.

Apparently, Winston had been very busy setting his plan into motion. He had contacted Mayra, asking to meet with her and Francisco. During this meeting, Winston had asked Francisco if he could marry Diego. Although it had taken a week for Francisco to settle down after such direct dialogue, he had seen that Winston had come to him out of respect.

When he had heard all of this for the first time, Diego initially wasn't sure how he felt about Winston asking for permission, as if Diego was a woman. Then he, too, saw the sweetness in this gesture.

Francisco stood there waiting for him. Diego could not deny that his brother loved him. Francisco raised a brow and smiled. He said in English, "We've been waiting, little brother. Are you ready to do this?"

Diego wrapped his arms around his brother, and the two embraced. Trying not to cry, a simple "*Sí*" was all Diego was able to get out.

On cue, the mariachi band that Winston insisted on hiring began to play for the processional. The soothing sound of the violin, matched with the vihuela and several guitars, instantly made Diego think of his father. Dressed in their traditional formal *charro* costumes, the eight-man mariachi band was the real deal. Diego fought even harder not to cry as he thought of his mother and father.

Reaching the front of the crowd, Diego joined Winston on a small platform. Ann stood by Winston's side as his best (wo)man, as Winston's mother took her seat in the front row. Diego smiled at her before resting his eyes on his soon-to-be husband.

Winston took Diego's hand and interlocked their fingers. Then the two turned and faced the minister.

When the music stopped, the silence was deafening. Diego could feel his body swaying as he waited. Seconds that seemed like minutes passed before the minister began the ceremony, starting in Spanish, and translating back and forth between Spanish and English.

"Diego and Winston, we are gathered here together to witness the love and respect that you have for each other . . ."

Diego's knees were shaking. Sweat beaded across the top of his forehead. The minister was talking to them, but it was all a blur. He heard the words but retained none of them. It wasn't until the moment came to exchange their vows that he checked back in. Scrambling, he remembered that he had them written down. He reached into his pants pocket, and pulled out a single sheet of paper and unfolded it.

He focused on the words as he tried to hold back the swell of tears in his throat. "Um . . . um, I . . . knew you existed long before you know of my desire. Our paths, they not just cross, they collided and intertwined." Diego swallowed as he found his voice. "You now my best friend, and today, I become your faithful husband. You are my one true love. I will forever be there for you, to lift you up and to love you unconditionally. I have to catch my breath to believe this is real, that I am marrying my true love, my heart's desire, and my best friend." Wiping a tear from his eye, he folded the paper and placed it back in his pocket. His hands remained in his pockets for a second before he remembered to take them out. Shaking, he smiled at Winston and whispered in Spanish, "I love you."

Winston smiled back. His eyes burned with nothing but love as he stared into Diego's. "All I have in this world, I give to you. I love you unconditionally and without hesitation. I vow to love you forever and forever, and to always respect you. Before we met, I was just a body, empty as I moved about in this world. Then one day, in the blink of an eye, it all changed for me. You, you walked into my heart and stole it. Since our first date, I have been helplessly lost in your eyes. You take my breath away, make my knees weak, and rattle my thoughts. Together, let us create a home filled with love, understanding, and laughter. Wherever our journey leads us, I promise to walk with you, arm in arm, hand in hand, to hold you as your husband and to learn from you, love you, and surprise you, forever."

Diego heard sniffling in the crowd, but he didn't dare look. He was on the brink of losing it. When the gold band slipped onto his finger, warmth spread throughout his body. Becoming present and in the moment, he felt his heart thump.

They stood gazing into one another's eyes. Diego felt his heart thump again, and again. His chest pounded as a warmth spread throughout his entire body.

"Diego and Winston—and all who have gathered here today, may the love in your hearts give you joy. May the greatness of life bring you peace, and may your days be good and your lives be long upon the earth. So be it, by the authority vested in me, I recognize you as united in marriage. Partners in life . . . for life. Ladies and gentleman, I present to you Mr. and Mr. Makena-Castillo."

ABOUT THE AUTHOR

Early in life, Bryan learned that he was different from everyone else in his world. As a young African American boy, he was the second to the youngest of seven children. Long before hormones kicked in and the realization of same sex attraction, it was his light skin and blond hair that made him different from those around him. Teased within his own race for being lighter than everyone else, the kids on the playground called him "Cornbread".

At the age of fifteen, he accidently stumbled over a book called 'The Front Runner' by Patricia Neil Warren on his mother's bookshelf. Admiringly, it was the cover that really caught his eye. However, it was Patricia's emotional tale of romance between two men that opened his eyes to a whole new world, not only in literature, but for his own life.

Bryan's love for poetry came many years later. It was Maya Angelou, Iyanla Vanzant, and yes, Jewel that taught him that you can put emotions on paper.

As a writer, Bryan has taken back the power once given up to those schoolyard bullies. He is committed to bringing his readers stories of real life, with multicultural characters, riveting plots, and where the underdog always wins. He is the founder of **Cornbread Publishing**: the name empowers him and is a constant reminder that life can have a *Happily-Ever-After.*

If you've enjoyed **Diego's Secret,** I'd love to hear about it. Honest reviews on Amazon, Barnes & Noble, and Goodreads are always appreciated.

Author's Official Website: http://www.btclark.com

E-mail-Bryanbrianx2@Yahoo.com

If you would like to explore some of my other novels, follow the links below.

Ancient House of Cards
http://www.amazon.com/dp/1494955172

Before Sunrise:
http://www.amazon.com/dp/0997056207

Come to the Oaks
https://www.amazon.com/dp/B01N5XNP2S/